CELTIC MYTHOLOGY:

LEARN ABOUT CELTIC HISTORY, MYTHS, GODS, AND LEGENDS

AMY HUGHES

© Copyright 2021 by Amy Hughes

All rights reserved.

This document is geared towards providing exact and reliable information with re-gards to the topic and issue covered. The publication is sold with the idea that the publisher is not required to render accounting, officially permitted, or otherwise, qualified services. If advice is necessary, legal or professional, a practiced individual in the profession should be ordered. From a Declaration of Principles which was ac-cepted and approved equally by a Committee of the American Bar Association and a Committee of Publishers and Associations.

In no way is it legal to reproduce, duplicate, or transmit any part of this document in either electronic means or in printed format. Recording of this publication is strictly prohibited and any storage of this document is not allowed unless with written per-mission from the publisher. All rights reserved.

The information provided herein is stated to be truthful and consistent, in that any liability, in terms of inattention or otherwise, by any usage or abuse of any policies, processes, or directions contained within is the solitary and utter responsibility of the recipient reader. Under no circumstances will any legal responsibility or blame be held against the publisher for any reparation, damages, or monetary loss due to the information herein, either directly or indirectly. Respective authors own all copyrights not held by the publisher.

The information herein is offered for informational purposes solely, and is universal as so. The presentation of the information is without contract or any type of guaran-tee assurance.

The trademarks that are used are without any consent, and the publication of the trademark is without permission or backing by the trademark owner. All trademarks and brands within this book are for clarifying purposes only and are owned by the owners themselves, not affiliated with this document.

TABLE OF CONTENTS

Introduction 1

Cap 1: Celtic History 8

Cap 2: The Gallo-Roman deities 41

    Mercury: The Inventor of All the Arts.. 42

    Jupiter Taranis: The God with the Wheel... 50

    Sucellus: The God with the Mallet 54

    Apollo: The God of Light and Water 57

Cap 3: Ériu, the Emerald Isle.. 62

    The Names of Ériu: Give the Land a Name..................................... 62

    The Circle of Time: From Darkness to Light 64

    The Invasions of Ériu: The Peoples Who Came from the Sea ... 72

    The Divisions of Ériu: The Space and the Territory 80

Cap 4: The Cycle of Invasion of Ériu 90

    The Story of Tuan: Immortality and Memory................................ 90

    The Creation: The Biblical Tale in the Irish Myth 95

    The Origins of Europe: Genealogy of the peoples of Ériu 104

    The Daughters of Cain: The Betrayed Invasions 110

    The People of Cessair: Ériu at the Time of the Flood 112

    The Shapeless Island: Ériu After the Flood 119

    The People of Partholon: The First Basics of Civilization........ 124

    The Nemedians: The Second Invasion.. 138

    The Fir Bolg: The Third Invasion 152

Cap 5: The Túatha Dé Danann 158

    The Túatha Dé Danann: The Tribes of the Gods of Danaan ... 158

    The Advent of the Túatha Dé Danann: The Fourth Invasion.. 170

The First Battle of Mag Tuired: The Defeat of Fir Bolg 179
The Kingdom of Bress: A Bad King 194
The Healing of Nuada: The Arm and the Throne 202
The Birth of Lugh: Prisioner on the Tower of Glass 205
The Arrival of Lugh: The Samildanach at the
Gates of Temair 214
Return From Tir Tairngiri: The Battle of Mag Mor
An Oenaig 220
The Fate of Delbaeth's Children: The Vengeance of Lugh 228
The Adventure of Dagda Mor: Meeting at the Wading 261
The Second Battle of Mag Tuired: The Defeat of
the Fomorians 266
The Prophecies of the Morrigan: The Happy Age and
the Cruel Age 281

Conclusion 285

INTRODUCTION

Around the beginning of the first millennium BC, the Celts made their appearance between the North Sea, the Rhine, the Alps, and the Danube. The period of their maximum diffusion was between the sixth and fourth centuries BC, during which, through France, they reached Spain and Portugal, then the British islands and Ireland, while in Italy they occupied the Po Valley, Puglia, and Sicily, finally reaching Greece, where, in 279 BC, they sacked Delphi. From there, they reached Asia Minor.

The term "Celts" had different meanings for the ancients. For the Romans, these were the Gauls; for the Greeks, they were the peoples of Anatolia. All their knowledge was handed down orally by the druids, often in poetic form, especially as it was considered essential to accustom the young aspiring druids to mnemonic training and, secondly, to not divulge the knowledge among the populace. In their expansion, they gave birth to very different ethnic groups. One of the first peculiarities that concerned them was the use of writing for purely practical purposes.

The Celtic deities were, as always, identified with the deities of the Roman pantheon. Studies on this have led to the conclusion that it may not be possible to affirm the existence of a Celtic pantheon valid for all ethnic groups. The druid is a central figure in this field, too; an approximate definition can translate the word "druid" into "priesthood"; even if other interpretations translate it instead into "expert" or "expert of the oak," it remains certain that this caste was a real intellectual elite who practiced knowledge.

The cultural training of the druids could last up to twenty years and was precisely based on mnemonic learning for two reasons: firstly, to accustom the neophyte not to rely too much on writings and therefore get lazy, and secondly, to prevent people from becoming acquainted with druidic "esoteric" knowledge.

Julius Caesar made it known that the most important center of Celtic cultural radiation was Britain. It also seems certain that metempsychosis entered the competence of the druids, who maintained a relationship of non-competition with the leaders, though they often inspired their actions: Their authority also allowed the druids to speak before the leaders themselves, and it was precisely this detail that worried the Romans to such an extent that during the Romanization process of Gaul, those Gauls who wanted to become Roman citizens had to abjure the "druidic religion."

Other important figures in Celtic society were the bards and the vati; according to some scholars, the bard would have been nothing other than the druid during the celebration of heroic deeds, just as the poet would have been the druid at the moment of the interpretation of the divine will. However, other scholars believe that the three castes represented instead three different hierarchical degrees of three distinct and respective social classes. Yet it was also and above all Christianization that dispersed the ancient cultural heritage transmitted orally by the druids, though, for example in Ireland, the converted princes did not give up the idea of being descendants of a god, as per traditional idea.

The Celtic religion was undoubtedly aimed at achieving success in this life and on this earth; good health, abundant herds, long life, and obedient children were required, and rites and sacrifices were practiced to obtain these favors from the gods. One type of human sacrifice involved thieves or murderers, but failing that, also common people, who were burned alive in huge human figures woven from wicker.

Due to the difficulty of giving a univocal anthropological definition of the Celtic type, it must be concluded that the Celts represented an aristocratic and warrior minority: this is, for example, the impression aroused by the Irish epic. Caesar left a description of the Celtic civilization that follows the traditional tripartite scheme of the Indo-Europeans: priests, warriors, craftsmen.

The priestly class of druids is at the top of the social ladder. The kings were generally elected and considered more the balancers of wealth than the holders of civil and military powers, and in any case, their authority was subject to the control of the druids. Also, for this reason, the king had a small number of officials. The archetype of the Celtic ruler is the one who, thanks to good administration, can afford to donate without any refusal, while the bad king is the one who charges his subjects with taxes and fees without any counterpart.

The Celtic state organization has always remained in the tribal state: Celtic patriotism has never exceeded the boundaries of the local territory. In fact, the Celtic tribes did not disdain alliances with the Romans or with the Germans to attack neighboring tribes. This is the greatest limit of the Celtic civilization and would determine its disappearance.

The Celtic territorial fragmentation derives from the fact that the Celts considered, as the fundamental social cell, the clan, which could count at most a few thousand people. Beyond the clan, only personal alliance bonds recalling those of the feudal world could be recognized. The Celtic settlement generally consisted of a village protected by a wooden palisade; the villages rarely took on the dimension of real cities.

Furthermore, the Celts had not developed a written law and relied on the norms of customary law; however, Irish literature has left evidence of intense discussions and subtle wits in legal matters. The financial organization was rather archaic, and mostly gold or copper bars were used as currency.

The Roman invasion of Gaul actually marked the end of Celtic autonomy: The Celtic tribes, fragmented and incapable of unitary organization, could not face a situation of total war like the one the Romans were leading. The Celts disappeared because the religious and political structure of their society was not adaptable to the Roman, then modern, notion of the state and Celtic culture, not having developed a script. They had to succumb to the Greek and Latin. The British Isles have left behind examples of Celtic literature, albeit from a late period compared to the time the language was formed.

From these testimonies, it can be deduced that the Celtic languages were rather simple. Moreover, the absence of the relative and the placement of the verb at the beginning of the subordinate clause prevented oratorial periods of some breadth. Celtic literature was intended for recitation, not for reading. Oral stories must have been widely used, and traces of them remain in the "matter of Brittany" that inspires the Arthurian tales of the Middle Ages. In particular, the symbolism of the Grail would be absorbed by Christian esotericism.

Celtic society assumed a theocratic character, being the reflection of the metaphysical conceptions of the druids, who shaped human society on the model of the divine society of which they were the representatives on earth. The studies that have shed light on Celtic religion outline a non-Aristotelian philosophy, a form of speculation independent of the logic of Greek reasoning and which essentially made use of symbols.

An operation of this type is not easy for the modern mentality, impoverished by the materialist culture, and research must make use of essentially comparative data. The parallel with Hindu and oriental culture finds an interesting confirmation in Celtic myths; in particular, a certain tendency stands out to bring the various divinities back to a single dimension of the sacred. When Caesar describes the religion of the Gauls, he tries to compare the Celtic gods to the Roman ones, but an operation of this type risks being approximate and arbitrary. Caesar himself, in fact, does not claim to be exhaustive on the subject.

Lug, the god of light, seems to have attributions that bring him closer to Mercury, while Brigit, the goddess of wisdom, is assimilated to Minerva. With a similar procedure, the Celtic gods transmitted some of their characteristics to the Christian saints. An emblematic case is that of Saint Brigit.

The powerful caste of the druids had within it further hierarchies that dealt with sacrifices, with poetry and literature (the bards), and with prophecy. Women were also admitted to the priesthood with the status of prophetesses. The druids taught the doctrine of the immortality of the soul: Upon the death of the body, souls pass to the Other World, or to the abode of the gods, called sid (a word that contains the etymology of peace).

The Other World is a place of peace and delights similar to the Germanic Valhalla. Its inhabitants enjoy delicious food, are loved by beautiful women, and have a high social rank. This paradise is reserved for those who, in life, behaved in a virtuous and heroic way. The Other World is described in the famous texts called "navigations" (*immrama*), which will find their continuation in the "navigations" of medieval monks, the most famous of which, that of San Brandano, will be a model for all medieval travel stories in the afterlife.

The Celts did not build temples in the classical sense of the term and celebrated their rites mostly in the sacred groves. Druidism also became extinct because, as we have seen, Celtic culture as a whole was incompatible with the written culture of the Romans. With the spread of Christianity, there was the coup de grace to any survival of Celtic paganism, whose influence, however, is present above all in the Irish Church, to the point that one speaks of a "Celtic Christianity" that has given peculiar traits to the religious literature of Ireland.

CAP 1:

CELTIC HISTORY

1. La Tene Culture

The Celts are traced by scholars to the people of the La Tène Culture, which developed during the Iron Age from the previous Hallstatt Culture, in an original area extended between southern Germany, eastern France, and northern Switzerland, where there was a continuous cultural evolution.

To the early 13th-century urnfield culture BC, followed at the beginning of the eighth century BC, was the Hallstatt Culture, with an agricultural base but dominated by a class of warriors, with a commercial network toward Greeks, Scythians, and Etruscans. From this Central-Western European civilization, around the fifth century BC, Celtic culture developed. The various populations had a cultural and linguistic unity, but not a political one. In fact, they were made up of tribes of which the most important were: the Britons (British Isles), the Celtiberians (Iberian Peninsula), the Pannonians (Pannonia), the Galatians (Anatolia), and the Gauls (Gauls).

The Celts were therefore neither a people nor a race, but a set of Indo-European peoples that expanded over a vast area of Europe, from the British Isles to the Danube and the Iberian, Italic, and Anatolian peninsulas. Caesar, Herodotus, Livy, Polybius, Tacitus, and others have narrated about them. They were an essentially nomadic population and, therefore, dedicated to raising livestock, in particular cows, sheep, and goats, from which they obtained meat, milk, and wool.

The most important groups were the Britons, the Gauls, the Pannonians, the Celtiberians, and the Galatians, settled respectively in the British Isles, Gaul, Pannonia, Iberia, and Anatolia. The Gauls in turn, constituted various groups, including the Belgians, the Helvetians, at the eastern end of Gaul, and the Cisalpine Gauls of northern Italy.

The expansion in the Iberian Peninsula and the French Atlantic coasts dates back to the eighth to seventh centuries BC. Later, in the La Tène culture, they reached the English Channel, the mouth of the Rhine, present-day northwestern Germany, and the British Isles; then they went to Bohemia, Hungary, Austria, northern Italy, partly central Italy (early fourth century), and the Balkan Peninsula. In the third century, the group of Galatians passed from Thrace to Anatolia, and the Senonian Gauls in central Italy, through the supremacy of arms.

2. The Tribes

Dislocation of the Gallic tribes before the conquest of Gaius Julius Caesar in 59 BC:

Allobrogi - Gaul between the Rhone river and Lake Geneva

Ambiani - Of Belgian Gaul

Ambibari - Of the Armorican people

Ambiliati - South of the Loire

Ambivareti - in the Aedui region

Andecavi or Andi - North of the lower course of the Loire

Aquitani - A mixture of Celts and Iberians from southwestern France

Arverni - Central Gaul, with King Vercingetorix

Atrebati - Of Belgian Gaul

Aulerci Cenomani - From Gallia Cisalpina, then also Lombardy and Veneto

Aulerci Eburovici - Normandy

Aulerci Diablinti - From Gallia Lugdunensis

Ausci - Aquitaine

Baiocassi - Lugdunense Gaul

Bellovaci - Northeastern Belgian Gaul

Betasii - In the Ardennes

Bigerrioni - Aquitaine

Biturigi - Bourges

Blannovi - In the Aedui region

Boi - Aquitaine

Cadurci - Close to the Arverni

Caleti - Close to the Armoricans (Belgians)

Carnuti - Chartres; they had the greatest power among the Celts

Catalauni - Châlons-en-Champagne

Caturigi - In the Cottian Alps

Ceutroni - In the Graian Alps

Cocosati - Aquitaine

Coriosolites - From the Côtes-du-Nord

Edui - Bibracte

Eleuteti - Close to the Arverni

Elvi - Bordered to the north with Narbonne Gaul

Elusati - Aquitaine

Elvezi - La Tene

Garonni - Aquitaine

Gabali - Bordered to the northwest with Narbonne Gaul

Gati - Aquitaine

Graioceli - Moncenisio area

Lemovici - Limoges

Lessovi - Lisieux of Normandy

Leuci - Between the Vosges and the Marne valley

Lingoni - Between the Seine and the Marne

Mandubi - Transalpine Gaul

Mediomatrixes - Metz

Meduli - Medoc

Meldi - Meaux

Menapi - Cassel

Morini - Boulogne-sur-Mer

Namneti - Nantes

Nantuati - Martigny

Nervi - Bavay

Nitiobrogi - Bordered to the northwest with Narbonne Gaul

Osisms - Of the Armorican Celts

Parisi - Paris

Petrocori - Périgueux, in Périgord

Pictoni - Poitiers

Ptiani - Aquitaine

Raurici - Basel

Redoni - Rennes

Remi - Reims

Ruthenians - Bordered to the northwest with Narbonne Gaul

Santoni - Saintes

Seduni - Martigny area

Segusiavi - Loire area

Senoni - Gaul-transalpine east of Orléans

Sequani - Besançon

Sibuzati - Aquitaine

Soziati - Aquitaine

Suessioni - Soissons

Tarbelli - Aquitaine

Tarusati - Aquitaine

Toulouse – Toulouse

Trier, Treveri – Trier

Tricassi – Troyes

Tungri – Tongeren

Turoni – Tours

Unelli – Normandy

Vangioni – Worms

Veliocassi – Rouen

Vellavi – Ruessium, in the Haute-Loire

Veneti – Vannes in Brittany

Veragri – Near Martigny

Viducassi – Vieux

Viromandui – Vermandois

Vocals – Aquitaine

Voconzi – Vaison-la-Romaine

Arecomic Volci – Gallia Narbonense

England, Ireland, Scotland, and Wales – Roman Britain and Celtic native tribes

Ancaliti – Hampshire and Wiltshire, England

Attacotti – Scotland or Ireland

Atrebati – Hampshire and Berkshire, England

Autini – Ireland

Belgians – Wiltshire and Hampshire, England

Bibroci - Berkshire, England

Brigands - Northern England, Ireland

Cereni - England

Caledoni - Scotland

Cantiaci - Kent, England

Carnonaci - West Scottish Highlands

Carvezi - Cumberland, England

Cassi - England

Catuvellauni - Hertfordshire, England

Cauci - Ireland

Corieltauvi - Leicestershire

Coriondi - Ireland

Corionotozi - Northumberland, England

Cornovi - Caithness, Cheshire, and Cornwall in England

Creons - Argyllshire

Damnoni - Strathclyde, England

Darini - Ireland

Deceangli - Flintshire

Decanzi - England

Demezi - Wales

Dobunni - Gloucestershire

Dumnoni - Devon, England

Durotrigi - Dorset, England

Eblani - Ireland

Epidi – Kintyre, England

Gangani – Ireland and the Lleyn Peninsula

Erpeditani – Ireland

Iberni – Ireland

Iceni – East Anglia, England

Lugi – England

Magnazi – Ireland

Manapi – Ireland

Novanzi – Galloway, England

Ordovici – Gwynedd, Wales

Parisi – East Riding, England

Regnensi – Sussex, England

Robogdi – Ireland

Segonziaci – England

Selgovi – Tweed, England

Setanzi – Lancashire, England

Torpedoes – Wales

Smerzi – England

Tassali – Aberdeenshire

Trinovanti – England

Vacomagi – England

Velabri – Ireland

Veniconi – England

Vennicni – Ireland

Vodie - Ireland

Votadini - Lothian

Cisalpine Gaul 391-192 BC

Boi - Emilia

Meat - Carnia

Galli Cenomani - Brescia

Galli Anari - Oltrepò Pavese

Gesati - Gallic mercenaries from the Rhone

Graioceli - Moncenisio and Lanzo Valleys

Insubri - Insubria

Lingoni - Ferrara, Lower Romagna

Salassi - Valle d'Aosta and Canavese

Senoni - From Romagna to the Ancona area

Taurini - Turin

Vertamocori - Novara

Central Europe - The Illyrian and Celtic populations

Anartii - Hungary

Arabiati - Illyria

Boi - Czech Republic, Slovakia, Hungary, and Germany

Cotini - Slovakia

Eravisci - Hungary

Ercuniati - Illyria

Osii – Slovakia

Scordisci – Croatia, Serbia

Taurisci – Noricus

Asia Minor (Turkey)

Galati: Volci Tectosagi, Tolostobogi, Trocmi

3. *The Costumes*

Caesar calls unfortified villages vici and Celtic strongholds oppidum. The Celts, on the other hand, indicated with the term dunum the fortress and with nemeton a sacred place. Especially in Gaul, their cities had very thick walls. They lived mainly in wooden huts, circular or rectangular, and in villages. With the influence of the Etruscans and Greeks, they built stone houses with small rooms. They loved to live outdoors, under the oaks, considered sacred, where sacred rites and processes were held.

It was a tribal society, with villages that had an average of 25 inhabitants, and with a village chief who led the male warriors. In this society, now already distant in the time of Caesar from the matriarchal and magical one which is talked about in the various sagas, such as that of King Arthur, which seems to draw on myths of 1200 BC, gradually modified with the advent of the Christian religion, which disqualified in a stroke only women, children, priestesses, foresight, the Great Mother, the concept of death and magic.

In the patriarchal Celtic society, there were only men or men capable of fighting. Everything else, including wives and children, could be sacrificed, as seen in the battle of Alesia.

Being a warrior people, the Celts used splendid plumed helmets and sometimes armor, such as medieval ones, but they almost always fought naked. In battle, they colored their faces and, after having danced to reach the right momentum, threw themselves naked at the enemy, screaming. They preferred the melee and the first assault. For this reason, they struck with their swords, making cuts, which never proved to be fatal blows. The Celtic sword was, in fact, short and used as a cutting weapon.

Polybius says their little swords bent after the first blows. This was one of the reasons why they lost against the Romans, who instead used the sword and spears, hitting with deadly blows and avoiding the melee.

The shields, then, well finished and engraved, were small compared to the body, again because the Celts trusted in the impetus of the assault. The Romans had long shields; this was also a reason for the Celtic defeat.

The Celtic armies were not well organized and their war tactics were based mainly on war fury. Later, longer ones were forged, all inlaid and adorned with stones, but only after 500 AD.

The only Celtic king who understood that, in battle, it was necessary to use a strategy in addition to fury was the rooster Vercingetorix, who, using the "scorched earth" tactic, undermined the supplies of the Romans, obtaining some success. In particular, he understood that if he accepted direct confrontation with the Romans, he would lose.

The basic difference between them and the Romans is that while the Celts, like any tribal people, had to get excited with drums and drugs or alcohol to launch into war, for the Romans it was enough to receive an order and will. They were used to controlling their emotions, to obeying and leaving, as they were well aware that only organization and obedience could give them the victory over the barbarians.

They loved to shave their faces and comb their blond hair upwards, hardening it with chalk.

As for burials, they first used the tumulus tombs, typical of the Indo-European culture, and then the inmentation.

4. The Capacites

They were experts in the art of weaving and dyeing and in the processing of minerals, especially iron. They introduced brass and, for a long time, worked with smithsonite, a particular mineral that replaces zinc. They were very familiar with the various casting techniques.

They were skilled in firing glass, both white and colored, in the use of enamel, and in the processing of amber. These practices were perfected during the transition from Hallstatt to Latenian culture.

In the maritime areas, they developed a skillful navigational ability. They possessed stronger ships than Roman ones, made of oak, with leather sails—ships that the Romans successfully copied.

They loved music very much, especially with the harp, which was used to celebrate sacred rites, in view of a war to set the spirits on fire, and to tell the deeds of heroes through ballads. For the Celts, fame was everything, especially because being remembered was considered a kind of immortality.

They traded and worked salt, in Celtic hal. In fact, many cities in the salt area have this term as an initial suffix.

They preferred the use of barrels to that of amphorae, and it seems they were the ones who invented the barrels. They were very fond of wine, but they also made beer.

5. The Celtibers

The Celts who settled in the Iberian Peninsula were indicated, since ancient times, with the name of Celtiberi. The term has long been understood as a symptom of a hybridization between Celtic groups and Iberian groups, as indicated in antiquity by Diodorus Siculus, Appian, Martial, and Strabo, who specified how the Celts were the dominant group. Among modern scholars, this interpretation has been supported by Johann Kaspar Zeuss. More recently, however, the hypothesis of a mixed population has been progressively discarded, and the term Celtiberi simply indicates the Celts who settled in Iberia.

The central nucleus of the Celtiberian settlement corresponds to an area of present-day central Spain, between the regions of Castile, Aragon, and La Rioja and between the middle basin of the Ebro and the upper course of the Tagus. The penetration in this area dates back to the eighth to seventh centuries BC. At a later time, the Celtiberians expanded southwards (in present-day Andalusia) and northwest, until they reached the Atlantic coasts of the peninsula (Galicia).

In the second century BC, the Celtiberians were subdued by Rome through a series of military campaigns, the Celtiberian Wars. The capitulation was marked by the fall of their last stronghold, Numantia, conquered in 133 BC by Publio Cornelio Scipione Emiliano. From that moment on, the Celtibers, like all the other populations of the Iberian Peninsula, underwent an intense process of Latinization, dissolving as an autonomous people.

6. The Gauls

Gauls was the name with which the Romans indicated the Celts who inhabited the region of the Gauls. From the original area of the La Tène culture, the Celts expanded toward the Atlantic coasts and along the course of the Rhine between the eighth and fifth centuries BC; later, starting from approximately 400 BC, they penetrated today's northern Italy. They continued to push south, so much so that in 390 BC, according to tradition, or more likely in 386 BC, the Senoni tribe led by Brenno sacked Rome itself, finally settling on the middle Adriatic side (Piceno).

The populations of Cisalpine Gaul 391-192 BC. Like all Celtic peoples, the Gauls were divided into numerous tribes, which in only rare cases were able to unite to face a common enemy, such as when, in 52 BC, numerous tribes led by Vercingetorix rebelled against the Caesarian conquest of Gaul. Among the Gallic populations, some groups of tribes were united by their own shared sub-identity: the Belgians, settled between the Channel and the Rhine and variously mixed with Germanic elements; the Helvetians, located in the upper Rhine and upper Danube areas and in contact with the Reti; the Aquitans, between the Garonne and the Pyrenees, mixed with Paleo-Basque peoples; and the Cisalpine Gauls, all the tribes that entered Cisalpine Gaul, on this side of the Alps. Among the populations of the central region of Gaul, Caesar attests that at the time of his campaigns, two factions were distinguished, headed respectively by the Aedui, traditionally from the second century BC, and by the Sequani, the latter soon ousted by the Remi.

The subjugation of the Gauls to Rome started in the third century BC: A series of military initiatives against the Cisalpine Gauls led to their complete submission, attested to by the creation of the province of Cisalpine Gaul around 90 BC. At that date in the once Celtic territory, there were already numerous Roman presences, in the form of municipalities and, above all, colonies. The conquest of transalpine Gaul began around 125-121 BC, with the occupation of the entire Mediterranean belt between the Ligurian Alps and the Pyrenees, subsequently constituted in the province of Gallia Narbonense. Northern Gaul came under the dominion of Rome following the campaigns conducted by Caesar between 58 and 50 BC.

Due above all to the testimony given by Caesar in his De bello Gallico, the Gallic civilization is by far the best known among those developed by the Celts in antiquity, even if the observations of the Roman statesman are likely to be extended—at least in general terms—to all the Celtic peoples. Cesare describes Gallic society as divided into family groups and divided into three classes: that of the producers, made up of farmers with formal rights, but politically subjected to the ruling classes; that of the warriors, holders of political rights, to whom the exercise of military functions was entrusted; and that of the druids, priests, magistrates and custodians of the culture, traditions, and collective identity of a people fragmented into numerous tribes.

7. The Britons

Celtic populations reached Great Britain, crossing the Channel, in the eighth to sixth centuries BC. From present-day southern England, they later expanded rapidly north, colonizing the whole of Great Britain and Ireland, although pre-Indo-European Picts have long survived in present-day Scotland. Caesar attests to the close ties, not only cultural but also economic and political, between the Britons and the Gauls: The dominions of Diviziaco, for example, extended on both sides of the Channel and on the island escaped exiles from Gaul, which in turn he obtained, in case of need, military aid from Britain. A first Roman expedition, led by Caesar himself in 55 BC, did not involve an immediate subjugation of the Britons. This was completed about a century later, in 43 AD, by the emperor Claudius.

The Romans occupied the area of present-day England and Wales, erecting fortified limes to the north: Hadrian's Wall (122), later moved farther north (Antoninus Wall, 142). Beyond the limes (in present-day Scotland and Ireland), both British tribes and the Picts remained.

The Latinization of the Celtic tribes subject to Rome was intense, but less than that suffered by the Gauls and the Celtibers: At the end of the Roman control of Great Britain (late fourth to early fifth centuries), the ethnic and linguistic identity of the Celts was still alive, and also survived, for a long time, the subsequent Germanic invasions. From the fusion of the three elements—Celtic, Latin, and Germanic—the modern populations of Great Britain and Ireland were formed during the early Middle Ages. The only direct heirs of the ancient Celts are those of the British Isles, preserving the linguistic tradition in the two branches, Goidelic and Brythonic.

8. *Pannoni*

The process of expansion of the Celts toward the east, starting from the original cradle of the La Tène culture, is historically much less attested to than that which occurred toward the Gauls. However, it is believed that the penetration into that region of central Europe later identified with the name of Pannonia dates back to the early fourth century BC. In that area, on the middle course of the Danube, the Celts came into contact with the Illyrian tribes already present; in part, they intermingled with them and in part, they remained separated into autonomous groups, ethnically and linguistically homogeneous.

That of the Pannoni is the branch of the Celtic family on which the testimonies are scarce and uncertain; nothing remains of their language (certainly, a variety of continental Celtic languages), except perhaps for some isolated element which served as a substratum for the languages that later developed in that region. Among the Celtic tribes present in Pannonia, that of the Boi stands out—probably the eastern branch of a tribe also present in Gaul and penetrated into central Europe at a later time, perhaps in 50 BC. To them, we owe the toponym "Bohemia."

Starting from 35-34 BC, the Pannonians began to enter the sphere of influence of the Romans, who later made Pannonia a province, although a significant portion of the Pannonians nevertheless remained included in the nearby province of Noricum. Subjected to Latinization and, later, to Germanization, Slavicization, and Magyarization, the Pannonians—both of Celtic and Illyrian lineage—dissolved as an autonomous people from the first centuries of the first millennium.

9. The Galates

The penetration of the Celts into the Balkan Peninsula is attested to by Greek sources, which testify to a migration that submerged Thrace in 281 BC. The Greeks, perhaps adapting a term employed by those same Celtic tribes, called the invaders γαλάται instead of κελτοί or κέλται—a term with which they identified the native inhabitants of the Greekized areas near the colony of Marseille.

Galatian incursions went as far as the heart of Greece. A horde, led by the leader Brenno, attacked Delphi, giving up only at the last minute to desecrate the temple of Apollo. Alarmed by portentous thunder and lightning, he also renounced to collect a ransom. Also in the third century BC, another fraction of the people, consisting of three tribes and ten thousand strong fighters accompanied by women, children, and slaves, moved from Thrace to Anatolia at the express invitation of Nicomedes I of Bithynia, who had asked for their help in the dynastic struggle that opposed him to his brother (278 BC).

The Galatians settled permanently in an area between eastern Phrygia and Cappadocia, in central Anatolia; following their settlement, the region took the name of "Galatia." San Girolamo attests to the survival of their language (Galato, a variety of continental Celtic) until the fourth century AD, after which the Hellenization process of the Galatians was completed.

10. Latinization and Germanization

Celtiberi and Gauls were entirely Latinized in the first centuries of the Common Era; the assimilation of the vanquished concerned both the linguistic side, to the point of leading to the disappearance of the continental Celtic languages, and the socio-cultural one, with the extension of Roman citizenship and integration into the imperial political structures. The same fate fell to the Galatians, even if, in their case, the assimilating agent was of Greek origin.

The Pannonians and the Britons, on the other hand, were only partially Latinized, and in the regions they inhabited, Germanic elements took over—as early as the third century. If in Pannonia the assimilation of pre-existing populations was complete, also due to the successive Slavic and Magyar migratory waves, in the British Isles the process followed a different path.

Great Britain underwent, since the fourth century, a process of re-Celtization by groups from neighboring Ireland, which never entered the domains of Rome. Starting with St. Patrick's mission to Ireland (432), the island lost much of its Celtic heritage, dissolving ancient religions and myths. The first testimonies of the insular Celtic languages date back to these years—a resumption of the attestations of the Celtic languages after the oblivion that followed the extinction, at least in the testimonies, of the continental Celtic languages.

The expansion phase of the Irish Celts characterized the last centuries of the first millennium and affected mainly Scotland and the Isle of Man. This activity, however, was exclusively cultural and religious: From a political point of view, in fact, Ireland was invaded and controlled by the Germanic Vikings from the eighth to the ninth centuries, generating a Viking-Gaelic cultural syncretism.

11. The Society

Celtic society traced the fundamental structures of the Indo-European one, centered on the patriarchal "great family." This model was preserved by the Celts even in historical times; the family group (clan, a Scottish term that entered Italian) included not only the family in the strict sense but also ancestors, collaterals, descendants, and in-laws, including several dozen people. Several clans formed a tribe, at the head of which was a king. The family and not the individual also owned the land.

The social structure, known mainly thanks to the testimony given by Caesar about the Gauls in his Commentarii, was divided into classes. The warrior aristocracy performed the tasks of defense and offense and elected, according to a customary scheme among the Indo-Europeans, a king with mainly military functions, while the prerogative of the free people was economic activities, centered on agriculture and livestock. Then there is news of the existence of slaves. Finally, there were the druids, priests, magistrates, and magicians—custodians of community traditions, of collective knowledge, and of the intertribal identity in which all Celts recognized themselves. This identity was not limited to the single subgroups of the great Celtic family, but embraced it in its entirety; Caesar, in fact, repeatedly certifies the bonds that the Celtic Gauls were aware of having, not only among themselves but also with the nearby Helvetians, Belgians, Cisalpine Gauls, and Britons.

The woman enjoyed equal rights within Celtic society. She could inherit like men and be elected to any office, including that of druid or commander in chief of armies; this last possibility is attested to by the figures of Cartimandua of the Briganti tribe and Boudicca of the Iceni at the time of the Roman emperor Claudius.

12. The Warriors and the Army

The armor of the Celts included wooden shields with bronze and iron finishes, with sculpted bronze animals. On their heads, they wore bronze helmets with large protruding figures like horns, forelegs of birds, or quadrupeds, which made those who wore them appear gigantic.

Their trumpets of war made a deafening and terrifying sound to the enemy. Some wore iron plates on their chests, while others fought naked. They used not only short swords similar to the Roman gladi but also long ones, anchored to iron or bronze chains, which hung along their right flank, as well as iron-tipped spears one cubit long and just under two wide. Their darts had points longer than the swords of other peoples.

13. Celtic Daggers

It is also said of them that they preferred to resolve battles with duels between leaders or among the most skilled warriors of each of the opposing sides, rather than clash in battle. They had the habit of hanging the heads of slain enemies around the neck of their horses, and, in some cases, of embalming them, when the vanquished was an important opposing warrior; in fact, they considered the head, and not the heart, the seat of the soul.

The warrior vocation of these people, together with the prospect of obtaining a regular penny or occasional loot, eventually resulted in an activity practiced by many of their tribes: becoming mercenary soldiers. The first indication of such a choice dates back to 480 BC, when it seems that some Celtic soldiers participated, alongside the Carthaginians, in the battle of Imera. Other Celtic mercenary holdings are mentioned during the Syracusan expedition to Greece in 369-368 BC; in 307 BC, when three thousand armed Gauls joined Agatocle of Syracuse, together with Samnites and Etruscans, to lead a campaign in northern Africa; and in the struggles that followed between the heirs of Alexander the Great (the Diadochi). This practice not only generated an expanding market for several tens of thousands of courageous, experienced, and less expensive soldiers than the Greeks but also allowed, on the return of soldiers from wars fought almost everywhere in the Mediterranean basin, the introduction of coinage to the interior of Celtic communities.

14. Nature and Physical Appearance

The Celts were described by their Greek and Roman contemporaries as tall, muscular, and robust; the eyes were generally light, the skin clear, the hair frequently blond (also due to the custom described by Diodorus Siculus of lightening his hair with chalk water). The average height among men was around one meter and seventy. From the character point of view, the same sources describe the Celts as short-tempered, quarrelsome, valiant, loyal, heavy drinkers, and music lovers.

15. Religion

Cernunnos, the "horned god" of the Celts

The main testimony of Celtic beliefs and religious customs is once again that provided by Caesar in the De bello Gallico, which, although referring specifically to the Gauls, probably attests to a situation largely common to the entire Celtic group at the time of the facts narrated (first century BC).

The Celts probably shared the same polytheistic religious vision and worshiped divinities linked to nature, the oak, and the warrior virtues. Caesar also refers to the belief in the transmigration of souls, which resulted in an attenuation of the fear of death such as to strengthen the Gallic military value. It is also known, always among the Gauls, that human sacrifices were practiced; the victims offered themselves voluntarily. Alternatively, criminals were used, but innocent people were also sacrificed in case of need.

In the Gallic pantheon, Caesar testifies to the particular cult attributed to a god that he assimilates to the Roman Mercury, perhaps the Celtic god Lúg. He was the inventor of the arts, the travel guide, and the divinity of trade. Other prominent figures among the Gallic gods were "Apollo" (Belanu, the healer), "Mars" (Toutatis, the warlord), "Jupiter" (Taranis, the thunder lord), and "Minerva" (Belisama, initiator of the arts).

16. Celtic Laws

There is very little evidence of Celtic law. Caesar testifies, speaking of the Gauls, of a matrimonial law which provided for the joint administration between the spouses of the family patrimony, constituted in equal parts at the time of the wedding. Justice was administered by the druids, who had full discretion over the secrecy of the sentences.

17. Economy

The Celts routinely hunted and pillaged the cities and populations on which their raids fell; this habit is attested to in the entire area occupied by the Celts in antiquity, as evidenced, for example, by the Gallic incursions into Italy (sack of Rome, 390 BC) and Galatian raids in Greece (sack of Delphi, 279 BC).

In the places where the Celtic settlement was more extensive and lasting (Gauls and the British Isles), flourishing agriculture developed, which accompanied breeding, and metallurgical craftsmanship, with a peculiar and refined goldsmith's art, of which they constitute a characteristic element of torque, rigid necklaces in bronze, silver, or gold. From these regions, the Celts developed an extensive commercial network; in particular, tin from Britain was imported to the continent, where it was conveyed to the Mediterranean Sea. Here, in the cities of Narbonne Gaul (Marseille, Narbonne), commercial transactions took place with the Carthaginians, Greeks, and Etruscans and, later, the Romans.

18. Agriculture

Skilled farmers, the Celts cultivated quadrangular fields, not very large; the average size was ten to fifteen ares, corresponding to what was possible to plow in a single day. The fields were bordered by hedges to protect them from the trampling of wild animals.

As early as the eighth century BC, the ability to work iron allowed the Celts to make axes, scythes, and other tools to clear out large-scale territories, previously occupied by impenetrable forests, and to work the land with ease. The growing skill in metalworking also allowed for the construction of new equipment, such as swords and spears, which made them militarily superior to their neighboring populations and enabled them to move with relative ease, as they did not fear other peoples. Extracted in a spongy form, the iron was subjected to a first forge processing and distributed in ingots, weighing five to six kilograms, with a bipyramidal shape. In a later period, the ingots were replaced by long flat bars, ready to be worked into long swords. Such bars were so popular that they were even used as money, along with copper and gold coins.

19. Monetation

The use of the coin spread in the Celtic territories starting from the areas colonized by the Greeks, along the Mediterranean coast of Gaul. Since the third century BC, the Gauls used Greek coins, then passed later to Roman ones. The Celts also minted their own coins, both in Gaul and in the Iberian Peninsula (part of the so-called Hispanic coinage), inspired by the Greek and Roman ones.

Even among the Celts, the coin was a convenient means for quantifying a precious metal such as gold or silver, in transitions of a certain importance. Its introduction is to be found in the pay that was given as compensation to Celtic mercenaries (such as the Gesati). Therefore, the first appearances of local emissions in the Rhone river basin, following the return by the Jesuit mercenaries of the first half of the third century BC, would not be due to mere coincidence. The subsequent variations, in particular starting from the second century BC, were a means of marking the difference between the different territorial communities, with the progressive affirmation of the city-states. The obligation to distinguish each subsequent issue of the same oppidum, while maintaining its main and distinctive features, led engravers to develop a rare capacity for variation in the processing of ever more original images.

20. Trade

In addition to the Mediterranean, the commercial relations of the Celts also developed toward the interior of the European continent; Celtic artifacts have been found in a large area of central Europe, at the time inhabited by Germans and other populations. For example, one of the finest examples of Celtic metallurgy, the Cauldron of Gundestrup (late second century BC), was found in Jutland.

The Celts were also responsible for the opening of most of the roads in northwestern Europe. The mere fact that Caesar, in his account of the conquest of Gaul, repeated several times that his troops moved so quickly through Gaulish territory, suggests how excellent the road system of this region was then. New confirmation of the excellence of Celtic road networks arrived in 1985, with the discovery, in the Irish county of Longford, of a stretch of road over nine hundred meters long, dating back to 150 BC. It had foundations of oak beams placed side by side, over bars of ash, oak, and alder. In the areas subjected to them, the Romans did nothing but replace the wood with stone, above the pre-existing paths built by the Celts.

21. Language

The main feature of the identification of Celtic peoples is their belonging to the same linguistic family, that of the Celtic languages. This family is part of the larger Indo-European group, from which it broke away in the third millennium BC. There are three main hypotheses that better specify the moment of separation of the common Celtic or proto-Celtic.

According to the first, the proto-Celtic would have developed in the area of La Tène culture starting from a wider "European whole." This linguistic continuum, extended in much of central-eastern Europe, was formed following a series of penetrations of Indo-European peoples in Europe, coming from their original Indo-European homeland (the steppes north of the Black Sea, cradle of the Kurgan culture). The detachment from the common trunk of this European ensemble is traced back to the first centuries of the third millennium BC, between approximately 2900 and 2700 BC.

The second hypothesis, which in any case starts from the same overall vision of the Indo-Europeanization of Europe, postulates a secondary penetration into central Europe (always in the area of La Tène, and always starting from the Kurganic steppes). This population movement, in this case exclusively Proto-Celtic, would be placed around 2400 BC. This postponement of the separation of Proto-Celtic from Indo-European is motivated by dialectological considerations, which underline some characteristics that Celtic languages share with later Indo-European languages including, in particular, Greek.

The third hypothesis moves from a radically different approach. It is the one, advanced by Colin Renfrew, which makes the Indo-Europeanization of Europe coincide with the spread of the Agricultural Revolution of the Neolithic (fifth millennium BC). The Proto-Celtic would, in this case, be the evolution that took place in situ, in the entire area historically occupied by the Celts (British Isles, Iberian Peninsula, Gallie, Pannonia), of Indo-European. This hypothesis is supported in the archaeological field, but contested by linguists: The size of the area occupied by the Celts, the absence of political unity, and the long period of separation of the different varieties of Celtic (three thousand years from the common Celtic to the first historical attestations) are a set of factors considered incompatible with the close affinity between the various ancient Celtic languages, very similar to each other.

22. The ancient Celtic languages

The Celtic languages attested to in antiquity, the first and direct result of the dialectal fragmentation of the common Celtic, are defined as continental Celtic languages due to the absence in this era of evidence of the varieties spoken by the Britons. Indirectly, however, it is possible to hypothesize that the differences between Gallic and British were not particularly profound: Caesar, in fact, testifies to close contacts—cultural, commercial, and political—between Gauls and Britons, describing them as extremely similar, even if not explicitly referring to their language. The ancient Celtic languages of which attestations are preserved (Gallic, Celtiberian, Lepontius, Galatian, and, to a very limited extent, Paleoironian) are testified to by a series of inscriptions and glosses in the Greek, Latin, and—limited to Celtiberian—Iberian alphabets, dated roughly between the fourth century BC and the fourth century AD.

The languages of the Celts in continental Europe all died out in the Imperial Roman age, under the pressure of Latin, the Germanic languages, and, in the case of Galato, Greek. The continental Celtic languages acted as a substrate in the formation of the new languages, Germanic or neo-Latin, which developed in the regions that hosted their speakers.

The Celts created their own heroic literature, of which, however, there is very little evidence. This literary tradition, in fact, was transmitted only orally, through the work of the bards and druids, according to what Caesar testified to the Gauls. The use of writing—in the Greek, Latin, or Iberian alphabet—was reserved for practical functions, as the transcription of wisdom (poetic and religious) was considered illicit among the Celts. Wishing to preserve its secrecy, the wise handed it down exclusively orally, dedicating many years of study and the use of mnemonics to this task. At a later age, however, part of the Celtic poetic corpus was still put in writing: The earliest evidence, in Irish, dates back to the sixth to seventh centuries.

Between the fourth and third centuries BC, the ornamental ironwork of the swords was very fine, incised, chiseled, die-forged. Cities, generally of modest size, were built on the tops of hills, which made them easy to defend.

The construction technique used by the Celts in the fortification of their citadels was that defined by the Romans murus gallicus. Caesar, in the De bello Gallico, describes it as a structure consisting of a wooden framework and stone fillings.

The goldsmith's art is the artistic branch of the ancient Celts of which the greatest testimonies have survived. Typical of Celtic craftsmanship, Gallic in particular, are the torques, necklaces, or bracelets made of gold, silver, or bronze. Other Celtic artifacts preserved are jewels, bowls, and cauldrons.

The metal objects, at the end of the processing, were embellished with applications of colored material. On numerous artifacts, in fact, starting from the fourth century BC, fusions of enamels, obtained with a particular red glass paste, were initially fixed using a fine iron mesh, together with the Mediterranean coral, directly on the objects, almost representing a magical form of blood, "petrified of the sea" and released from fire. Starting from the third century

BC, polychrome glass bracelets were developed, with direct application and fusion of the enamel on swords and sets, without the use of support structures. New colors, such as yellow and blue, were introduced starting from the second to first centuries BC, although red remained the predominant color.

The Celts had a notable taste for bright colors, even on the fabrics that they used to make their clothes, as the modern Scottish tartans still testify to today. Diodorus Siculus says that "the Celts wore surprising clothes, dyed tunics in which all colors bloom, and trousers that they call 'breeches.' Above they wear short cloaks with multicolored stripes, tightened by fibulae, of furry fabric in winter and smooth summer."

Thus was born the Empire of the Gauls by the general Posthumus (260). However, he was soon killed by his own troops (268) and the secession of the Gallic provinces was repressed by Aureliano in 273. In the same period, the state of economic and social crisis pushed bands of bagaudi in revolt against the imperial authority to take refuge in wooded or less populated regions.

The Roman Empire managed to overcome the crisis and present itself with greater force under Diocletian (284 - 313 or 316) thanks to the institution of the Tetrarchy. The resistance of the Gallic bagaudi was weakened by Maximian, general of Diocletian and future emperor.

23. Vandals 457-461

On the night of December 31, 406, the Roman Empire suffered a devastating invasion; favored by the cold that had closed the waters of the river in its grip, groups of Vandals, Suebi, Alani, and other Germanic peoples en masse crossed the imperial limes spanning the frozen Rhine. Despite the efforts and good military results of Flavius Ezio against the invaders, the imperial power in Gaul continued to lose ground and the cadres of the Empire disintegrated until the transfer of political power into the hands of the "kings"; this process continued until the fall of the Western Roman Empire in 476 AD.

CAP 2:

THE GALLO-ROMAN DEITIES

Regarding the Celtic pantheon, let's start by saying that the Celts worshiped a multitude of gods and goddesses, although these differed according to the nation of origin. The Irish worshiped deities other than the Gallic ones, who themselves were different from the Gaelic ones. Another point to consider is that not only were the gods known by different names but also that many of these names were considered too sacred to be pronounced aloud. It is important to remember that in pre-Christian times, people worshiped complex and imperfect deities, who, like men, had their own personalities, interests, and feelings. For this reason, a "professional" religious was absolutely necessary, capable of knowing all these things and able to avoid their anger, which would seriously endanger the health of the whole tribe. Because the gods were similar to men in nature and temperament, they were much more accessible than men themselves. The idea that the gods are the architects of man's morality and judgment was a concept foreign to most of the European populations of the time.

Amy Hughes

Mercury: The Inventor of All the Arts

The Gauls paid the highest cult to a god that the Romans identified with Mercury. Despite the abundance of dedications and monuments that the Gauls raised to their Mercury in late ancient times and the large number of epithets attributed to him, the original identity of this important Celtic deity continues to elude us.

The god that the Gauls worship above all others is Mercury. This news might be surprising to a Roman citizen, who knows well that it is Jupiter, the king of the gods, who must be given the supreme cult. Evidently, the Gauls do not think so, as Caesar testified in the commentaries on his campaigns. The image that these barbarians have of Mercury does not differ much from ours. Also in Gaul, Mercury is the god who shows the way to travelers, who guides and protects them along the roads, and who takes care of trade and financial activities. He is the most able to ensure good earnings. It is also to Mercury that the Gauls attribute the invention of all the arts and techniques. The Gauls raise the greatest number of monuments to Mercury, such is the devotion they bring to him. This devotion (*pietas*) was noticed by Caesar at the time of his campaigns but, still today, the traveler who crosses the Gauls can easily see, along the roads, the many statues and inscriptions dedicated to the god of travelers and artisans. Since they were Romanized, the Gauls have taken to represent Mercury according to the classic image: a young naked man with a shaved beard, with a caduceus in his hand, a petasus on his head, sandals on his feet, and a purse for money in his hand. However, if necessary, one can encounter very different images of a Mercury, dressed in the Gallic style, with a bearded chin. Sometimes animals accompany him: a rooster, a goat, a lizard, or a tortoise. A Greek may perhaps recognize in the tortoise the one from which the very young Hermes drew his first lyre, but the rooster and the goat remain symbols completely foreign to the classical figurations of the god. Other times, next to Mercury we find a snake with ram horns. Mercury is often joined by a goddess called Rosmerta, the "provident". The Romans identify her with Maia, Fortuna, Felicitas, and Salus. The Gauls also call her Visucia, the "wise one". In the city of Lugdunum, which the Romans made the capital of Gaul, the cult of Mercury is particularly cared for and placed in close relationship with that of the emperor Augustus.

The traveler who crosses the Gauls, admiring the numerous monuments that the Gauls have dedicated to Mercury and stopping to read the dedications, will notice how many and which epithets, both Celtic and Latin, the god is called and invoked in those lands. Some of these names are widespread, while others attest to small local cults. It is difficult to say how many of these epithets are actually addressed to the supreme god of the Gauls, Mercury, the inventor of all the arts, and which ones conceal other deities that, for some reason, have come to be identified with the Roman god. These names have different meanings and different origins. Many of them are simple epithets of Gallo-Roman Mercury, some of Celtic origin, others purely Latin. Some of these epithets are evidently related to local cults of various tribes. Among these names, there are also those of Gallic divinities in their own right that have been identified with the Roman Mercury: the case of Cissonius, a god worshiped by the Treveri, but also known in Aquitaine, and of Gebrinius, a god of the Germanic tribe of the Ubii. The list also contains the names of two great Gallic deities, Esus and Teutates, which our theologians have identified with both Mercury and Mars.

Mercury is not only the supreme god of all the Gauls but also the protector of many individual tribes. One of the many Gallic names of Mercury is Teutates, "father of the tribe" (although some associate this name with Mars). In fact, Mercury sometimes assumes the appearance of a warrior god and, as such, watches over the territory of the tribe and safeguards its borders. Defensor and Finitimus are precisely two Latin names that the Gauls willingly associate with Mercury in his aspect of tribal god. Very devoted to Mercury are the Segusiavi, whose city Lugdunum was founded under the auspices of the god. The Arverni, who worship Mercury in a temple erected on Mount Domus, are considered particularly close to the god. However, many Gallic tribes worship Mercury on mountaintops. Mediomatrici and Leuci, for example, worship Mercury Clavariates on the peaks of Vosges. With the same name, the god is known by the Lingones and the Tricasses. Mediomatrixes worship a Mercury Vosegus. Mercury Vellaunus, the "valiant", is adored with this epithet throughout Gaul, but above all by the Vellauni tribe. He is also a warrior god, so much so that in Britain one speaks rather of a Mars Vellaunus. In Belgic Gaul, the Treveri identified Mercury with their god Cissonius. However, the Gallic cult of Mercury is also boundless among the Germanic peoples who live on the two banks of the Rhine. Mercury Visucius, the "wise man", is the name by which the god is known in Superior Germany. The Cimbri, people of Germanic origin, although Celtized, worship a Mercury

Cimbrianus or Cimbrius. The same can be said for the border Germans: The Ubii identify their god Gebrinius with Mercury. The Nemetes likewise address a Mercury Seno. Yet even the Germans, as confirmed by Publius Cornelius Tacitus, see Mercury as a supreme god.

Particularly devoted to Mercury is the tribe of the Arverni, who have always had a particular bond with the god, so much so that throughout Gaul, right up to the *limes* of the Rhine, it is customary to invoke Mercury Arvernus, as if the god belonged to the Arverni, or rather, as if a holier and deeper cult was rendered to their Mercury. Elsewhere, he is invoked as Arvernorix, "king of the Arverni". The Arverni have dedicated a famous temple to Mercury, erected on the top of Mount Domus (the Puy-de-Dôm), shining with precious marble and with a lead-covered roof. Here is the imposing bronze statue of Mercury Dumiatis. It was forged under the reign of Emperor Lucius Domitius Nero, the famous Greek sculptor and toreutics Zenodorus, who worked on it for ten years and received a salary of forty million sesterces from the Arverni. The statue, more than 100 feet (30 meters) high, portrays the god crouched on a stone; he is depicted according to classical models, naked, with a winged petasus on his head and a purse for money. At his feet are a rooster, a goat, and a turtle. This statue is so well known among the Gauls that they made many small copies of it, which they keep for devotion. After giving such a fine proof of his talent, Zenodorus was summoned to Rome by Nero, and there he outdid himself by making the 119-foot-tall colossus representing the emperor.

Among the numerous epithets that the Gauls have attributed to Mercury, there are two—Mercury Moccus and Mercury Artaius—

in which the god is close to two animals: the pig and the bear. Such epithets may perhaps surprise us, but they should not lead us to hasty accusations of impiety. For the Celts, the pig (*moccos*) is a symbol of wisdom, as it feeds on acorns and hazelnuts, fruits of trees that the druids consider sacred because they are associated with deep and occult knowledge. The cult of Mercury Moccus is particularly felt by the people of the Lingones, in whose capital, Andematunum, one can admire dedications and monuments devoted to this curious porcine Mercury. The bear (*artos*) is, for the Celts, a noble beast—a symbol of strength and royalty. Many Gallic personal names refer to this animal: Articnos, Artomagus, Arctorix. And because the bear cuts down the hives and feeds on the honey distilled by bees, it is perhaps related to the idea of immortality. The Celts believe that the gods drink a special mead that keeps them eternally young. The cult of Mercury Artaius is widespread among the Allobroges, settled along the Rhodanus River; monuments dedicated to him are found in the cities of Gallia Narbonensis and Cularo (today Grenoble). But this is not the only cult that the Celts dedicate to the bear. In Britain, the bear-god Matunus is worshiped and may be the local equivalent of Mercury Artaius. The goddess Arduinna is depicted riding a boar. The Helvetii instead worship Artio, the goddess of bears.

The streets of Magna Graecia are lined with images dedicated to Hermes, called "herms". Even in Gaul, images of Mercury are placed along the streets. These images may have marked phallic characteristics. The Belgae sometimes present a curious Mercury with three penises, the second on the nose and the third on the top of the head. Thus, they combine the magical meaning of triplicity with the symbolism of fertility and luck traditionally linked to the phallus.

In many images, Mercury is accompanied by a female figure. Sometimes this goddess is defined with a Roman name: It can be Maia, the mother of the god, or Fortuna, Felicitas, Diana, Salus, or Minerva. However, it often bears the Gallic name of Rosmerta, the "great dispenser". The cult of the divine couple formed by Mercury and Rosmerta is practiced in most of the Gallo-Roman regions, but is particularly widespread in central and eastern Gaul, along the Rhone, Meuse, and Moselle rivers, and on both banks of the Rhine. The tribes of Lingones, Treveri, Mediomatrici, and Leuci are devoted to Rosmerta. In the figurations, Rosmerta is usually standing and holding a cornucopia or a bag. She often has the caduceus, like her companion Mercury, with whom she forms a couple aimed at material profits and distributions. The Gauls invoke her so that prosperity will favor them and so that they will never remain without anything. The divine couple is even worshiped in Britain, where Rosmerta is represented with a wooden bucket and ladle. There are temples dedicated to them among the Dobunni, and some of these temples are found in the Roman colonies. Another place of worship dedicated to Mercury and Rosmerta is located in Aquae Sulis. Variants of the name of Rosmerta are Atesmerta and Cantismerta. All these names contain a Celtic root whose meaning is "to dispense"; the same one is found in the name of Adsmerius or Atesmertus, with which Mercury is honored among the Lingones tribe. Thus, Adsmerius and Rosmerta, or, with still closer correlation, Atesmerius and Atesmerta, come to be the "dispensing god" and the "dispensing goddess". At other times, Mercury and his companion are instead called Visucius and Visucia, the "wise man" and the "wise woman", again with a perfect symmetry of roles and attributes.

We have so far talked about the god to whom the Gauls attribute the supreme cult and who in Roman times was identified with Mercury. However, we don't know the original Gallic name of this god. Identification problems are quite complex. For example, the gods Teutates and Esus have both been associated with both Mercury and Mars. It is suspected that our informants did not have very clear ideas! So, what was the Gallic name of Mercury? Some say it is Lugos, the "shining one". This name, as far as we know, is never attested to in the epigraphies or in the surveys of our writers, but many localities scattered in Gaul, in Germany, in Britain, and even in Hispania—places often sacred to Mercury—have a name that derives from a "Lugos". One of these is precisely the city of Lugdunum, which in the time of Augustus became the capital of all Gauls.

On a hill, not far from the place where the Rhodanus and Arar rivers mix their waters, stands the city of Lugdunum. At first the center of the Segusiavi tribe, Lugudunum then became, in Roman times, the political, cultural, and religious capital of all the Gauls, who gather here in their assemblies, the *Concilia Galliarum*. It is a beautiful and populous city, located in a pleasant place, from which one can enjoy a wonderful view of the Alps. It is also a large commercial emporium and the Roman governors have gold and silver coins minted there. It is said that this place got its name when two Gaulish chiefs, Atepomaros and Momoros, arrived there. Driven out by Seseroneos, they came here, obeying the order of an oracle, to found a city there. Ditches were being dug for the foundations when a flock of crows appeared. The birds fluttered over them and covered the trees. Momoros, an expert in the science of augur, called the new city Lugdunum, because—the Hellenic authors say—in the Celtic language, the crow is called *lugos* and a fortified place *dunum*. As evidence of these facts, medallions were wrought depicting the god of the city with a crow at his feet. However, it must be said that the Greeks are wrong: "crow" in Gallic is not lugos, but *brennos*. Indeed, Lugdunum means "shining fortress" or, perhaps, "fortress of the shining (god)". Later, the emperor Augustus, in placing a capital at the center of the now subjugated Gaul, chose Lugdunum. Facing the city, at the confluence of the two rivers, the Gauls wanted to dedicate a magnificent sanctuary to Augustus. There, they placed a splendid altar on which they wrote the names of the 60 Gallic tribes and placed a statue for each tribe. When the emperor wanted to place his annual feast, the *Feriae Augusti*, he chose as a recurrence the first of August, the day that, to the Gauls, was sacred to Mercury.

In Hispania, the Celtiberians worship the Lugoves gods, patrons of shoemakers. Is it a plural form of the god Lugos plus several protectors of this profession? We do not know. Mercury was certainly the inventor of every technique, and therefore could also be the inventor of shoemaking.

Jupiter Taranis: The God with the Wheel

The Gauls considered him the king of the gods, and the Romans did not take long to identify him with Jupiter. His Celtic name was likely Taranis, the lord of thunder, and his image that of the "god with the wheel".

The place that the Gauls reserve for Jupiter is curious. They consider him the king of the gods, but they do not give him great importance in myth and worship. Caesar testified to this in the commentaries on his campaigns. Citing the five main Gallic gods, Caesar says that Mercury is the god whom the Gauls worship above all others and that only after him do Apollo, Mars, Jupiter, and Minerva follow. It may seem bizarre that these barbarians assign a secondary place to the lord and master of all the gods, but this should not lead us to consider the Gauls ignorant in terms of religion—a subject in which, indeed, they appear to be very versed. The minor importance that they assign to Jupiter is not to be considered impiety, but a different approach to the spheres of the sacred. Much revered from Gaul to Hispania, from Helvetia to Noricum, the Celtic Jupiter does not differ much from ours. He is a heavenly god in his most sublime and terrifying aspect, but also a god of thunder and life-giving rain. His sacred tree is the oak, and even in this, the Gauls agree with the Greeks and Romans. Since the Gauls have been subdued, Jupiter is represented with the usual classical attributes: the scepter, the lightning bolt, and the eagle. Typically Gallic, on the other hand, is the wheel that the god carries with him, which he sometimes holds, and which at other times he seems to lean on. This wheel, which has a variable number of spokes, perhaps represents the thunder rumbling in the clouds.

The Gauls have not attributed many epithets to Jupiter, their king of the gods, above all compared to all those attributed to Mercury or Mars. Of these epithets, some are of Gallic origin; among these, the name Taranis, the "thunderer", is very important. The Gauls have drawn other epithets from the Roman cult, such as the one, well known in the Romanized areas, of Jupiter Optimus Maximus.

We do not know the exact name of the Gallic Jupiter, but many think it is Taranis, the "thunderer". With this name, Jupiter is worshiped throughout the Celtic territory: in Gaul, in Britain, and in Germany. Along the Rhine, the god is known by the name of Jupiter Taranucnus. There are traces of a cult of Jupiter Taranucnus even in distant Dalmatia. Taranis is the lord of thunder, whose rumble is evoked by his own name, and as such has power over him among the powers of heaven. Storms and bad weather come from him. From him comes the rain, which brings fertility and abundance. The poet Lucan states that sacrifices no less ferocious than those that the Scythians give to Diana take place on the Taranis altar. His scholiasts add that the Gauls consider Taranis a god similar to Jupiter, lord of wars and maximum of the gods, but also similar to Dis Pater, god of darkness and death. When Taranis has the appearance of Jupiter, he is appeased by the sacrifice of human lives to him in bloody rites. When he looks like Dis Pater, his victims are burned alive in large wooden vats. Caesar also agreed that some Gallic peoples sacrificed numerous human victims burnt alive in large vats or wooden simulacra. However, with the Christianization of the

Gauls, these barbarian customs partially ceased and the Gauls began to replace men with animals in their sacrifices. Even today, in fact, the custom of making large bonfires remains among them, with dogs, cats, foxes, and other animals, enclosed in wooden or wicker baskets, thrown on them.

In Cisalpine Gaul, Jupiter was worshiped on the peaks at the top of the mountains. For this, he was called Poeninus, the god of the peaks. In the year 218 BC, the leader Ḥannibal, at the head of the imposing Carthaginian army, crossed the Alps and descended from Gaul to Italy, threatening the power of Rome on its own territory. The Second Punic War reached its most dramatic moment. Two centuries later, however, Roman historians were still debating which Alpine pass the Carthaginians had passed through, and there was a tendency to indicate a certain passage near Mons Poeninus (Mount Pennino). Indeed, it was thought that this mountain had taken its name from the Poeni, or the Carthaginians themselves. Titus Livius, in his historical work, refutes this argument. If Ḥannibal had taken the Poeninus pass, he would not have reached the territory of the Taurini Celts, as he later did. In reality, says Livius, the origin of the name of the mountain is different, as the Celtic tribe of Seduni Veragri, which inhabited those mountains, knew well. Indeed, they traced the name of the Pennine Alps not to the passage of the Carthaginians but to the god they worshiped on the highest peak of those mountains—a god that the Romans identified with Jupiter and Silvanus, but which they called Poeninus, the lord of the peaks.

Sometimes the Gauls refer to Jupiter with the epithet of Baginatis, god of oaks. And, in fact, the Celtic people, who still have great respect for all trees, consider the oaks to be particularly sacred. Apparently, they worship Jupiter precisely in the image of an oak. However, this is nothing new. Many peoples worship the god of thunder in oak and beech, especially when the tree is struck by lightning—the Thracians and the Germans, for example. However, the Greeks and Romans also believe that the oak is the sacred tree to Jupiter.

We do not know of any myth concerning the Gallic Jupiter. One of them, however, seems to be suggested by certain pillars and columns widespread in many places in the Celtic area: among the Lingones, the Treveri, the Arverni, and especially in the Rhine valley, but also among the Helvetii and even in Britain. At the top of a high column stands the image of a god on horseback, standing above a bearded giant with a snake or fish tail: The Anguiped lies on the ground, its face contorted with terror, crushed under the hooves of the horse. In other cases, the god is standing erect and the monster is lying at his feet. The god is armed; he often wields a javelin or a flash of lightning, but at other times he holds the wheel, and only for this reason can he be identified with Jupiter. What history, myth, or symbolism is the basis of this figure, we do not know.

Amy Hughes

Sucellus: The God with the Mallet

Progenitor of the Gauls, he was a god in which the Romans saw Dis Pater, lord of the dead and king of the underworld. This divinity may be identified in the images of the so-called "god with mallet", whose Gallic name was Sucellus.

Caesar states, in a passage of his commentaries, that the Gauls claim to be descendants of Dis Pater, the lord of the underworld, and add that this was handed down to them by the wisdom of the druids. This is also why they do not calculate time by counting days, but nights; Christmas dates and the beginning of the months and years are counted by making the day begin with the night. According to the Gauls, Dis Pater is the progenitor of humanity—the first man to be born, but also the first to die, and as such, he became the lord of the underworld. In his honor, the Gauls practice human sacrifices, burning men alive in wooden vats. The inscriptions and dedications to Dis Pater come from southern Germany and the northwestern Balkans. The god appears next to his wife Erecura, whom the Romans consider a local form of Proserpina and who has the emblems of the great mother.

When Caesar speaks of the Gallic Dis Pater, he is perhaps referring to the "god with the mallet", whom the Gauls call Sucellus, "the good hitter" or "he who strikes well". The cult of Sucellus has its center in Gallia Narbonensis, in the Rhodanus and Sauconna valley, where it is revered by the Vocontii, Allobroges, and Sequani tribes. From here, his cult goes north; Sucellus is well known and revered in Belgic Gaul and in Superior Germany. Traces of his cult can even be found in distant Britain. In the figurations that the Gauls make of this deity, Sucellus appears as a mature man, mild-looking, with a thick, curly beard and hair. He is dressed in the Gallic manner, in simple, peasant clothes: a tunic tight at the waist and sandals on his feet. In his left hand, he holds a long shaft, one end of which points to the ground, while the other, higher than the god's head, ends in a large mallet. Some have described it as a hammer or maul, but then the handle would have been shorter and sturdier. Rather, Sucellus appears to be holding it like a scepter, giving an impression of calm royalty rather than strength. On the right, the god carries a small vase similar to an *olla*, which seems to serve as a symbol of wealth and fertility. In other and different figurations, Sucellus holds a *falx* or money bag. In other figurations, widespread above all in Alesia, he appears leaning against a large vat. The goddess Nantosuelta often accompanies Sucellus, as dignified and regal as her consort. Very often, Sucellus is escorted by a small dog or, sometimes, by a crow.

The Romans identified Sucellus with Hercules, but also and above all with Silvanus, the Roman god of the woods and agriculture. With this name, the god is honored throughout the Celtic area but seems to have the center of his cult in Gallia Narbonensis. In Britain, Silvanus is equated with various local deities; along Hadrian's Wall, he is honored as the god of hunting, and his name is sometimes added to that of Sucellus. Still, in Britain, he is invoked as Silvanus Callirius, the "king of the hazelnut forest", and deer seem to be sacred to him. The Gallic Silvanus retains the typical attributes of Sucellus: a mallet higher than his head, which he holds majestically in his left hand, and the small *olla*, which he holds out with his right hand. These attributes—the mallet and the vase—also appear alone in the commemorative plaques dedicated to Silvanus. In the role of Silvanus, Sucellus has a somewhat different appearance: He wears only a short tunic of skin, perhaps of a wolf, which leaves his legs and right shoulder uncovered, and on his head is a crown of laurel leaves. Attributes of the Gallic Silvanus (besides the mallet and the vase) can be fruit trees, flutes, knives, and axes. He is sometimes depicted with a falx in his hand, indicating the domestication of the wilderness.

In Gaul, a few epithets are attributed to Silvanus, which we report here: Callirius, Cocidius, Sinquatis, Sucellus, Vinotonus, "god of wine". In particular, Callirius and Vinotonus were widespread among the Britons and Sinquatis among the Belgians.

It should be noted, however, that some of these epithets Silvanus has in common with other deities. For example, Cocidius is elsewhere an epithet of Mars.

In other places, the "god with the mallet" appears in a third, completely different aspect. He is naked, with a wolf skin draped across his back and arm. In some cases, five minor mallets seem to branch out from his mallet, in a sort of emanation and multiplication of divine power. Here, the "god with a mallet" can be identified with Pluto or Dis Pater, who, for the Romans, is the god of the dead but whom the Gauls consider the father of their race. The bride of this Gallic Pluto is Proserpina or Erecura. A three-headed dog often accompanies them.

A goddess with a majestic and regal bearing often appears next to Sucellus, dressed in a long tunic, according to Roman custom. Her name is Nantosuelta, the lady of the sunny valleys. She holds a cornucopia, or sometimes a small patera. At the Raurici, she holds a long shaft surmounted by a sort of *fanum*. The Romans identified her with Diana. When Sucellus has the appearance of Dis Pater, his companion's name is Erecura, although, of course, the Romans call her Proserpina.

Apollo: The God of Light and Water

The Romans indistinctly identified with Apollo a host of different Gallic deities, associated with light and spring waters, linked to thermal centers and able to heal from all diseases. Grannus, Borvo, and Belenus were some of them.

In second place among the five main Gallic gods, Caesar mentions Apollo, and says of him that he hunts down disease. We can imagine Caesar's perplexity in front of this Gallic Apollo—so similar to the Apollo that centuries earlier the Romans had derived from the Etruscans and then from the Greeks, yet so inextricably different. In Rome, Apollo was never a very important god; instead, the Gauls hold him in the highest regard. His cult, very ancient and rooted, is widespread in even the most peripheral areas of the Celtic area. While the Greek Apollo is known for spreading diseases and plagues with arrow shots, the Gauls see, in Apollo, a divinity linked to the brightness of the light and the transparency of the waters, a healing god with great healing abilities. The great feast of May 1st is dedicated to him; during it, the Gauls light large fires to welcome summer, but also to hunt diseases and purify livestock. Horses are sacred to Apollo, as they are animals traditionally linked to the cult of the solar chariot. However, it cannot be generalized, as Apollo became, after the Roman conquest, a generic name that covers many different yet similar divinities, generally related to thermal springs and their healing powers. Belenus, Grannus, and Borvo are just some of these gods with similar shades, identified with Apollo. An infinity of temples have been dedicated to these "Apollos" throughout Gaul, and for the most part, they are located near the springs and thermal springs. Some of these temples are very large and pilgrims from all over Gaul meet there. In these places, Apollo is worshiped with a large number of names and epithets and is often flanked by a consort goddess with whom he forms a divine couple. Pilgrims bring, to Apollo, images depicting sick body parts, for which they hope for a quick recovery: hands and feet, internal organs, breasts, and genitals. The Apollo Vindonnus of the Lingons, for example, specializes in eye care; he is presented with images of hands offering fruit and bread. In these temples is an *abaton* or dormitory, with many small cubicles in which pilgrims retire to sleep, hoping that the god appears to them in a dream to heal them. Skilled doctors and priests are consecrated to the god.

Many different Gallic deities, especially if related to light and thermal waters, were identified with the classical god Apollo—so much so that today it is not easy, in analyzing the many epithets to which Apollo has been referred in Gallic countries, to distinguish which of these hide the names of small local deities later identified with the Greek-Roman god, or which of them were actually epithets of the great Apollo Celtic of which Caesar spoke.

Grannus is a god linked to the sun and the thermal springs, to which great healing powers are attributed. Identified with Apollo, he is worshiped in the vast region between the Seine and the Rhine, especially by the Lingoni and Treveri tribes, and then even farther north, in the upper course of the Rhine. Among the various centers dedicated to him is the thermal town of Aachen, which later became the capital of the kingdom of the Franks. However, his cult also extends to other regions: to the northwest, toward Armorica and then to Britain, and to the southeast, along the course of the Danube, up to Szőny in Hungary. Grannus' bond with the sun is very strong. The Treveri call him Phœbus and in figures, they put him at the helm of the solar chariot. Grannus is well known as a healing god and his fame has extended far beyond the Celtic world. In his temples and shrines, pilgrims can purify themselves in sacred waters; after making offerings and praying to the god, they enter the dormitories, hoping that the god will appear to them in sleep. At his peak of popularity, Grannus was worshiped even in Rome. In 215, the emperor Caracalla, who fell ill, visited the temples of the Gallic god Grannus, the Greco-Roman god Asclepius, and the Egyptian god Serapis, hoping to recover from his illness. However, despite all his efforts, he did not get what he hoped for. The wife of Grannus is Sirona, the goddess of the stars. Generally represented with fruit or spikes in hand, but also with a crescent on the forehead, or holding a snake symbol of regeneration on the arm, she is closely associated with Grannus. Her cult has its center between the Rhine and the Upper Moselle.

Another god identified with Apollo and linked to the thermal waters is Borvo, the boiling one. His name is linked to ancient thermal towns, as well as to many waterways. It is especially worshiped in central Gaul, in a band that includes the tribes of the Arverni, the

Aedui, the Lingoni, and the Treveri. *Paredra* (the one who sits behind) of Borvo is the goddess Ritona, the goddess of fords and waterways, who is especially adored by the Treveri. However, the Lingons attribute, as his wife, the goddess Damona, who elsewhere is associated with Apollo Moritasgus or Albius. Elsewhere, the god and his paredra are called Bormanus and Bormana.

Many of the Gallic deities identified with Apollo, gods of light and thermal waters, are closely associated in worship and myth with a goddess. We have seen that Grannus's bride is Sirona, the goddess of the stars and rebirth, with ears in her hand and a crescent on her forehead. Borvo's bride is Ritona, the goddess of the fords honored by the Treveri. However, in the territory of the Lingoni in Borvo, an important healing goddess is associated: Damona. Damona's name means "divine cow", perhaps regarding her character as the goddess of fertility. In Alesia city, she is paired with Apollo Moritasgus. Here, a temple is dedicated to both. Damona is represented there in a stone image; she has spikes on her head and holds a coiled snake in one hand, which perhaps symbolizes rebirth. As the snake sheds its skin and becomes young again, so the pilgrim hopes to recover from his illnesses and return to health. In one of the Damona sanctuaries in this region, there is an incubation room; here, the sick spend the night hoping that the goddess will visit them in a dream and heal them. Also in the territory of the Lingons, Damona is mated with the god Albius, the "White", also a transparent local form of Apollo. Here, there is a votive pit where pilgrims throw ex-votos and other objects in honor of the goddess, especially small statuettes that represent her.

Belenus, the Shining One, is the god of light, assimilated by the Romans to Apollo. He is a young and radiant god. His cult seems to originate in a not-very-large area whose center is around the Eastern Alps. It seems that the Norics adore him as a god of their province; one of his centers of worship is Aquileia. From here, the cult of Belenus extends southward on the east coast of Cisalpine Gaul. Other ramifications lead instead to southern Gaul, where he is venerated in Nemausius (Nîmes) and Narbonne. One of his temples seems to be in Burdigala (Bordeaux). In Tivoli, the emperor Hadrian could not ask for anything better than to enhance the beauty of his favorite Antinous by comparing it to the splendor of Belenus. Cunobeline, leader of the Trinovanti, seems to have been particularly devoted to him. This is revealed by his very name: "dog of Belenus". It was he who minted coins bearing the image of the god on the front, surrounded by a crown of flaming rays to represent the splendor of the sun, while on the reverse appears the figure of a boar. The Celtic festival of May 1st is dedicated to Belenus.

Maponos, the Divine Son, is a god of the Celts of Britain, especially worshiped by the Brigantes tribe. The god is known, among other things, for his skill in the art of music. Hence, he has been identified with Apollo citharode. The cult of this Divine Son should perhaps be combined with that of a Divine Mother, called Matrona. In fact, the Celts say that the goddess Latona, mother of Apollo, was born on an island opposite Gaul, and therefore in Britain. And indeed, in Britain, near the city of Verolam (St. Albans in Herefordshire) stands a large and famous circular temple, the *Fanum Maponi*, which the Celts consecrated to the radiant Divine Son.

CAP 3:

ÉRIU, THE EMERALD ISLE

The Names of Ériu: Give the Land a Name

The first and absolute protagonist of the Irish myth is Ériu, the Emerald Isle, with its plains and lakes, hills, and rivers. Ireland, with its five provinces and its proud people, its furious heroes and its melancholy poets.

Throughout its history, Ériu, the Emerald Isle, has had a large number of names. The first name was *Inis na Fidbagh*, "Island of the Woods", and was given to her by Adna mac Bith, because, when he arrived there, he found the island covered by only one immense wood, except through the bare plain of *Mág nElta*. Three times, indeed, Ériu covered herself with woods, and three times she undressed completely. The second name was *Crioh na Fuinedah*, the "Land of Remote Limits", because Ériu stood out in front of the ocean, at the ends of the world. The third name was *Inis Elga*, "Noble Island". Thus, Ériu was called in the time of the Fir Bolg and during the dominion of the Túatha Dé Dánann. The next name was *Inis Fáil*, "Island of Fál", and it was the Túatha Dé Dánann who gave Ériu this name. It derived from the Lía Fáil, the stone that uttered a cry when the legitimate supreme king of Ériu stepped on it. However, that stone has cried no more since the time of Conchobar mac Nessa, as the false idols of the world were silenced when Christ was born. *Ériu, Banba,* and *Fódla* were the three names that gave her the Clann Míled, in honor of the queens of the Túatha Dé Dánann. In fact, they were called Ériu, Banba, and Fódla, the wives of the three supreme kings who, at that time, shared the sovereignty on the island, each reigning, in turn, for a year. Because it was the husband of Ériu who reigned the year when the Clann Míled arrived, it was the name of Ériu that prevailed over the other two. (Others, however, say that this name came from Aeria, the ancient name by which the island now called Crete or Candia was known, as it was in that land that the people of Gaedal Glas stopped for some time after fleeing Egypt.) The next two names of Ériu were *Inis Ceoí* and *Muic Inis*, that is, "Island of the Mists" and "Island of Pigs". These names were also given by the Clann Míled when, in their attempt to land in Ériu, they saw a misty island in the shape of a pig's back, due to the spells that the druids of the Túatha Dé Dánann had cast on them to prevent them from landing. The Greeks called it *Ogygia*, as Plutarch testifies. Indeed, this name means the "most ancient island", a very appropriate title given that Ériu was inhabited since the time of the universal flood. The Romans called it *Hibernia*, a name that, in classical sources, appears in several lessons, although none of the ancient authors ever understood the origin and meaning of this name. Though its etymology has little foundation, Cormac mac Culennáin states that it came from a Greek root meaning "western island". Others say that the island had this name because the Gaels descended from the Clann Míled, who had come from Iberia. *Inis Naom*, "Island of the Saints", was called Ériu after the arrival of Pátraic and his conversion. And, indeed, there was no other place, besides Ériu, where faith in Christ was felt more deeply and sweetly. During the Middle Ages, it was called *Scotia*, from the name of Scota, daughter of the pharaoh Nectonibus and ancestor of the Clann Míled, and the Scoti were also called its inhabitants. *Irland*, "land of the Iri", from the name of Ír, the first of the Clann Míled to die and be buried in Ériu, was the Germanic name that the Lochlannaig (the Vikings) spread at the end of the eighth century. With this name, Ériu was later known by the Sasanaig (the English), who occupied and held it long and hard. Today, after having suffered and struggled for a long time, and finally having conquered its independence, the island has returned to its old name: *Poblacht na hÉireann*, "Republic of Ireland". And Ériu will call her too.

The Circle of Time: From Darkness to Light

The calculation of time, among the Gaels, reflected very ancient conceptions that nights preceded days and winters preceded summers. The result is a metaphysical idea of time that progresses incessantly from the darkness of death to the light of life.

   1. *From Darkness to Light*

As Caesar already testified in his commentaries, the Gauls claimed to descend from Dis Pater, the lord of the underworld, as had been handed down by the wisdom of the druids. Their world was therefore something that proceeded from below to above, from darkness to light, from the cold of death to the warmth of life. The Gallic calendar centered on this dichotomy, dividing the days, months, and years into two halves, one of which was characterized by darkness, torpid latency, and the absence of life, and the other by light, movement, heat, and the presence of life. For this reason, the Celts measured time starting from the dark and then moving up toward the light. The days began at sunset, and therefore the night preceded the day. Christmas dates and the beginnings of the months and years were counted, making the day always start from the night. This is why the celebration of the holidays began at sunset of the previous day. Similarly, the years began in winter. The Celtic New Year was celebrated in November when the world plunged into winter darkness. The year died during the dark and cold months before being reborn in May, maturing in the long and hot summer semester and still dying in the winter. The Celtic idea of time was an eternal and repeated sequence of death and rebirth, a continuous evolution from darkness to light. Thus, the life of man on this earth was the continuation of a dark pre-existence. As they descended from Dis Pater, the Celts originated from the underworld. Death preceded life. Human existence followed a cycle no different from that of the day or year. It began in the dark season of death and continued in the bright season of life: infancy, youth, maturity, old age. The moment of passing was a sort of sunset; the long night of death would be followed by the rising of a new morning.

2. Night and Day

Of the many cycles of time, what immediately marks the experience of man is the alternation of night and day, of darkness and light. For the Celts, sunset and sunrise were, like all moments of transition, delicate passages in which not only light and darkness, but also sun and stars, were replacing each other. Day and night, rather than periods of time, were two "worlds" that continually faded into one another. It is said that when Aengus asked his father, the Dagda Mór, to borrow his home in Bru na Bóinne for "a day and a night", he then refused to give it back. Lending it to him for a day and a night, in fact, the Dagda Mór had granted it to him forever, because, as Aengus observed, "the world is consumed in a day and a night". Time is therefore made up of a diurnal world and a nocturnal world that are constantly replacing each other. Thus, while the day belongs to men, the night belongs to the beings of the "other world". Men should return to their homes after sunset; those who linger in the night away from home risk disturbing the supernatural people. It is good not to stay up late because our night is their day. During the darkest hours, the dead silently approach the houses and wish to find peace and quiet there; the way to show them respect is to retire early, leaving the house clean and the chairs lined up around the hearth, where the hot embers rest under the ashes. When dawn comes to dispel the darkness, the crowing of the cock sends the spirits and supernatural creatures back to their homes. The day begins with sunset and the night hours precede the hours of light. Night and day are two opposing realities: the supernatural and the natural that eternally swap places, with the silence and stillness of darkness preceding the brisk daytime activities of mortals. Just as a tree rises from a small seed stuck in the earth for a long time, so, too, from the world of the dead is the living born, while in the night the day ripens.

3. Seasonal Holidays

The year was a kind of wheel that turned incessantly, spending six months in the depths of winter (*giamos*) and six months in the light of summer (*samos*). Only these two seasons formed the ancient Gaelic year, which was marked by four important holidays that fell 45 days after the two equinoxes and the two solstices. In Ériu, these recurrences were called:

November 1: Samhain

February 1: Imbolc

May 1: Beltane

August 1: Lughnasadh

Samhain and Beltane were the two most important parties because they were the transition points between one and the other season. Samhain marked the beginning of the long winter, the time when the year died, sinking into frost and darkness; Beltane marked the end of winter, the time when the year was reborn, rising to new life, ascending toward the light and warmth of summer. Imbolc and Lughnasadh were, instead, the culmination of the two seasons. In particular, Imbolc marked the deepest, darkest, and most mysterious point of winter, but it was the moment when the long descent into darkness stopped and the slow ascent toward life began. Lughnasadh, on the other hand, marked the height of summer, the moment when the year had reached the peak of maturity, before it entered its waning phase. Of course, the Gaels also knew spring (*earrach*) and autumn (*fómhar*), but these were considered only transitional periods between one season and the other.

4. The Wheel of the Year

The year began the moment it died, in Samhain. It was the end of summer and the beginning of the long winter, when the days got shorter and the world was sinking into darkness. The beasts were led down from the summer pastures, rounded up and locked up in the stables to winter; the excess animals were slaughtered, as they could not be kept alive during the difficult cold months. Men retreated to homes, doing small jobs and telling each other stories in the firelight. Military expeditions were closed; actions of war and raids were suspended. The proud *fianna* left their lives in the woods and jungles of Ériu and returned to settle down with the sedentary population. At one point, Imbolc arrived, the mid-winter party. This was the time when the long six months of winter came to a head. Yet, in this dark period, the lambs were born and the sheep began to give milk. This time was dedicated to the goddess Brigid, who was celebrated by the lighting of virgin candles and small flames, which glowed in the dark, as if to announce the hope of a new spring. The seeds were blessed and the plows and agricultural tools were consecrated, which would soon be used once again. After reaching its deepest point, winter began to rise toward the light. Women and men came out of their houses to spy, in the snow-white fields, for the first signs of summer. Beltane marked the rebirth, the resurrection, the beginning of summer. The trees had put forth leaves, flowers covered the moors, and the sky was full of wings and songs. The end of the long winter isolation was celebrated with unbridled joy, and wreathed young men and maidens danced around the poles of May while the fires of Beltane lit up the countryside. The animals were purified after their long confinement in the stables by being forced to pass through the fires. Then they were carried up to the summer pastures. With the onset of summer, the warriors gathered under their rulers and resumed their raids and battles. The fíanna left their winter quarters and returned to their wooded existence, where they lived hunting and fishing all summer. At the height of summer, the Lughnasadh, the festival dedicated to the god Lug, arrived. The worries about the hay harvest were over and the prospect of the wheat harvest loomed. Large fairs were held, with games and sports competitions. The most important took place in *Óenach Tailten* in the Ulaid. The party started two weeks before the Lughnasadh and ended two weeks later. Athletics competitions were held in *Óenach Tailten*, during which it was possible to show the speed of the horses and show the athletes' skills in archery, throwing the spear, swimming, and wrestling. In the evening, the bards, the storytellers, the poets, and the musicians entertained the people with their skill. Lughnasadh was also the time when weddings were celebrated, as young people were the first to perform. There were love marriages and arranged marriages in which, depending on the condition of the boy or girl, the interest of the c*lanna* was at stake. However, it was probationary marriages that took place in Lughnasadh. Placing their hands in a perforated stone, the young couple committed themselves to living together for a year and a day. If children had come, they would have been born in Beltane at the beginning of the summer, when the warmest months would be ahead of them. If the couple decided to split up, at the next Lughnasadh the man and the woman would return to the fair site, put themselves back to back, and go in opposite directions. Lughnasadh was also the moment when, having reached its maximum splendor, summer entered its waning phase: The golden colors of autumn followed to mark the decline of summer. When the days had visibly shortened, with the bad weather and the bitter cold of autumn, Samhain arrived again: the anniversary that celebrated the end of summer, the death of the year. The Ard Ríg, the supreme king of Ériu, announced the Feis of Tara: a solemn assembly lasting seven days (three before and three after Samhain), in which all the princes and warriors subjected to him participated. In the banquet hall, each profession had its predetermined place; members of the aristocracy, warriors, and champions put away their weapons in light of the long winter; poets recited songs and ancient sagas. Thus, the supreme king recognized the role and prerogatives of each, and the subjects recognized the supremacy of the king. Samhain was the New Year celebration, the last and first holiday of the year. The druids tried to light a new sacred fire, whose flames were carried in all the houses. Yet, if Samhain was a delicate period, the night vigil was even more so. It was the moment of transition between light and darkness, life and death, and, as such, it belonged not to time but to eternity. Everything that happened on Samhain's night took on a profound meaning. The great epochal moments of the Irish myth, the magical encounters, the solemn battles, the loves, and the metamorphoses, took place in Samhain. On this day, the boundaries between our world and the other one disappeared; the doors of the *síde* were opened, supernatural beings came into our world, and men fell into the afterlife without realizing it. Few left the house on Samhain's night. There was always the risk of running into supernatural beings, the ranks of the people of the dead. People left small offerings on the doorsteps of the houses to satiate the spirits; they avoided putting bars on the doors so that the souls of the dead could return to their homes, and the benches lined up around the hearth were left for them. However, Samhain was also a moment of unbridled disorder; the young people themselves masked themselves as ghosts, whitening or blackening their faces and wearing veils or covering themselves with straw. At dusk, they went around the villages. combining jokes and pranks, opening the stables, blowing smoke in the crevices of the houses, and bombarding the houses with vegetables plucked from the gardens. On Samhain's night, space and time vanished and the social order was suspended. Then time began to flow again and everything returned to the way it had been before. The long winter began again...

Amy Hughes

The Invasions of Ériu: The Peoples Who Came from the Sea

The history of Ériu is marked by the invasions of six populations that, over time, came to occupy, populate, and dispute the Emerald Isle, at the same time defining its territory and the basis of civil life.

1. The Gaels in Ériu, and Those Previous to Them

According to the tradition handed down by the Irish bards and genealogists, the Gael people who now populate Ériu would descend from the invasion led by the sons of Míl Espáine, who landed there with their fleet about 3,700 years ago, coming from Hispania. Tradition still says that the sons of Míl—or *Milesians*—were the last of a series of peoples who, in even more remote antiquity, came from the sea to invade Ériu. Indeed, most Irish chroniclers agree in speaking of five invasions that, from times which can be traced back almost to the flood, would have occurred on Ériu's soil. Tradition reports their names: the People of Partholon, the Nemedians, the Fir Bolg, the Túatha Dé Danann, and the Milesians. One after the other, each of these peoples came to occupy the Noble Island and then disappeared to make way for the following peoples. Each of these peoples contributed to defining the territory, society, and customs of Ériu. Other chroniclers say that before these five invasions, indeed, even before the flood, there was an even older invasion, that of the People of Cessair, who, however, would not have left any trace on Ériu's soil.

2. The Invasions of Ériu, According to the Britanians

The first to pass on the tradition of the Ériu invasions was not an Irish historian, but a British one, Nennius. He writes—in good Latin—that the Scots arrived in *Hibernia* at a time following the invasion of Britain by the Picts. A certain Partholon arrived first, at the head of 1,000 men and women, who grew to become four thousand. However, an epidemic hit them and they all died in a week, with no one escaping. Later, a certain Nemed, son of Agnoman, arrived, who is said to have sailed for a year and a half. With the ships now failing, he docked in Hibernia and remained there for many years before returning to Hispania. Then came the three sons of a Míl Espáine with 30 ships, each of which contained 30 men with their wives, and they remained there for only one year. They saw a glass tower in the middle of the sea, on which men could be seen, but when they tried to call them, no one answered. So, they prepared an assault on the tower with all their ships, except one that was damaged in a shipwreck. However, when they landed on the beach, ready to storm the tower and take it, the sea rose all around the island and submerged them. Nobody was saved. The crew of the damaged ship, who had not been able to take part in the assault, got stuck in Hibernia, and it is those people who populated the island to this day. Then Damhoctor arrived in Britain and his offspring reside there to this day. Istoreth, son of Istorine, took possession of Dál Riata with his people. Builc and his men took the island called Eubonia (the Isle of Man) and the neighboring islands. Liethan's sons had possessions in the Demetii region and other areas, including Caer Cydweli, until they were driven out of Britain by Cunedda and her sons. If anyone wanted to know how long Hibernia remained uninhabited and deserted (this was reported to Nennius by competent scholars of the people of the Scots), it is necessary to start from the day when the Israelites crossed the Red Sea and the Egyptians who pursued them were submerged, as in the Holy Scriptures. There was, among the Egyptians, a noble from Scythia with his large family. Having been expelled from his kingdom, he was at that time with the Egyptians. In the Red Sea disaster, the most talented Egyptians died, but he survived. Thus, the surviving Egyptians gathered in council and expelled him from the country along with his family, fearing that he might take advantage of their weakness and take power. For 42 years, he wandered through Africa and came across the Salt Lake to the altars of the Philistines. Then he wandered between Rusicada and the mountains of Azaria. Along the Malva River, he passed through Mauritania to the columns of Hercules, sailed across the Tyrrhenian Sea, and reached Hispania. There he lived with his people for many years. His lineage grew and multiplied. And so it was that, much later, his descendants arrived in Hibernia, 1,002 years after the Egyptians had been submerged by the Red Sea.

3. *The Invasions of Ériu, According to the Scots*

The Irish chroniclers provide a version of the tale of Ériu's invasions that is substantially similar in many places to that recalled by Nennius, but that, in others, differs significantly from it. According to the Irish, the first invasion touched Ériu even in antediluvian times. It was, in fact, 40 days before the flood that Cessair and his companions landed in Ériu. Cessair was the daughter of Bith, the fourth son of Noah; she and her companions had not been able to take their places on the Ark and had set out to sea by their own means, trying to escape the flood. The people of Cessair were badly balanced in sex (50 women and only three men: Bith, Ladra, and Fintan) and disappeared, overwhelmed by the cataclysm. They left no trace of their arrival, if not the memory of their existence, handed down by Fintan mac Bóchra, who became immortal. After the flood, for about 300 years, Ériu remained deserted until a group of people arrived, led by Partholon. He was the son of Sera, son of Srú, son of Esrú, son of Braiment, son of Aithecht, son of Magog, son of Iapheth, son of Noah, and had fled from his homeland, Mygdonia, the Scythia, as guilty of the murder of his own father and king. The People of Partholon were farmers. First, they worked the land of Ériu; they introduced trades in what they called the Island of Far Limits. They built buildings, millstones, and churns. Upon their arrival, Ériu was bare and empty; there was only the one barren plain of Mag Elta, leveled by the very hands of God, and only three lakes and 10 rivers. However, at the time of Partholon, four more plains were cleared and seven lakes arose that were not there before. The People of Partholon fought a battle against the Fomorians (*Fomóraig*), a people of deformed giants from the sea. They were finally exterminated by a plague, but the memory of their deeds was handed down by Tuán mac Cairill, who became immortal. For a long time, Ériu remained uninhabited until Nemed arrived there with his people, also from Scythia. Nemed was the son of Agnoman, son of Piamp, son of Tait, and the latter was the brother of Partholon. He therefore belonged to the same lineage as Partholon but, unlike the latter, who had fled his country for a crime, Nemed was a free man. His descendants, the Nemedians, cleared 12 more plains and built two royal fortresses. They, too, fought a series of battles against the Fomorians and won them but were then subdued and enslaved. Eventually, they rebelled and stormed the enemy stronghold, *Tor Conainn*, which stood on an island not far from the coast of Ériu. The two groups engaged in a terrible naval battle, in the course of which an immense wave arose that destroyed both fleets. Reduced to a few, sparse survivors, Nemedians split into various groups and left Ériu. A group of them returned to their homeland, where they were enslaved again, and remained so for several generations. After a long time, their descendants decided to flee and return to Ériu. Their leaders—Slaine, Rudraige, Gann, Genann, and Sengann—were the five sons of Dela mac Lóich, the descendant of Nemed. This new wave of settlers was divided into three groups who landed in Ériu at different times: the Fir Domnann, the Gaileoin, and the Fir Bolg. It is from the name of the latter that everyone is called Fir Bolg. They divided the island into five provinces and gave it a military and political organization. Among other things, they introduced the institution of kingship; the kings of the Fir Bolg were the first rulers to reign over Ériu. From the northern islands of the world came the Túatha Dé Danann, the "tribes of the gods of Danann", a lineage of druids and warriors endowed with supernatural powers. Their common ancestor was Tat, a descendant of Nemed. Their king, at the time they came to Ériu, was Núada mac Echtaich. The Fir Bolg and Túatha Dé Danann boasted a common ancestry and spoke the same language, yet they fought each other in a bloody battle, in which the Fir Bolg were defeated and the Túatha Dé Danann took over Ériu. During their stay on the Noble Isle, however, the Túatha Dé Danann also had to clash with the Fomorians and managed to defeat them in a second epic battle. Lastly, the Milesians came to Ériu from Hispania. Their leaders were the five sons of Míl Espáine, the Hispanic soldier, whose ancestry went back to Goidel Glas, son of Nel, son of Fenius Farsaid, son of Baath, son of Ibáth; some say he was the son of Gomer, son of Iapheth, son of Noah, while others say he was the son of Magog, son of Iapheth, son of Noah. Fenius Farsaid had been the one who created the Gaelic language by drawing it out of the 72 languages that had formed from the confusion of Tuir Nebróid (the tower of Babel); his son Nél had emigrated to Egypt, where he had married Scota, daughter of the *Forainn*. Accused of having taken the side of the Israelites, who had fled from Egypt while the Forainn army had perished in the waters of the Red Sea, Nél had left the Egypt with his son Goídel Glas and returned to his native Scythía. His descendants, after a long pilgrimage, had settled in Hispania. It would have been from Hispania that the sons of Míl Espáine went to sea with their fleet and invaded Ériu. After a series of battles, fought with the forces of weapons and magic, they defeated the Túatha Dé Danann and drove them into Ériu's underground. The Milesians took over the island, and their descendants, the Gaels, still hold it.

4. Chronology

Irish annalists are very precise with dates, although several calculations differ from each other. This is the calculation of the *Annála Ríoghachta Éireann* (Annals of the Kingdom of Ireland).

Anno Mundi 2242 (2956 BC). The flood, the scriptures say, flooded the whole earth in the year of the world. Forty days before the flood, Cessair and his companions landed in Ériu.

Anno Mundi 2520 (2678 BC). From the flood until Partholon took possession of Ériu, 278 years passed. For 300 years, the People of Partholon lived in Ériu, then all died from an epidemic. It was the year of the world 2820 (2378 BC). After that, Ériu remained uninhabited for 30 years.

Anno Mundi 2850 (2348 BC). Nemed came to Ériu with his men. The Nemedians remained on the island for 216 years, until the destruction of Tor Conainn, then abandoned it. It was the year of the world 3066. Ériu remained uninhabited for 416 years.

Anno Mundi 3266 (1932 BC). The Fir Bolg came to impose kingship on Ériu.

Anno Mundi 3304 (1895 BC). The Túatha Dé Danann came to wrest the kingship over Ériu from the Fir Bolg.

Anno Mundi 3500 (1698 BC). The Milesians came last from Hispania to wrest the royalty from the Túatha Dé Danann.

5. Fomorians

We cannot speak of the peoples who colonized Ériu without speaking of the race that fought with them for dominion on the island and fought them in terrible wars, the Fomorians. While the other bloodlines of Ériu descended from Iapheth, son of Noah, the Fomorians descended from Ham. They were originally from Africa, from which they had departed aboard a fleet that they had built themselves, for the sole purpose of separating from the lineage of Ham, cursed by Noah, for fear of being subjugated by the lineage of Shem. After a long voyage, the Fomorians arrived in Ériu. Cichol Gricenchos was called the leader who led them to the new land. When the People of Partholon landed there, the Fomorians had already been on the island for 200 years; they lived by hunting birds and fishing. Among them, women were more numerous than men and all had one arm and one leg. In the battle they fought with the People of Partholon, and that was fought with magical arts, not a single man died. When Nemed came to Ériu, the Fomorians, who at that time inhabited the surrounding islands, were much more aggressive and menacing. They were first enslaved by the Nemedians, then later rebelled and subjugated the newcomers in their turn. Their leader, Conand mac Febair, resided in the fortress of Tor Conainn, on an island not far from the coast. From there, he controlled the whole of Ériu. When the sons of Nemed rebelled, as we have said, they fought a battle with them so terrible and bloody that both races were nearly exterminated. The Nemedians was unable to rise again and preferred to abandon Ériu to the Fomorians. These remained undisputed masters of the territory until the Fir Bolg arrived, although no battles between the two peoples are recorded. In this period, the Fomorians controlled a vast territory that stretched from Lochlann (Norway) to Alba (Scotland) and were based on all the isles around the British Isles. The Túatha Dé Danann met the Fomorians in Lochlann and joined them to generate a mixed race. When the Túatha Dé Danann later settled in Ériu, after driving out the Fir Bolg, the Fomorians tried to place loyal men in key posts of the Danann government. Their leaders at that time were Indech mac Dé Domnann, Elatha mac Delbáeth, and Balor mac Néit. Their project failed; the Fomorians fought with the Túatha Dé Danann in the Mag Tuired plain, in a battle that remained historic in the Irish annals, at the end of which they were finally defeated and driven into the *síde* at the bottom of the sea.

The Divisions of Ériu: The Space and the Territory

Ériu was divided many times in the course of its history, but the traditional division of its territory is into five provinces, or more precisely, into five "fifths", a word that, more than any other, designates the transcendent unity of which each province is an integral and inseparable part.

1. The Airt

The ancient Irish, like many other peoples, oriented themselves by facing the direction in which the sun rises: the east. In this way, the south was on the right, where the sun is, the direction from which positive energy came. The north was on the left, a direction with negative connotations. Behind it was the west, the great ocean where the sun sinks into the night. In this way, space was marked by the polarity of the four directions. Each of the four cardinal points (*airt*) was associated with a wind, a color, a province, and an evangelist. The fifth direction was the center, the meeting point of the four poles, a privileged place of sacredness and royalty.

Oirth. It is the east, the direction from which the sun rises. Here lies the province of Laigin with its wealthy landowners. Its color is brownish yellow or a speckled brown.

Deis. It is the south, where the course of the sun turns. There is the province of Mumu, with its musicians. Its color is a bright, beautiful, and luminous white.

Tiart. It is the west, the direction in which the sun sets. There is the province of Connacht, with its druids and seers. Its color is a dull blue-green.

Tuais. It is the north, the direction of darkness. There is the province of Ulaid, with its warriors. Its color is black.

Lár. The center is the point where everything converges and is harmonized. There is the province of Meath, in whose capital of Temáir reside the Supreme Kings of Ériu. Its color is red, a symbol of royalty.

Because space is the intersection of these directions, the geographic axes of Ériu ended up defining the various provinces of the island according to their physiognomies and peculiarities. The cosmic polarities traced by the diurnal course of the sun and redesigned by the nocturnal rotation of the stars, in turn, marked a dynamism in which clockwise movement was favored, bringing beneficial influences. Conversely, the anticlockwise turn, performed in the direction opposite of the movement of the sky, caused unbridled negative influences.

2. The Earliest Partitions of Ériu

The island of Ériu was divided many times throughout its history. The first to do so were the Partolonians, who divided Ériu into four parts. After them came the Nemedians, who divided it into three. However, these two partitions did not survive. The first division was therefore made at the time of the Partolonians. It was Partholon himself who divided Ériu between his four children, who had the names Er, Orba, Fearon, and Feargna. To Er, he gave the first part, the whole territory between *Ailech Néit* in the north of Ulaid to *Áth Cliath* in Laigin. He gave to Orba the second part, the territory between *Áth Cliath* to *Oilén Árda Neimed*. To Faeron, he gave the third part, from *Oilén Árda Neimed* to *Áth Cliath Medruide* in Gallway (*Gaillim*). Finally, he gave to Feargna the fourth part, from *Medruide* to *Ailech Néit*. The second division was carried out in the times of the Nemedians. Three chiefs, among the sons of Nemed divided Ériu into three parts. Their names were Beothach, Semon Brecc, and Britán Mael. Beothach took the territory from Tór Inis to the Boyne River for himself. Semon took the part from the Boyne River at Belach Chonglais near Cork (*Corcaigh*). Finally, Britán Mael took everything from Belach Chonglais to Tór Inis.

3. The "Five Fifths" of Ériu

The most important and lasting division that was ever made of Ériu, this time into five parts, was carried out in the time of the Fir Bolg. It was the five sons of Dela, who led the three tribes of the Fir Bolg in Ériu, who divided the island into five parts so that each would have a "fifth". In his book about this division, Gerald of

Wales writes: "*In quinque enim portiones fere æquales antiquitus hæc regio divisa fuit; videlicet, in Momoniam duplicem, Lageniam, Ultoniam, et Conaciam.*" "In ancient times this country was divided into five parts, which were the double Mumu, the Laigin, the Ulaid and the Connacht." These are the five chiefs of the Fir Bolg who became the chiefs of the five provinces: Slaine, Sengann, Gann, Genann, and Rudraige. Slaine took the "fifth" of Laigin for himself, Gann took the "fifth" of the eastern Mumu, Sengann had for himself the "fifth" of the western Mumu, Genann had the "fifth" of Connacht, and Rudraige got the "fifth" of the Ulaid.

4. Five Times Five

Other and further divisions were made over time, although mostly based on that in fifths made by the Fir Bolg. The five "fifths" of Ériu were, in fact, divided into five parts each by King Ugaine Mór (627-588 BC), who further divided the territory of Ériu into 25 parts, dividing them among his 25 sons. In this way, each of the five provinces ideally became a small replica of the whole country, complete in itself as well as part of a larger whole.

5. The Creation of the Center

The division of Ériu implemented by the Fir Bolg, which lasted in various forms for many centuries, was not very clear, not only because the four cardinal points corresponded to five "fifths" of the island but also because, while the provincial kings had vast territories, corresponding to the four provinces (Ulaid, Connacht, Mumu, and Laigin), the supreme king of Ériu, who resided in the palace of

Temáir, somehow lacked a comparable land. In 56 AD, in the course of a revolt of the Irish tribes, Fíachu Finnfolaid, supreme king of Temáir (56 AD), fell. Its downfall was caused by the four provincial kings of Ulaid, Connacht, Mumu, and Laigin. After 20 years of anarchy, the legitimate dynasty was restored in the person of the slain king's son, Túathal Techtmar mac Fiachach, who defeated the rebel tribes in each of the four provinces and, in turn, assumed supreme kingship. He again established the borders of the four provinces and associated with them a fifth province, central to the other four: the Meath, which he created by removing parts of the territory from the other four provinces. Before that, the Meath had been only a minor kingdom around Uisnech Meath, but since then it has become the heart of Ériu, the seat of supreme royalty, the territory of the palace of Temáir, seat of the supreme kings of Ériu.

6. *The Tradition of Borders*

It is also said that, sometime later, when Diarmait mac Cerbaill reigned (545-565 AD), the nobles of Ériu rose again due to the extension of the royal domain, so that the king summoned the wise Fintan mac Bóchra to Temáir to judge the matter. Fintan's authority on historical and genealogical matters was justified by the fact that he had arrived in Ériu before the Great Flood and, made immortal by divine work, had witnessed all the invasions that had occurred since then on Irish soil. Fintan came from his home in Mumu. Taking his place in the Temáir judge's seat, he went over the story of Ériu da Cessair to the Milesians and told of a strange character called Trefuilngit Tre-eochair, who had suddenly appeared at a gathering of Ériu's men on the day Christ was crucified. This giant, blonde stranger seemed to control the rising of the sun and moon. He held stone tablets in his left hand, a branch with three fruits—nuts, apples, and acorns—in his right hand. He had inquired about the ancient chronicles of Ériu, but the men had replied that they had no historical accounts.

"Then I'll give them to you!" said Trefuilngit. "I will establish for you the progression of the stories and the chronicles of the house of Temáir with all the men of Ériu; for I am the wise witness who explains to all things unknown." And he continued: "Bring me seven men from each of the four provinces, who are the wisest, the most prudent and the most crafty, and the king's own archivists who are in the house of Temáir; because it is right that all the provinces are present at the partition of Temáir and its chronicles, so that each can have the part due to it." When Ériu's men had gathered around Trefuilngit, and Fintan mac Bóchra was among them, Trefuilngit had asked him, "Oh Fintan, how was the division of Ériu done, how were things arranged?" "Easy to say," Fintan replied. "Knowledge in the west, war in the north, prosperity in the east, music in the south, and royal sovereignty in the center."

In approving the answer, Trefuilngit had detailed the attributes of each quarter and center. Ériu had therefore been divided into four parts plus one. The four parts belonged to the provincial kings, the center to the supreme king. Upon leaving Ériu's men, Trefuilngit had given Fintan some berries from his branch. Fintan had then planted them where he thought they had grown and five trees originated from them: the Tortu Ash, the Ross Trunk, the Mugna Oak, the Dathi Branch, and the Uisnech Ash.

After finishing his tale, Fintan mac Bóchra went to Uisnech Meath, the central hill of Ériu, and all the nobles went with him. He erected a stone pillar with five protruding reliefs and assigned a relief to each of the five provinces of Ériu, judging it right to derive the five provinces from Meath, as here were Uisnech and Temáir, which were for Ériu like the two kidneys of an animal. However, he added that it was just as right to derive them in turn from each of the other provinces of Ériu.

7. Half of the Chief and Half of the Servant

Without prejudice to Ériu's division into five "fifths", there is also a second division, known throughout Irish literature, in which Ériu is divided into two parts, of which the northern half is known as *Leath Cuinn* and the southern half as *Leath Moga*. This division originated in the time of the Milesians from a dispute that arose between two of Míl's sons, Éremón and Éber, regarding the royal power. Their brother Amergin, who was a poet and judge, declared that the chief's inheritance should go to Éremón, who, after Donn's death, was the eldest among them. However, because Éber still insisted on a partition between them, Ériu was divided along the *Esker Riada*, a broken chain of hills running from east to west, separating the northern half of the country from the southern one. Éber took the southern half, and six clan chiefs went with him. Seven chieftains went instead with Éremón, who took the northern half along with the supreme royalty. Before separating, the two brothers also split a poet and a harpist. The poet, a learned man of great power, went with Éremón to the north, to whom he ensured from then on dignity and wisdom. The harpist went with Éber to the south, giving the southern part of Ériu the sweetness of music. Thus, the division of Ériu into halves conferred different attributes on the north and south of the island, and so it will be until the day of judgment.

But then a new dispute arose between the two brothers regarding three mountain ranges, as the north had two and the south only one. Dissatisfied, Éber rebelled but was killed, so that the whole of Ériu returned to Éremón's hands. The feud was perpetuated over the centuries, between the descendants of the two brothers. There were still reasons for friction at the time when the kings Cermna Finn and Sobairce jointly ruled over Ériu (1526-1487 BC), as they replicated once again the ancient division between Éremón and Éber. The country was once again divided from east to west, along a line from Inber Colptha to Luimnech in the Mumu. Sobairce took the northern half, where he built a fortress called Dún Sobairce. Cermna Finn took the southern half and, near the south coast of Ériu, built the fortress called Dún Cermna. Upon their death, however, the entire island returned to one king. Many years later, the ancient Milesian division into two parts was again implemented. When this happened, Conn Cétchathach (123-157), also called Conn of the Hundred Battles, reigned in the northern half, while in the south reigned Éogan Mug Núadat, the ancestor of the Eoganachta, the future lords of the Múmu. The latter had conquered the southern kingdom for himself by setting aside food for an impending famine.

It was from them that the two parts took the names Leth Cuinn and Leth Moga, the "half of Conn" and the "half of Moga". However, because "conn" means "chief" and "mug" means "servant", the two

87

halves of Ériu—Leth Cuinn and Leth Moga—were also understood as the "half of the chief" and the "half of the servant".

8. A Hierarchy of Provinces

The division of Ériu into its five provinces, or "fifths", was therefore not only the geometric projection on the Irish territory of the spatial directions, with the central province as the meeting place of the cardinal points. The distinction between Ulaid in the north and Mumu in the south, between Laigin in the east and Connacht in the west, and with, in the midst of these four provinces, the Meath, was also a distinction of quality, as each of the provinces had its own character and attributes; it excelled in some things and in some other things was scarce.

The north-south axis was not only that which led from the "half of the chief" (Leth Cuinn) to the "half of the servant" (Leth Moga), but also the confrontation between poetry and music, between wisdom and art, between war and prosperity.

However, the division of qualities between the five provinces was even more precise, as Fintan mac Bóchra had asserted when he said, "Knowledge in the west, war in the north, prosperity in the east, music in the south, and royal sovereignty in the center." Trefuilngit Tre-eochair had asserted and given a more precise vision of the nature of the five provinces.

Laigin. East. It is the seat of prosperity. Its main qualities are wealth, abundance, elegance, hospitality, poise, splendor, nobility, dignity, art, and work.

Mumu. South. It is the seat of music. Its main qualities are harmony, music, sentiment, the game of chess, ritual, subtlety, honor, and law.

Connacht. West. It is the seat of wisdom. Its main qualities are knowledge, teaching, judgment, science, history, eloquence, beauty, and modesty.

Ulaid. North. It is the seat of the war. Its main qualities are struggle, combat, conflict, battle, assault, courage, arrogance, pride, and toughness.

Meath. In the center. It is the seat of the Supreme Kings of Ériu. Its main qualities are royal sovereignty, stability, institution, honor, war, poetry, opulence, prosperity, mead, fame, and notoriety.

CAP 4: THE CYCLE OF INVASION OF ÉRIU

The Story of Tuan: Immortality and Memory

The problem of how the memory of people who disappeared into thin air could be passed on must have fascinated the Irish chroniclers, who came up with various figures of immortals who lived through the centuries perpetuating the stories of their people. I choose the myth of Tuan mac Cairill as a "frame" through which to focus on the Cycle of Invasions.

1. *The Guest of Finnian of Clonard*

It is said that one day (we are at the beginning of the 6th century), saint (*noíb*) Finnian of Clonard left the monastery he founded in the Ulaid and went to find an old warrior who lived not far from there. However, Tuan, son of Cairill, was very rude to the saint, refusing to receive him. Then Finnian sat outside the door of the surly warrior's house and fasted all Sunday. Faced with such obstinacy, Tuan finally welcomed the monk into his home. Good relations were established between the two and Finnian returned to his monks in Ulaid.

"Tuan is an excellent man," he told them. "He will come to you to comfort you and tell the ancient stories of Ériu." In fact, the warrior soon arrived in the monastery and proposed that the monks go with him to his hermitage. The monks followed him and celebrated the Sunday offices, complete with psalms, prayers, and mass. When the monks asked him what his name was and what his lineage was, he gave an astonishing answer:

"I'm a man from Ulaid," he declared. "My name is Tuan, son of Cairill. However, once I was called Tuan, son of Starn, brother of Partholon. This was my name in the beginning." Then Finnian asked Tuan to tell his story and added that none of the monks would accept his food until Tuan had told what he remembered.

So Tuan began to tell.

2. The Story of Tuan mac Cairill

Tuan told of five invasions which, after the flood, came to occupy Ériu – and, indeed, he never mentioned anyone who had arrived in Ériu before the flood. Three centuries after the flood had reached Ériu, he said, Partholon, son of Sera, had settled there with his people. However, following a plague, in the space of two Sundays, the entirety of the People of Partholon had been annihilated. Now, because it was the law that at least one person could survive every massacre afterward, by divine decision, Tuan had survived the epidemic, the only survivor of all his people. For years, Tuan had wandered alone among the cliffs and hills, guarding himself against wolves, until he was so old that, unable to walk comfortably, he retired to Ulaid, where he found refuge in a cave. For twenty-two years, Tuan had been alone on the empty island of Ériu, until he saw new people land on the island from the top of a hill. It was Nemed, a distant descendant of Partholon himself, who came with his people to colonize the island. Old and miserably naked, with gray hair and long nails, Tuan did not have the courage to meet the new arrivals, so he fled to hide in his cave, where he would await death. However, one night, while Tuan was sleeping, his body changed shape. When he awoke, he found that God had turned him into a deer, restoring his youth and cheerful mood at the same time. And Tuan sang these verses:

- They come to me, sweet Lord,

the Nemedians son of Agnoman;
mighty warriors in battle,
ready to seek my blood.
However, they rise on my head
two stages bristling with sixty points:
new shape, coarse and gray hair
when I was deprived of strength and defense.

And Tuan was prince of the deer of Ériu. Great herds surrounded him no matter what path he followed. He spent this new life of his at the time when Nemed and his descendants inhabited the green Ériu. By the time the Nemedians also disappeared, Tuan, transformed into a deer, had already reached extreme old age. His horns were worn out and his once agile legs could no longer escape the packs of wolves. So Tuan retired to his cave in Ulaid to die. However, one morning, when he woke up, he realized that his body had changed shape again. He had transformed into a black boar. Tuan sang:

- Today boar among the herds,

mighty lord of great triumphs,

I was once among the People of Partholon

in the assembly that regulated the judgments.

My song was pleasant to everyone,

pleasing to young and beautiful women;

I had a majestic and shining chariot,

grave and sweet voice in the long journey;

quick pace, without fear

to combat and assault:

yesterday I had a beautiful and radiant face,

today I'm a black boar!

Young again in this new form, Tuan regained his good humor. He was the king of Ériu's boars and proudly roamed the island. Another people came from the sea to occupy Ériu. They were the Fir Bolg. Meanwhile, Tuan's life had come to an end: The spirit was weary, powerless to do what it was capable of doing before. The old boar lived only in dark caves and between cliffs. Then Tuan returned to his cave in Ulaid, to that same place where he returned every time the load of the years made him fall back into old age, so that his appearance would change and he would find his youth again. This time he came out transformed into a sea hawk. His spirit became happy and he was capable of anything again. He became restless and lively; he flew all over the island and sang these lines:

- Today sea hawk, yesterday boar,
God who loves me
gave me this form.
I lived among the herds of wild boars,
today they are among the flocks of birds.

And then a new people came to take over Ériu. It was the Túatha Dé Danann, who won the Fir Bolg, who at the time occupied the green island. As for Túan, he remained for a long time in the form of a hawk and was still in that appearance when a further invasion arrived: that of the Milesians, who tore the island from the Túatha Dé Danann. Now old, the hawk was in the hollow of a tree above a stream, his spirit struck down, unable to fly. After he fasted for nine days, sleep took hold of him and he was transformed into a river salmon. Later, God placed him in the water, where the salmon lived and was comfortable, vigorous, and well-fed. Skilled in swimming, he escaped dangers and traps: the hands of the fisherman, the talons of the hawk, the fishing lances. One day, God decided it was time to put an end to the state of Tuan and that was how a fisherman ended up catching that big salmon.

3. Reborn

The salmon was brought to the court of King Cairell, son of Muiredach Muinderg. The salmon was placed on the grill and roasted.

The king's wife, as soon as she saw the salmon, was overcome by an irresistible temptation; she wanted it served, and she ate it greedily. Not for this Tuan ceased to be conscious. He kept a memory of the time he remained in the womb of the woman and from there he heard all the conversations that were held in the house, of what was going on in Ériu in those days. Then the queen gave birth and he was born, and was called Tuan again. As soon as he was born, Tuan could speak perfectly and told of the very ancient events he had witnessed. Throughout his life, Tuan mac Cairill had been a prophet until Pátraic came to bring faith in Ériu. Tuan was already very old, but he had been baptized. He was very old now, and this was the story he told Finnian and his monks: the chronicle of the ancient invasions of Ériu.

It is thanks to Tuan mac Cairill that the historians of Ériu still have the memory of Partholon and its people today.

The Creation: The Biblical Tale in the Irish Myth

The Celtic creation myth was never handed down; Christian monks conveniently replaced it with the biblical story. The result is a Genesis full of extra-canonical news, endowed with a bizarre sense of the marvelous and subtly oriented in an "Irish" sense.

   1. *The Creation of the World*

The world was created, according to the calculation of the most attentive Irish annalists, 5194 years before the birth of our Lord, Christ.

In principio fecit Deus Caeum et Terram...

In the beginning, God made heaven and earth, He who has no beginning and no end. This happened on the fifteenth day of the calends of April, according to the Hebrews and the Latins, although until then the world had never seen either sunrise or sunset. That first Sunday, God made formless matter - fire and air, earth and water - and the light of the angelic hierarchies. On Monday, he made the seven heavens and the firmament. On Tuesday, he made the land and the sea. On Wednesday, he made the sun and the moon and the stars of the sky. On Thursday, he made the birds of the air and the reptiles of the sea. On Friday, he made the beasts of the earth and then created man to govern and administer them. On Saturday, God stopped at the completion of his creation and blessed it. However, that doesn't mean he turned away from governing it. In this way, God made creatures: some with a beginning but without an end, like the angels; others with a beginning and an end, like animals without reason; and still others with a beginning and an end but without an end, like men, who have a beginning when they are born, a term in their mortal bodies, and no term in their immortal souls.

2. The Heaven on Earth

God made a paradise on earth, in the plain of *Arón* (which others call Eden), on the southern coast of that land which is located in the east of the world (just as Ériu is in the extreme west of the earth, on the northern side). In paradise is the *Pairtech* mountain, which the sun illuminates as it rises. Not far away is the source of *Nuchal*, from which four free and mighty rivers flow. The Pishon is the first river, made of oil, which flows eastwards. The Tigris is the second, of wine, which goes west. The Euphrates is the third, with honey, flowing south. The Gihon is the fourth, made of milk, which heads north.

In the center of paradise, in the plain of *Arón*, rises the forbidden tree, whose name is *Daisia*, and which produces many kinds of wonderful fruit.

3. Adam and Eve

When God created the first man, he did so in this guise: the body of common earth, the head of the earth of Garad, the chest of the earth of Arabia, the belly of the earth of Lodain, and the legs of the earth of Agoria.

Others say that God took the land of the Malón region for the head, the land of Arón for the chest, the land of Babylon for the belly, or that of Byblos, and the land of Laban and Gogoma for the legs. For three days the splendid semblance of Adam remained lifeless, after it had been shaped by the earth. His blood and sweat came from water, his breath from air, his heat from fire, and his soul from the breath of God.

It was on the eastern side of Pairtech, the mountain of heaven, that Adam first stood up and welcomed the rising sun. It was then that he raised a hymn to the Lord. "I adore you, I adore you, oh my God!"

These were the first words that were ever spoken. Adam's body was strong and perfect. He moved, and then ran toward the springs of

Paradise. God presented all the animals to Adam so that he could give each one a name.

However, Adam was overcome with great sadness because every animal had a mate and he was alone. Then God made sleep fall upon him, took a rib from him, and created Eve. As soon as the woman was introduced to Adam, he laughed with joy. That was the first laugh.

And Adam said: "Here are the bones of my bones and the flesh of my flesh." And this was the first prophecy that was uttered, as God, when he put Adam to sleep, gave him the gift of prophecy.

4. The Downfall

God assigned the rule of heaven to Lucifer, with nine orders of angels under his command, and gave the land to Adam and Eve, and their offspring. However, then, blinded by presumption and pride, Lucifer rebelled and attacked heaven, supported by a third of all the celestial hosts.

God struck him down and hurled him and all his angels to Hell, saying: "Arrogant is this Lucifer; so let's go down and confuse his decisions." This was the first judgment that was ever pronounced.

Lucifer had jealousy and hatred toward Adam, to whom God had promised heavenly bliss in his stead.

Using the power that came to him from the ineffable name of God, Lucifer assumed the appearance of a serpent, his body as thin as air, and placed himself in the path of the first man and the first woman.

The snake persuaded the woman and then the man to sin, causing them to eat an apple from the forbidden tree. The reason God forbade eating the fruit of that tree was that if Adam did, he would understand that he was under the power and authority of the Lord.

5. The Fratricide

At the age of thirty, Adam was created, and Eve looked twenty when God took her from the rib of man. So Adam was only fifteen years old when he fathered Cain and his sister Chalmana. In the thirtieth year of Adam's life, Abel and his sister Delbora were born. One day, Cain and Abel offered two rams to the Lord. However, God did not like Cain's offer, while he accepted Abel's.

Behold, seized by jealousy and pride, Cain brandished a camel's jaw and struck his brother, just as the victims of sacrifices are struck, killing him. Abel's blood stained the stones of the earth, which since then ceased to grow. Some say that it was Seth, seeing the blood of sin, who collected the camel bone, but this is not possible because it was only long after Abel's death, in the hundred and thirtieth year of Adam's life, that Seth was born, from which Adam's posterity would descend. Others say that Cain's hatred of Abel was dictated by jealousy, as they were both in love with Chalmana. However, Adam, judging the relationship between Cain and his twin too close, had supported Abel's claim against Cain's, provoking the latter's murderous reaction. Others say that Pendan, son of Adam, was later the husband of Chalmana, and this led Cain to a second fratricide.

After the killing of Abel, seven sores appeared on Cain's body: two on the hands, two on the feet, two on the cheeks, and one on the forehead. And it was precisely in the wound on his forehead that Cain, much later, would be hit by the apple thrown by Lamech, thus ending his wretched days.

The ram that Abel had offered to the Lord would later replace Isaac, son of Abraham, on the altar of sacrifice. The same skin would be seen later, when Christ washed the feet of his disciples.

6. The Age of Patriarchs

After the killing of Abel, God decided to send the flood on the earth to wipe out humanity, who lived in sin. The only one to be saved was Noah, aboard his ark. This is the genealogy of Noah: Noah, son of Lamech, son of Methuselah, son of Enoch, son of Jared, son of Mahalel, son of Kenan, son of Enos, son of Seth, son of Adam.

There were three sons of Adam who had descendants, but only the lineage of Seth survived the flood, while the race of Cain was wiped out, as was the race of Sile.

According to the Jewish annalists, who summed up the years of the generations of the patriarchs, between the creation of Adam and the flood, one thousand six hundred and fifty-six years passed. This calculation is confirmed by the verses of the ancient poets of Ériu:

The first age of the melodious world

from Adam to the flood,

fifty-six years, clear calculation,

plus six hundred plus a thousand

7. The Flood

When, indeed, God saw that the people of Seth's clan were transgressing his command, that there was no relationship or alliance with the people of the race of wicked Cain, he decided to send the flood to wipe out mankind. Only Noah had continued to obey the divine command and had avoided joining the clan of Cain. God decided that Noah would be saved with his family and commanded him to prepare an ark so that he could escape the catastrophe.

The ark was made of wood, coated inside and out with bitumen. Thirty cubits was its height, three hundred cubits its length, and fifty cubits its width. The door opened on the eastern side. Noah brought a pair of all unclean animals and three pairs (or seven) of the pure into the ark so that he could dispose of the victims for sacrifice once they had come out of the ark.

Noah had Coba for his wife, who was his sister. He had three children, Shem, Ham, and Japheth, who had married their three sisters. Six hundred years was the age of Noah when he entered the ark. He went aboard, with his family, on the seventeenth day of the May moon, Friday, and God closed the door behind him. It rained continuously for forty days and water covered the earth. The flood engulfed all men and beasts except the eight who were on the ark and the animals that had been loaded into it. (However, the antiquarians remember that Enoch, who was in heaven fighting the Antichrist, and Fintan mac Bóchra, who was locked up in his cave in Ériu, were also saved, as God had chosen him to tell men the stories of the ancient times.) Twelve cubits was the level of the water on the highest mountains and this for an obvious reason: The ark was immersed for ten cubits and emerged for twenty. In this way, the tops of the highest mountains would remain two cubits under the keel of the ark, without damaging it.

After a hundred and fifty days, the waters began to dry up. For seven months and twenty-seven days, the ark was tossed from wave to wave until, finally, it rested on the mountains of Armenia. The waters receded until the tenth month, and on the first day of the tenth month, the tops of the mountains began to be seen. At the end of another forty-seven days, Noah opened the window of the ark and sent out the crow, which never came back. The next day, he let go of the dove, and it returned because it had not found a place to rest. Noah sent out the dove again after seven days, and in the evening the dove returned, carrying an olive branch with leaves in its beak. After another seven days, Noah sent it out again and the dove never came back. Noah came out of the ark on the twenty-seventh day of the May moon, Tuesday, in the six hundred and first year of his life. The first thing he did when he got out of the ark was to raise an altar to God and offer him a sacrifice.

8. The Second Age of the World

The second age of the world began. Noah was the first man to undertake agricultural work in the first year after the flood. He began to plow and reap, and planted a vineyard. His wife Coba was the first to sew clothes for the small community.

Shem, son of Noah, was the first blacksmith, the first craftsman, and the first carpenter after the flood. Japheth was the first to play the harp and organ after the flood. Ham was the first poet and the first bard.

It is said that, before the flood, Ham had erected three four-sided columns, one of lime, one of clay, and one of wax, and had written on them the stories of the antediluvian times to be known after the catastrophe. The lime column and the clay column were destroyed by the flood, but the wax column remained intact: and it was thus that the stories of the time before the flood were passed down and survived into the later ages of the world. Noah divided the world into three parts among his children:

Shem took up residence in pleasant Asia, while Ham went with his children to Africa. The noble Japheth and his offspring settled in Europe.

It is also said that Ham was cursed by Noah, and was enslaved by his two brothers. From him then descended deformed and grotesque lineages, such as the Lupracanaig, the Fomorians, and the horse-headed *Gaburchinn,* perhaps to be identified with the *Pucai.* This was the origin of the monsters.

Others say that a fourth child was born to Noah after the flood, named Eoinitus. Ethan was called the territory he received, chosen away from the other three, in the far east of the world. He was a good astrologer, having learned the art of observing the stars from his father Noah.

Noah was six hundred years old when the flood came. After the flood, he still lived for three hundred and fifty years. He was, along with Adam, Jared, and Methuselah, one of the four men who had the longest life.

The Origins of Europe: Genealogy of the peoples of Ériu

Nothing is left of the ancient theogonies and anthropogonies of the Celts of Ireland if not the names of some mythical forefathers who, in the biblical rereading of the ancient traditional genealogies, ended up being grafted onto the descendants of Japheth, son of Noah.

1. The Division of the World

In the global flood, the entire seed of Adam drowned, except those who were on the ark: Noah and his wife Coba, his three sons, Shem, Ham, and Japheth, and their three wives. For this reason, Noah is said to be the second Adam: because, from him, all the men of the earth descend.

Noah divided the world into three parts. To Shem he assigned Asia, to Ham Africa, and to Japheth Europe. Each moved to the part that had been assigned to him. Soon their offspring filled each of the three divisions of the earth.

Shem's lineage occupied all of Asia, from the Euphrates River to the eastern regions of the earth. That of Ham spread throughout Africa and in the southern belt of Asia. That of Japheth occupied all of Europe, from the River Don to the ocean, including the island of Britannia in the north and Spain in the south, and also the islands of the Mediterranean; and again it occupied the whole northern belt of Asia, Scythia, Asia Minor, and Armenia, up to the distant buttresses of the Taurus. Each of Noah's three sons died in the portion of the earth allotted to him.

2. Descendants of Noah

Ham, son of Noah, had four sons: Cush, Mizraim, Put, and Canaan. Thirty nations would descend from them and their descendants.

Shem, son of Noah, had five sons: Elam, Ashur, Arpachshad, Lud, and Aram. Twenty-seven nations would descend from them and their descendants (some say thirty, but that's not correct). The Jewish people belong to the lineage of Shem.

Japheth had seven children: Gomer, Magog, Madai, Javan, Tubal, Meshech, and Tiras. Fifteen nations would descend from them and their descendants.

In all, they make up seventy-two nations, which would be divided at the foot of the Tower of Nemrod, when God gave each its own language.

3. Japheth's Sons

Antiquarians provide several calculations of the number of Japheth's sons and cite different lists of their names. The Irish scholars claim that Japheth had fifteen children and that Gomer, Magog,

Danaus, Graecus, and Hispanus were five of them. They probably misunderstand that fifteen were the peoples descended from Japheth, which do not necessarily correspond to the number of children.

In these matters, however, it is appropriate to refer to the high magisterium of the Bible, according to which the sons of Japheth were seven: precisely, Gomer, Madai, Javan, Tubal, Meshech, Tiras, and Magog. Gomer had three sons: Ashkenaz, Riphath, and Togarmah. Javan had four: Elishah, Tarshish, Kittim, and Dodanim. This is what the scriptures say.

From Gomer descend the Galatians, who are none other than the Gauls of Greece. From Ashkenaz, son of Gomer, descend the Sarmatians, from Riphath the Paplagons, and from Togarmah the Phrygians and - it seems - the Trojans.

From Madai descend the Medes, eight kings of whom assumed the kingship of the world.

From Javan, which the ancient Irish chronicles call Graecus, descend the Ionians and the Aeolians, who had Greece, Little Greece, and Magna Graecia. Even the Ionian Sea was named after him. The lineage of Alexander, son of Philip, king of the Macedonians, is traced back to Javan.

From his son Elishah descend the Aetolians, ancestors of the Sicilians. The inhabitants of Cilicia descend from Tarshish, and the city of Tarsus took its name. The Cypriot population of Kiti descends from Kittim and their capital, Kition, is named after him.

From Dodanim, the inhabitants of the islands descend: Rhodes, Karpathos, Kythera, and all the islands of the Aegean Sea, Crete, Sicily, and the islands of the Mediterranean Sea. The Irish chronicles mention another son of Graecus, Thessalus, who founded the city of Thessaloniki and gave its name to Thessaly.

From Tubal, which the ancient Irish chronicles call Hispanus, descend the Iberians, Celtibers, and Italics.

From Epirus, of the seed of Tubal, the Epiroti descend. To this lineage belonged Ianus, the first ruler of Lazio, the one who gave his name to the month of January.

From Meshech descend the inhabitants of Cappadocia. From Tiras descend the Thracians. From Magog descend the Scythians, while others say the Goths.

Irish sources sometimes quote - erroneously - an eighth son of Japheth, Maisechda, about whom, however, they do not provide information.

4. Lineage of Magog: The Invaders of Ériu

Scholars point to Aithecht, son of Magog, son of Japheth, as the ancestor of the various peoples who invaded the island of Ériu after the flood: the People of Partholon, the Nemedians, the Fir Bolg, and the Túatha Dé Danann. In fact, Partholon was the son of Sera, son of Sru, son of Esru, son of Braiment, son of Aithecht, son of Magog.

Nemed was the son of Agnoman, son of Piamp, son of Tait, son of Sera, son of Sru, etc. From Nemed, the three tribes of Fir Bolg (the

Gáilióin, the Fir Bolg, and the Fir Domnann) and the Túatha Dé Danann descended.

5. Lineage of Gomer: The Gaels

Regarding the lineage of the people of the Gaels or Scoti, who last invaded Ériu, snatching her from Túatha Dé Danann, there is no uniformity of views. Some claim they are descended from Japheth's son Gomer, although the exact genealogy is controversial. Although the Scriptures state that Gomer had three sons, Ashkenaz, Riphath, and Togarmah, Irish sources refer to two of his sons, named Emoth and Ibath.

This Ibath is identified with Riphath, who is also called Riphath Scot, as he was the ancestor of the Scots or Gaels. (Others say that Riphath Scot was a fourth son of Gomer, distinct from Riphath, but this does not seem likely.)

Emoth was the progenitor of the people who inhabited the far north of the world. Ibath had two sons: Bodb and Baath. Bodb was the father of Dothe, who was the father of Alanus, ancestor of the peoples of Europe.

Baath fathered Fenius Farsaid, father of Nél, father of Goidel Glas, from whom the Gaels took their name.

6. Elinus: The First European

Seventeen years before the division of languages, the first man of the lineage of Iapheth came to Europe. He was Elinus, son of Dothe, son of Bodb, son of Ibath, son of Gomer, son of Japheth, son of Noah.

Elinus had three sons: Airmen, Negua, and Isacon.

Airmen had five sons: Gothus, Gebidus, Valagothus, Burgundus, and Longobardus.

Negua had three sons: Saxus, Boguarus, and Vandalus.

Isacon had four children: Romanus, Francus, Britus, and Albanus.

Gothus was the ancestor of the Goths, Gebidus of the Gepids, Valagothus of the Viligotes or Goths of Italy, Burgundus of the Burgundians, and Longobardus of the Lombards. Saxus was the ancestor of the Saxons, Boguarus of the Bavarians, and Vandalus of the Vandals. Romanus was the ancestor of the Romans, Francus of the Franks, Britus of the Britons, and Albanus of the people of Alba (Scotland). Later, Albanus led his brothers across the Channel and arrived in Italy. the Albans of Lazio descended from him.

7. Other Genealogical Traditions

As we have seen, all the peoples who invaded Ériu after the flood belonged to the lineage of Japheth. The most authoritative among the Irish scholars affirm that the People of Partholon, the Nemedians, the Fir Bolg, and the Túatha Dé Danann descended from Aithecht, son of Magog, son of Iapheth, and that the Gaels descended from Goidel Glas, son of Nel, son of Fenius Farsaid, son of Baath, son of Ibath (Riphath Scot), son of Gomer, son of Iapheth. However, the antique dealers report other traditions. Some argue that the Gaels also descended from Magog and report different genealogies in which the lineage of Baath and that of Aithecht appear closely intertwined.

Some claim, for example, that Aithecht was the son of Baath, son of Magog. Others claim that Partholon and Nemed descended from Goidel Glas, son of Nel, son of Fenius Farsaid, son of Baath, son of Magog.

Some antiquaries record a tradition according to which Magog had five children: Baath, Ibath, Barachan, Emoth, and Aithecht. According to them, Baath was the father of Fenius Farsaid, ancestor of the Scythians; Ibath was the father of Elinus, ancestor of the peoples of Europe; Barachan was the father of Tai, who was the father of Bai, who was the father of Etheor, who was the father of Goidel, regarding whom, however, it is uncertain whether he should be identified with Goidel Glas, ancestor of the Gaels; Emoth was the progenitor of the people of the north of the world; and Aithecht was the ancestor of the peoples who came to Ériu before the Gaels.

The Daughters of Cain: The Betrayed Invasions

Very ancient tales, not well integrated into the mythical cycles, tell of three women who, in antediluvian times, first came to this island at the edge of the world to give it their name.

1. *The Three Daughters*

Some say that it was three virgins, the daughters of evil Cain, who were the first to reach the green island at the edge of the world. With them was Seth, son of Adam.

According to others, three times fifty were the women who came with *Banba*, and only three men. Ladra was the name of one of them, who was the first man to die in Ériu, It is from him that the place called Árd Ladrann took its name.

They stayed twice twenty years on the island, until a disease struck them and they all died within a week. After that, the island remained deserted and empty, with no one living there, for two hundred years. Then the flood came.

From Banba came the first name that was given to that land.

2. The Three Hispanic Fishermen

Others say that three fishermen, who went out for a fishing trip on the high seas, were blown by a storm from Hispania to the uninhabited island that would one day be called Ériu. Their names were Cappa, Lavigne and Luasad. Apparently, they were a craftsman, a healer, and a rude fisherman. Having landed at Tuad Inber, the mouth of the River Bann, at the northern tip of the island, they explored the new land from one end to the other and were able to appreciate the beauty of the landscape and the richness of the soil. Incredulous about their discovery, sovereigns could already be seen at the head of many proud fortresses perched on the hills.

Thus, they returned to Hispania to take their wives and brought them to the excellent Ériu. However, their plans were destined to clash against an ineluctable fate: Cappamu, Laigne, and Luasad had been on the island for only a year when the universal flood swept them in Tuad Inber and submerged them.

The People of Cessair: Ériu at the Time of the Flood

The People of Cessair, three men and fifty girls, arrive in Ériu forty days before the flood. A tale sometimes excluded from the Invasion Cycle, it is instead an integral part of it.

1. The Announcement of the Flood

When God saw that the people of Seth's clan were transgressing his command, that there was no relationship or alliance with the people of the race of evil Cain, he decided to send the flood to wipe out mankind. Only Noah, son of Lamech, found grace in the sight of God.

A prophet and divine messenger thus approached the patriarch and told him: "Build an ark of light wood, because a flood will come and submerge every living thing, due to the serious murder that Cain, son of Adam, committed against his brother Abel.

"And no man of the seed of Adam will escape that catastrophe, apart from you, your wife, your three sons, and your three daughters, because you did not go with the clan of Cain. In fact, just as you took your sister as your wife, your daughters married your sons."

2. The Lineage of Bith

However, although the Holy Scriptures ignore his existence, Noah also had a fourth son, Bith. Knowing of the arrival of the flood, he approached his father: "And what will I do?" he asked him.

"I don't know," replied Noah. "Because of the gravity of your sins, I am not allowed to take you onto the ark." Shortly after, the patriarch was approached by his relative, Fintan mac Bochra. It is not clear whether he was the son or grandson of Lamech; Bochra was, in fact, the name of his mother.

"What am I going to do?" Fintan asked Noah.

"I'm not your keeper," Noah replied. "And I will not challenge divine power by taking you to the ark with me."

Ladra, son of Bith, arrived. "What am I going to do?" he asked Noah. "I don't know," replied the patriarch. "However, I'm not allowed to take you to the ark."

Last came Cessair, daughter of Bith. "What am I going to do?" she asked Noah.

"I don't know," Noah replied once more. "The ark is not a ship of thieves, and it is not a den of evildoers."

3. The Origin of Idolatry

Then Bith, Ladra, and Fintan met in consultation and said to each other: "What are we going to do? What decisions will we make? It is now certain that the flood will come on earth. How can we be ready?"

"Easy!" Cessair intervened. "Give me your obedience and submit to me. If you do, I'll give you some great advice."

"We'll give it to you!" promised the three men.

"Then take an idol yourself," she said. "Worship him and turn away from the God of Noah." The people of Cessair built an idol and began to worship it. This was the first time in the world that anyone abandoned faith in God to turn to false gods. At one point, the idol spoke up and said to the tribe of Bith: "Embark and set out on the sea journey." However, they did not know, nor did the idol, when the flood would come.

4. The Journey to Ériu

By mutual agreement, Cessair's comrades obeyed the idol's advice and built three ships. "Flee to the western ends of the world," Noah advised them. "The flood may not reach you down there." In fact, it was necessary to find a place where no one had ever arrived until then, where no crime or sin had ever been committed, a place free from reptiles and all the monsters of the world. Only such a place, Cessair believed, could offer them escape and safety from the flood. The druids she consulted confirmed that only the distant island of Ériu, on the western edge of the world, met these requirements.

On a Tuesday, the fifteenth of the month, the people of Cessair set out from the islands of Meroe, on the River Nile, and came to Egypt.

For seven years, perhaps ten, Cessair's ships skirted Egypt. Then the fleet set off again, and Ladra was their pilot. They sailed through the Caspian Sea for twenty days. It took another twelve to reach the Cimmerian Sea in the icy north. One day, they stayed in Asia Minor, then entered the Tyrrhenian Sea. They had a twenty-day voyage before seeing the Alps mountain, and after another nine days, they reached Hispania. At that point, having entered the ocean, they required nine days of navigation to cover the journey from Hispania to Ériu.

However, as they approached the rugged coast of western Mumu, two ships were wrecked on their landing. The remainder landed in Dún na mBárc, in Corco Duibne. It was Saturday, the fifth of the month, in the year 2242 after the Creation of the World (2956 BC). There were only forty days before the flood.

5. The Division of the Women

There were three men and fifty women on board the ship. The men were: Bith mac Noah, Fintan mac Bochra, and Ladra mac Betha. Among the girls were Cessair, leader of the expedition, as well as Bairrfhind, wife of Bith, and Alba, wife of Ladra. The "people of Cessair" were the first human beings to touch the soil of Ériu. Some say that there was also a child with them, Bath mac Betha, who, however, drowned in the well of Dún na mBárc on the day of the landing, from which came the ancient, enigmatic called "part Bith, not Bath."

The three came with their women to Miledach, at the confluence of the Suir, Nore, and Barrow Rivers. Here, the three men divided the fifty girls. Fintan chose Cessair, and with her they touched seventeen women in all. Bith took his wife Bairrfhind with him, and seventeen women in all went with him.

Ladra took his wife Alba with him, and sixteen women in all went with him.

6. The First to Die in the Land of Ériu

Disgruntled and angered by the unequal sharing, Ladra left with his sixteen girls and died of sexual abuse (although others say he was penetrated by an oar in the backside). The place where he was buried was named *Árd Ladrann*.

Ladra's sixteen women turned back. Cessair sent for his father Bith, who arrived at the place where his daughter was with Fintan. The two men decided to split the girls equally. Bith went north with his women and was the second to die. With great effort, the women buried him under a *carn*, a mound of stones, near the mountain that took the name of Slíab Betha from him.

After Bith's death, his girls returned to place themselves under the authority of the only man left. However, as Fintan found himself in front of all those women, he ran away. He left *Bun Súainme*, crossed the *Siúr*, and came to *Slíabh gCúa*. He passed farther, still heading west, until he reached the top of *Cenn Febrat*.

At this point, he turned north, reached the *Sínnan*, and, having forded it, skirted it, keeping the river to the left, until he reached *Duthaig Arad*. A hill stood by Loch Dergdeirc, and Fintan climbed to the top and hid in a cave.

Cessair followed him along with her companions and her heart - already severely tried for the death of her brother and father, and now also for the escape of her husband - broke in the center of her chest. The place where she died was named *Cúl Cessrach*, in Connacht, and the mound under which she was buried was called Carn Cessrach.

It was only seven days before the flood.

7. Fintan in the Hill of the Wave

Fintan was still hiding in his cave when the flood broke out. Overflowing waters engulfed Ériu, sweeping away all the women, and the wave roared up to the top. Fintan was now certain that he, too, would perish in the cataclysm, but God mercifully closed the mouth of the cave where he was. So, when the huge wave engulfed the hill, Fintan was now safe inside the cave.

Fintan remained for a whole year locked up in the cave at the top of the hill, which would be known as *Tul Tuinde*, the "hill of the wave." He had nothing to eat and drink, but God caused him to fall into a long and deep sleep. For a whole year, Fintan remained asleep in his stone ark, and only when the floodwaters returned did he awaken and leave the cave.

He had found true faith.

8. Fintan the Immortal

Made immortal, Fintan spent the centuries taking the shape of a salmon, an eagle, and a hawk from time to time, and witnessed all subsequent invasions that touched the shores of Ériu. Favored by his very long life, Fintan was thus able to pass on the memory of his people, the People of Cessair, who otherwise would have been forgotten by history.

It seems that Fintan mac Bochra was still living in the seventh year of the reign of Diarmait mac Cerbaill (± 551 AD), when he was questioned by the court poet, Amargin mac Amlaí, who, in order to force him to reveal his memories, fasted for three days and three nights before him and in the presence of the men and women of Temáir. From these tales, the *Dindśenchas* would be born. Thus sang Fintán: "In Ériu, whatever you ask me, I know the answer. I know everything that happened there from the beginning of the melodious world.

"Cessair came from the east. The woman was the daughter of Bith, with her fifty maidens, and only three men. The waters of the flood covered Bith in Slíab Betha, it is no secret; Ladra in Árd Ladrann, Cessair in Cúl Cessrach.

"However, as for me, God himself buried me, high above my companions. In Tul Tuinde, he saved me from the flood. One year I remained under the waters in the mighty hill; I had nothing to feed myself, better sleep without awakening."

And after having handed down the memories of all the peoples who, in the centuries after the flood, had invaded Ériu, Fintán concluded, proud: "A long life was given to me, I will not hide it, by the King of the cloud-covered sky. I am Fintan the white, the son of Bochra, and after the flood, here I am, noble and great among the wisest."

According to another tradition, Fintan died around the third century. A.D., when, in the form of a salmon, he was captured and broiled by Finn mac Cumaill, the future leader of the Fianna. Finn was just a boy then, but, burning himself from cooking the salmon, he put his finger to his mouth and suddenly had the ancient wisdom of Fintan.

9. The Four Who Survived the Flood

Whether or not Fintan survived the flood is a controversial issue, as the Holy Scriptures clearly state that no man, except the eight who were on the ark, escaped the cataclysm. Only Noah, his wife, his three children, and the wives of three children were saved. No one else, according to the true Canon, could survive.

However, some antiquarians claim that God allowed four men to escape the flood, and each was in one of the four corners of the earth. They were: Fintan to the west, Ferón to the north, Fors to the east, and Andóid to the south. However, the question is hotly debated because, as mentioned, this tradition is contrary to the Scriptures.

The Shapeless Island: Ériu After the Flood

After the flood, a still nameless island, silent and covered with woods, waits for men to come to populate it. A peoples of deformed beings come to you from the sea to escape a curse, a young man disembarks to tear you a tuft of grass.

1. Ériu After the Flood

When the flood wiped out humanity, the island of Ériu remained uninhabited for a long time. At first, Ériu was filled with an uninterrupted forest. Spoglia remained a single plain, leveled and tilled by the very hands of God the creator, without even a tree or blade of grass.

This first remote plain would be called Senmág, "ancient plain," in Étar, but later also "plain of flocks," because all the birds of Ériu came down there to bask in the sun, it being the only place on the whole island without trees.

2. The Original Lakes and Rivers of Ériu

In the green and silent Ériu there were, at that time, only three lakes and nine rivers. Neither one nor the other still had a name, but later the three lakes would be called like this:

Loch Luimnig, in Tír Finn in Des-Múmu (Desmond);

Loch Fordremain in Tráig-lí, near Sliab Mis, in the Mumu;

Finnloch Cera in Irrus Uí Fiachrach (or Irrus Domnann), in Connacht.

The history of Ériu's "original" rivers is still today, for the few able to understand it, a sure indication of the level once reached by the waters of the universal deluge.

They were nine in number:

the Buas, between Dál nAraidi and Dál Riada;

the Lifé, between the territory of the Uí Néill and the men of Laigin;

the Luí in the Mumu, which flows through Muscraige toward Corcaig;

the Samáir at Ess Rúaid, between the Uí Fiachrach and Cineal Conaill;

the Modorn in Tír Éogain;

the Finn, between Cinéll Éogain and Cinéll Conaill;

the Bann, between Lí and Elle, in the Ulaid;

the Muad in Connacht, which crosses the territory of the Uí Fiachrach going north;

the Slicech in Connacht.

3. Origin and Arrival of the Fomorians

About seventy years after the flood, the Fomorians arrived in Ériu. This race was descended from Ham, son of Noah. Bound to the sea and of powerful stature, with only one arm and one leg, and with only one eye in the middle of the forehead, they were later confused with demons or giants. After the flood, when Ham had been cursed by Noah, his offspring had spawned all possible deformities of the human species.

They were born tiny beings like the Leprechaun, or massive and cruel like the Fomorians, or horse-headed, like the Gaburchinn, perhaps to be identified with the Pucai.

And because Noah had given Shem authority over Ham, the latter's descendants - such as the *Canaan* - had become slaves of the sons of Shem. Therefore, the Fomorians wanted to separate themselves from the rest of the Ham lineage, fearing that they, too, would fall under the same curse.

The Fomorians set out from *Tír Émóir*, or *Slíab Émóir*, aboard a fleet they had built themselves. Their leader was Cichol Gricenchos, the "footless" son of Goll, son of Garb, son of the fiery

Túathach, son of Gúmór (or according to others, Cichol, son of Níl, son of Garb, son of Túathach, son of Úathmór).

The Fomorians fleet consisted of six ships, and each ship had fifty men and fifty women on board. However, Cichol's mother alone equaled the strength of all: The rough and shaggy Loth Lúamnach, daughter of Ner, was both splendid and terrible, with her mouths on her breasts and four eyes behind her neck.

She came from Slíab Chaucais and perhaps belonged to the Túatha Ithier, the tribes descended from Adam, and settled north of that mountain, whose appearance was very similar to hers. It was said that, despite their monstrous appearance, the Ithier appeared so irresistible and sensual that no one, to any other people they belonged, could resist them.

After a long voyage, the Fomorians arrived in Ériu and landed in the bay of Inbir Domnann Cícal. For over two centuries, they remained in Ériu, where they survived by hunting birds and fishing until the People of Partholon came to fight them.

4. The Shortest Employment of Ériu

It is said that one hundred and forty years after the flood, a young man arrived in the still deserted Ériu. He was of the lineage of Nín, son of Bél, emperor of the world after the collapse of the tower of Nemrod.

This young man's name was Adna, son of Bith. He did not stay long in Ériu. He made a quick survey and then came back, telling his people of his discovery and bringing them, as proof, a tuft of grass ripped from the ground.

Adna called *Inis na Fidbad*, the "island of the woods," the land he had discovered.

Sang Cormac mac Culennáin in his *Psalter of Cashel*:

Adna, son of Bith, with a prophetic spirit,

warrior of the lineage of Nín, son of Bél,

came to Ériu to explore it

and plucked a tuft of grass from the island of the woods.

He brought a handful of this herb with him

and returning, he reported the great news:

was clearly his complete invasion,

the shortest in duration among those who occupied Ériu.

Ériu remained uninhabited for a long time until the People of Partholon arrived two hundred and seventy-eight years after the flood.

The People of Partholon: The First Basics of Civilization

Partholon mac Sera, a man fleeing punishment. The first real invasion arrives in Ériu after the flood, to leave a lasting imprint and found there the customs of civil life.

1. Three Centuries After the Flood

After the flood, Ériu remained almost uninhabited for two hundred and seventy-eight years until the people led by Partholon first arrived there. This happened in the Anno Mundi 2520, or 2578 years before the birth of Christ. It was the sixtieth year of the third age of the world, sixty years after the birth of Abraham. Of course, not all annalists agree with this calculation (and those who follow the magisterium of the Greek translation of the Scriptures affirm that a thousand and two years had passed since the flood at the time of Partholon).

2. Partholon, the Parricidal Son

This is the genealogy of Partholon: Partholon, son of Sera, son of Sru, son of Esru, son of Braiment, son of Aithecht, son of Magog, son of Japheth, son of Noah. If you want to know why Partholon left his homeland, it's easy.

Partholon's father was the ruler of Mygdonia, the ancient Gréc Becc or "Little Greece" (although others say it was actually the island of Sicily, or Gréc Mór or "Magna Graecia").

Partholon had tried to oust his father, claiming sovereignty for his brother Becsomus. As punishment, his father had pulled out his left eye and chased him away, sending him into exile. After seven years, however, Partholon had returned to Gréc Becc, together with the crew of a ship, and had set fire to the royal residence, burning his father and mother alive. His brothers also perished in the stake.

Some say that Gréc Becc's ruler was actually Sru, and that Partholon was only later called mac Sera, as this last word, in Greek, means fingalach, "parricide."

3. After the Crime, the Exile

Having committed such a horrendous crime, Partholon escaped punishment by abandoning his homeland in the company of the few who had dared to follow him. Once at sea, within one month Partholon had arrived in Dalmatia, where he spent nine days in Septimania and, after, another month in Hispania. Then, keeping Hispania on the right, Partholon reached Ériu after another nine days.

In *Callann Mái*, on the fourteenth day of the moon, Partholon and his companions finally landed in *Inber Scéne (Kenmare)*, on the west coast of the Mumu.

4. Búadach!

Others say that Partholon and his entourage landed instead at Inis Saimer, an island at the mouth of the Saimer River. However, once the supplies ran out, and unable to support themselves, Partholon and his people moved elsewhere. They came to the mouth of a river so full of fish that Partholon exclaimed: "How rich he is!" (búadach!), and hence the name of *Inber mBuada*.

5. The People of Partholon

Four were the *airig* who led the People of Partholon, namely, Partholon himself and his three sons: Slaine, Laiglinne, and Rudraige. Each was accompanied by his own wife. Delgnat, daughter of the rude Lochtach, was Partholon's wife; Nerba, Cerbnat, and Cichba were the wives of his children. A couple of servants followed Partholon's family. The man was called Topa and he was Partholon's *gilla*.

Another name seems to have been Íth, which would later give name to the plain he tilled: *Mag nÍtha* nel Laigin.

These ten - eight noblemen of splendid appearance and two servants not as pleasant in appearance - were the crew of the *curach* who landed in Ériu.

Partholon had ten daughters: Aífe, Aíne, and the eminent Adnad; Macha, Mucha, and Melepard; Glas and Grennach; and Auach and Achanach. And these were their husbands, ten stalwart champions: Aidbli, Bomnad, and Bán; Caerthenn, Echtach, and Athchosán; Lucraid, Ligair, Lugaid the warrior, and Gerber.

Others say that Cerbnat was Íth's wife and that Laiglinne married her sister Aífe. It's possible. However, we believe that those who claim that Aífe married a certain Fintan, who actually belonged to the People of Cessair, are confused.

There is no doubt that Aífe's marriage was the first ever celebrated in Ériu. Later, Aífe would have given name to the plain of Mag Aífe in Osraige, while Cichba would have given name to the mouth of Inber Cichmuine.

It is not easy to define exactly the number of those who followed Partholon in Ériu, as historians and poets disagree with them. Some say there were only Partholon, his three children, and their four wives - eight people in all, from whom a population of four thousand and fifty men and a thousand women would later descend.

Tuan mac Cairill says the whole group was made up of twenty-four men, each accompanied by his woman, and he was present. Others say that Partholon arrived in Ériu with a retinue of a thousand men. It is difficult to determine which of these versions is the most truthful. Tradition recalls the names of many of those who were part of Partholon's entourage.

Brea, son of Senboth Seroll, son of Partholon, was the one who first built a house in Ériu and made a cauldron to cook the meat. He was a violent man, ready for revenge, who lived on war and robbery; he was the first to fight a singular fight and established this crude custom, destined to persist. His home, Dún mBrea, a fortress covered with a wicker roof, was built near a river estuary; there, Bree died, along with all her family, and there they all were buried.

Samailiath introduced the brewing technique and was the first in Ériu to drink fern beer. He was also the first to offer himself as a guarantor, and he invented adoration, offering, and supplication. Beoir, the steward of Partholon, instead built the first hostel where travelers were welcomed and refreshed for free.

Then, among the People of Partholon, there were seven chief farmers: Tothacht, Tarba, Eochair, Aithichbel, Cuailli, Dorcha, and Dam. There were two plowmen: Rimad the tail plow and Tairrle the head plowman. They used a plow with two iron parts: Fodbach was named the ploughshare and Fetain the coulter. There were four oxen of Partholon: Liac, Lecmag, Imair, and Etrige; these were the first to plow the soil of Ériu.

Fis "vision," Fochmarc "question," and Eólas "knowledge" were the three druids of Partholon. Milchú, Meran, and Muinechán were his three *trénfir* ("champions").

Bibal and Bebal were the two merchants, who introduced bartering in Ériu. The first exchanged gold, the second cattle. Furthermore, Bacorp was the healer and Ladru was Partholon's *fili and ollam*; they were the first to grant hospitality in Ériu.

6. The Death of Fea Mac Tortan

Seven years after the conquest of the island, the first man of Partholon's lineage died. It fell to the brave Fea to be chosen, the one who had accomplished numerous deeds - Fea, son of Tortan, son of Sru, son of Esru; Partholon's cousin.

The plain of Mag Fea took its name from Fea, and Oilbre Maige Fea took the name of the place where Fea was buried. It is said that his was "the first birth in Laigin" because he was born there, on top of the hill.

7. The Battle Against the Fomorians

When Partholon arrived in Ériu, the Fomorians had already resided there for two hundred years, and lived, not unlike the People of Partholon, hunting birds and fishing.

Cical nGricenchos was the leader of the Fomorians. When the People of Partholon met them, the Fomorians were eight hundred in number: Each quarter of their company consisted of fifty men and three times fifty women. They each had one eye, one arm, and one leg; they were not men but demons in human form.

The People of Partholon initially coexisted with the Fomorians. Then, three years after the death of Fea, the two peoples confronted each other to decide which of them should belong to the island.

For this reason, the People of Partholon and the Fomorians confronted each other in the *slemne* of Mag nÍtha. All the warriors of Partholon went into battle with one eye bandaged, one arm tied behind the back, and one foot tied to the thigh. The fighting lasted a week and no man received fatal wounds or was killed because druid arts were used. The Fomórians were defeated and Cical died. Some say that the Fomorians were all killed; others say they were driven out of Ériu and went to dwell in distant islands in the ocean or in fairy lands under the sea. However, they never gave up on the green Ériu and would later return to win it back.

8. The Death of Slaine mac Partholon

Of Partholon's three sons, the first to die was Slaine, thirteen years after the landing. Slaine had been a skilled healer and had treated his brother Laiglinne, who was wounded in his stead in the battle of Mag nÍtha. Slaine was buried under a *carn*, a mound of stones, on the mountain that took the name *Slíab Slánga*.

Others tell a different story regarding the name of the mountain. One day, Rudraige was chasing a wild boar, together with three times fifty warriors. However, the beast, after killing fifty people, broke two of the spears that Rudraige threw at it. Then he ran to the aid of his father Ross, son of Rudraige; the young man pierced the boar and skillfully retrieved the spear without breaking it.

"Long live you!" Partholon praised him. "Whole you tore off the spear." And from those words comes the name of Slíab Slánga.

9. The First Married Betrayal in Ériu

At that time there were no houses or farms. Partholon had camped on an islet at the mouth of the River Samáir, near a cove very rich in game. There weren't many ways to get food, and they mostly practiced hunting, fishing, and catching birds.

When Partholon went hunting or fishing, he used to leave his wife Delgnat - daughter of the ferocious Lochtach - and the young disciple (*gilla*) Topa to guard the camp. One day, the woman invited the gilla to make love to her. Topa tried to refuse, but Delgnat immediately began to insult him, to call him inept and cowardly.

To not suffer the shame, Topa ended up giving in and lay with the woman, without any pleasure. This was the first adultery in Ériu and, due to so much indecency and madness, the place was thereafter called *Ess Dá Éconn*, "the swift of the two fools." After the betrayal, Delgnat and Topa were seized by a terrible heat. Partholon possessed a jar of very sweet beer; no one could draw from it, except with a red gold cup. However, the two drank from the cup to quench that boundless and guilty thirst.

Back at the end of the day, Partholon asked for a drink. Bringing the cup to his lips, he, who was an educated man, tasted the mouths of Delgnat and Topa, and knew that he had been betrayed.

He stared at Delgnat: "No matter how short the time I was away, woman, I have a right to complain about you!"

"One with one" is always a good risk," she pointed out, not at all contrite. "Did you really think that it is possible to put a woman and a jar of honey, some fresh milk and a baby, some food and a hungry one, some fresh meat and a cat, weapons and tools and a craftsman, or a man and a woman close together alone without anything happening between them?"

And she quoted these verses:

Look at your mottled herds: in their clinging, they feel desire.
Look at the white-coated sheep: they don't take long to find a master!
Watch the placid herds for anyone: they seek the bull against all reason.

Look at the lambs in heat: they accept the authority of the first ram in the stable.

Constraints are imposed on the calf so that it does not follow the dairy cow.

Fences are placed in front of the sheep so that the grown lamb does not suck.

The frothy milk of the horned cow cannot be entrusted to a kitten!

A sharp ax, difficult to protect, cannot be entrusted to a woodcutter!

"Great shame on you, woman," Partholon said. "Your behavior is excessive for anyone. Each will correctly judge your guilt. Since Eve stained herself with the sin of the apple, enslaving mankind and cutting it out of heaven, the kind of guilt you committed had never been committed. However, I think Eve's sin is even lower than yours, Delgnat, or worse still."

Seized by a fit of jealousy, he struck his wife's dog, which was nearby, with his open hand, killing him. The cub was called Saimér and he gave his name to the islet where he died: Inis Saimér.

"The shame is not on us, but on you," Delgnat replied. And he added: "My Partholon, reason is on my side, not yours. You've left me in a one-to-one situation, and when the desire to mate comes, it's not easy to stifle it. I am innocent, and I am entitled to compensation."

This was the first judgment uttered in Ériu, Delgnat's right against Partholon. Some say that Partholon killed Topa; others say that

Topa fled and ended up devoured by dogs and birds. What is certain is that Partholon was the first husband betrayed in Ériu and hers was the first jealousy. This was sixteen years before his death.

10. The Death of Laiglinne mac Partholon

Fifteen years after the landing, Laiglinne, son of Partholon, captain (*airech*) of Ériu, died. That day, Laiglinne had gone with fifty men to the *Tipra Dera meic Scera,* the spring of Dera, son of Scera.

Suddenly, a flood wave erupted from the spring and the noble *airech* drowned in that shoreless lake, which took the name Loch Laiglinne.

Delgnat, wife of Partholon, went with fifty women to the *carn* that had been erected in memory of her son and there she died of pain.

Others say, however, that water erupted from the excavation of the tomb of Laiglinne, in the Uí mac Úais Breg, and thus Loch Laiglinne was formed.

11. The Death of Rudraige mac Partholon

Ten years later, Ériu's third *airech*, Rudraige of Partholon, also died. As his grave was being dug, water gushed out. That was how Loch Rudraige was formed, in Ulaid.

Others say it was under his feet - and not under Laiglinne's - that the lake water erupted, and he drowned in it.

12. The People of Partholon Change the Order of Ériu

During their stay in Ériu, the People of Partholon multiplied and filled the island. They established many trades and arts for the first time and were the first to establish laws.

They were mainly farmers. They practiced techniques such as bartering, milling, cooking meat, and brewing beer. They built the first buildings and the first hostels. They were the first to use a churn and a millstone. When Partholon had landed in Ériu, the island was different from what it is today: There were only three lakes and nine rivers and only the ancient plain of *Senmag nÉlta nÉtair*, the territory where today Baile Átha Cliath (Dublin) stands, which was said to have been leveled by the hands of God the creator, and in which grew neither a tree nor a blade of grass.

However, during their stay, the People of Partholon cleared four other plains: Mag Lí in the Uí mac Úais, between Bir and Camus; Mag Ladrann in the Dál nAraide; Mag nEthrige in Connacht; and eMag nítha nel Laigin (not to be confused with the homonymous plain where the battle against the Fomóraig took place).

It was the ox called Etrige, they say, that tilled Mag nEthrige, and his effort was such that the poor beast died after finishing the job. Therefore, his name was given to the plain. Later, however, it would be called Mag Tuired. Mag nítha was instead cleared by Íth, *gilla* of Partholon.

Similarly, in addition to the three ancient lakes present in Ériu, seven others were formed during the period in which the People of Partholon remained on the island.

In the twelfth year after Partholon's arrival, Loch Con and Loch Dechet erupted – both in Connacht.

The following year, Loch Mesc, abundant with mead, erupted. (Others say that Loch Mesc was the first lake to form, three years after the Battle of Mag nÍtha; but they, getting confused, believe that the Fomorians were defeated in the third year after Partholon's arrival in Ériu.)

Two years later, Loch Laiglinne erupted in Uí mac Úais Breg, on the tomb of Laiglinne, son of Partholon, as we have already said. Later, Loch nEchtra was formed between Slíab Modorn and Slíab Fúait, in Airgíalla.

Finally, ten years after Laiglinne's death, Loch Rudraige gushed under the feet of Rudraige, son of Partholon, in the Ulaid. In the same year, the sea flooded the land in the Bréna area and thus also formed the seventh lake, Loch Cúán.

13. The Death of Partholon

Although no one had been killed in the druid battle of Mag nÍtha, Partholon had sustained severe injuries. It was precisely those wounds, caused by bloody darts, that led to his death, exactly thirty years after the battle. Partholon died in Senmag nÉlta nÉtair, in the "ancient plain" of Élta, in Étar, thirty years after the landing of his people in Ériu, and was buried there.

14. The First Division of Ériu

The first territorial division of Ériu was implemented at the time of the People of Partholon. This division was stipulated by four children of Partholon, born, it is said, after his arrival in Ériu, and called Er, Orba, Fearon, and Feargna.

This tradition has aroused the perplexity of historians, as the names of these children of Partholon correspond to the names of the four children of Éber, who lived in the time of the Milensians, so that one could also think of a confusion between the two stories, if not that some of the most attentive historians assure us that it was indeed an extraordinary case of homonymy. At the time when the People of Partholon dwelt in Ériu, there was honesty among men, respect for covenants and property, and each knew the wealth that he kept in his own homes was secure. It was then that Er, Orba, Fearon, and Feargna divided Ériu among themselves into four parts, and no one was dissatisfied with their portion or threatened the part that fell to their brother.

He gave the first part to Er, the whole territory between *Ailech Néit* in the north of Ulaid to *Áth Cliath* in Laigin. He gave the second part to Orba, the territory between *Áth Cliath* to *Oilén Árda Neimed*. He gave the third part to Faeron, from *Oilén Árda Neimed* to *Áth Cliath Medruide* in Gallway (*Gaillim*). And he gave the fourth part to Feargna, from *Medruide* to *Ailech Néit*.

15. Coire mBreccain

A sea eddy roars in the icy Sea of Orkney, between Ériu and Alba. There, all the seas meet, from east to west, from north to south, and each one hurls with the others in a vortex that plunges into the abyss. The roar of the water is heard from afar, thunderous.

It is said that here came Breccán, son of Partholón, who, proud and obstinate, had left his father's land and, under the command of fifty *curaig*, headed north, determined to cross the world from one border to another. However, all fifty boats were sucked into the whirlpool and Breccán drowned. A third of Ériu's hosts died with him.

Therefore, the whirlpool is called *Coire mBreccáin*, the "cauldron of Breccán".

16. The End of the People of Partholon

The people of Partholon lived in Ériu for five hundred and fifty years, say the oldest chroniclers. Three hundred years, however, are the estimates of the most careful historians. What we do know is that they all disappeared, due to a plague, within a week. The disease manifested itself in Callann Mai, on Beltain Monday, in Mag mBreg.

Nine thousand died by the following Monday: five thousand four men and four thousand women, in Senmag nÉlta nÉtair. This was the same plain where Partholon himself had met his death. From then on, that place was called *Tamlecht Muintire Partholóin*, "pestilence of the People of Partholon" or *Tamlecht Fer nÉrenn*, "pestilence of the men of Ériu."

It was the year 2820 from the Creation of the World.

The only one to survive was a certain Tuan, son of Starn, son of Sera. Transmuted by God into various animal forms, Tuan survived in solitude from the time of Partholon to the time of Finnian and Columba. Reborn in the time of the saints, he would have handed down the memory of the invasion of the People of Partholon.

The Nemedians: The Second Invasion

A second people comes to Ériu looking for a new life. They will find oppression and slavery on the part of the Fomorians, but they will leave their mark forever.

1. The Arrival of Nemed

After the demise of the Partholon lineage, Ériu remained uninhabited for thirty years before the people led by Nemed arrived. They were Greeks originally from Scythia, a land located between Asia and Europe.

This is Nemed's genealogy. Nemed, son of Agnoman, son of Piamp, son of Tait, son of Sera, son of Sru, son of Esru, son of Friamaint, son of Fathochta, son of Magog, son of Japheth, son of Noah. Therefore, Nemed belonged to the same lineage as the one who had preceded him on the soil of Ériu, Partholon, son of Sera. The two branches of the family seem to have separated in the time of Sru, although some historians claim that Nemed was rather a direct descendant of Partholon, the great-grandson of one of his sons, named Adla.

However, even if they were of the same lineage, there could be no greater difference between Partholon and Nemed. Partholon had fled from Mygdonia because of his crimes, while Nemed and his companions were free men looking for a land where they could settle and live in peace.

After leaving Scythia, Nemed and his men headed north. Some say they made the long overland journey, keeping the Ural Mountains to their right. However, it is more likely that they had set sail with a fleet of boats on the waters of the Caspian Sea, heading north, to finally arrive where the cliffs of the Riphean Mountains mark the northern limit of the world.

Having entered the Boreal Ocean, the Nemedians had turned west and, keeping the northern coast of Europe on the left, had reached the British Isles after a year and a half of navigation. When the cliffs of Ériu were already looming on the horizon, the Nemedians had spotted an immense tower in the distance, the top of which was lost in the clouds. This rose from a rocky island that stood not far off the coast of Ériu. Hoping to find a treasure there, the Nemedians had approached those rocks to look for a landing place, but suddenly waves had risen so high and powerful that many ships were wrecked, while strong currents had repelled the surviving boats far from the island and its tower.

Of a fleet of thirty-four ships, each carrying thirty men, only the one on which Nemed and his relatives were traveling landed on the shores of Ériu.

It was the year 2850 after the Creation of the World, that is, 2348 years before the birth of Christ.

2. The Nemedians

With Nemed were his wife Macha and his four captains, who were his own sons, called Starn, Iarbonel the "Prophet," Fergus of the "Red – Side," and Annind. Each of them was, in turn, accompanied by his wife: Medu, Macha, Íba, and Cera. In all, the group consisted of thirty people. From this first nucleus would have descended that great people whom the Irish chronicles would have known as "*People of Nemed*" or Nemedians.

3. The Death of Macha

The first of the Nemedians to die on Ériu's soil was Nemed's wife Macha. She died only twelve days after the landing. She was a seer; she foresaw in a vision the destruction that would result, in the distant future, from the Cattle Raid of Cúailnge and her heart broke inside her. The place where Macha was buried took from her the name of *Árd-macha* (Armagh). In that place, twenty-seven centuries later, Pátraic would have founded the first place of worship in Christian Ireland.

4. The Nemedians Change the Order of Ériu

As long as Nemed lived, his people enjoyed security and prosperity.

If the Partolonians cleared four plains, the Nemedians cleared twelve: Mag Cera, Mag Eba, Mag Cuile Tolad, Mag Luirg in Connacht, Mag Tochair in Tír Eoghain, Leccmag in Mumu, Mag Bernsa in Laigin, Mag Lugaid in Uí Tuig, Mag Seired in Tethbae, Mag

Selmne in Dál nÁraidi, Mag Muirthemne in Brega, and Mag Macha in Airgíalla.

At the time of the Nemedians, four other lakes also formed: *Loch Cal* erupted in the plain of Mág nAsail in Uí Nialláin; *Loch Munremair* in Mág Sola, near the land of the men of Laigin; and *Loch Dairbrech and Loch Annind* in the plain of Mág Mór in the Meath, the tenth year after the arrival of the Nemedians in Ériu.

The latter lake took its name from Annind, son of Nemed. A pit was being dug to bury him and his body was already on the point of being placed there when the waters of an underground spring erupted from the excavation and formed the lake.

5. Mide Lights Eriu's First Fire

The first fire was lit in Ériu at the time of the Nemedians. It was lit by the druid Míde, son of Brath, and he did it on the sacred hill of Cnócc Úachtair Forcha, in the precise center of the island. That fire remained lit for six years and from it all the fires of Ériu were subsequently lit. The other druids regarded the lighting of that fire as an insult and gathered at the hill to discuss the matter. However, Míde cut off everyone's tongues, buried the tongues under the hill, and sat on that hill with satisfaction. His mother then said: "Proudly (*uaisnech*) you sit up there tonight."

From the woman's words, the sacred hill of Cnócc Úachtair Forcha also took the name of *Uisnech Míde* (Hill of Uisneach). And from the name of the druid came that of the entire province of Meath, which is the central province of Ériu, the future seat of the Supreme Kings of Ireland.

6. The Fight Against the Fomorians

At the time the Nemedians dwelt in Ériu, the Fomorians roamed in their ships along the coasts of the country, plundering the Nemedians.

The Fomorians had their base in *Tor Inís*, a rocky island that stood off the northwestern coast of Ériu, and between those cliffs they kept their fleet. It was the same island that the Nemedians had seen from afar when they were about to land in Ériu. The tower that stood there was the fortress where the two fearsome Fomorian leaders lived: Conand mac Febair and Morc mac Dela.

For a long time, the Nemedians resisted the assaults of the Fomorians in every way. Between them, a series of bloody fights broke out.

A battle was fought in *Sliab Bádgna*, and it ended victoriously for the Nemedians. Another was won by Nemed at *Ros Fraechain* in Connacht.

In the latter, Gann and Sengann, two Fomorian captains, were killed. Gann was shot down by Starn, son of Nemed. Sengann fell by the hand of Nemed himself.

Another battle was fought in Murbólg, in *Dal Riada*, in Ulaid. Starn, son of Nemed, fell to the hands of Conand mac Febair at Leithed Lachtmaige, but this time, too, the Nemedians were victorious.

Particularly bloody was a battle that took place at *Cnamoss* in Laigin, which resulted in veritable carnage. Artur, son of Nemed, who was born after their arrival in Ériu, and Iobcan, son of Starn, son of Nemed, died there. Despite the heavy losses, however, the Nemedians managed to prevail once and for all. Heavily defeated, the Fomorians were enslaved.

7. The Construction of the Royal Fortress

The Nemedians testified to their victory by building two royal fortresses (*ríográith*): Rath Chindeich in Uí Nialláin and Rath Chimbaith in Semne. The construction of Rath Chindeich was completed by four Fomorian slaves. They were called Boc, Roboc, Ruibne, and Rotan, and they were the four sons of Matan Muinremar. Nemed forced them to build the fortress within a single day. At dawn the next day, he had them killed for fear that they would destroy what they had just built. In Dáire Lige, the four brothers were killed and buried in the same place. However, because there were no kings among the Nemedians, it has been wondered for whom they had built the two royal fortresses.

Some historians think that they built them not for themselves but for their distant descendants, who would one day return to Ériu to bring the institution of royalty. So, the Nemedians had already foreseen the coming of these future peoples and had provided to honor them by giving them the two fortresses of Rath Chindeich and Rath Chimbaith.

8. The Death of Nemed

Twelve years after the arrival of the Nemedians, a terrible plague broke out in Ériu in which Nemed died along with three thousand of his people, men and women.

Nemed was in Múmu when the pestilence killed him. He died on the island of Oiléan Mór an Barraig, which was later also called Ard Nemid, in Crích Líathan (the future territory of the Uí Líathan).

9. Slavery of the Nemedians

As long as Nemed was alive, the Fomorians had not dared to rebel. However, when the leader of the Nemedians died, they decided that the time had come for the revival and rose up in arms against their masters. The Nemedians, with their leaders and best champions having perished in the battles and in the epidemic mentioned above, were soon overwhelmed.

From lords of the island, they became subjects of the Fomorians, whose leaders, Morc mac Dela and Conand mac Febair, soon proved to be tough and ruthless rulers. From the rocky cliffs of Tor Inís, where Conand's Tower rose, they kept the people of Ériu in subjugation.

It was a sad slavery, that of the Nemedians. Every year, on Samain's Eve, two-thirds of the grain, milk, and birthright were to be handed over to the Fomorians.

The delivery of the taxes took place in a clearing between the Drabaois and the Erne, which is why it was called Mág Cétne, "Same plain."

Each family gave the Fomorians a measure full of milk cream, a measure of wheat flour, and one of butter, which were brought to Morc and Conand in Tor Inís. They no longer dared to let smoke be seen from the roof in any house.

It was for this reason that the Fomorians earned this name, which in Gaelic means "Those who come from the sea," because from their island they got rich at the expense of the people of Ériu. While the Nemedians suffered under the play of the Fomorians, a woman named Liag traveled from one end of Ériu to the other to remind the sons of Nemed how hard and unfair was the tribute that the Fomorians had imposed on them.

In this way, she kept the spark of resentment alive in the hearts of the Nemedians, not ceasing to remind them how shameful it was for a free people to submit to such a sad subjection.

10. Revolt of the Nemedians

The ignominious tax, a cause of misery, ended up unleashing the indignation of the Nemedians. Gathered in assembly, the Nemedians resolved to go to Tor Inís, where the great fleet of Fomorians was, and to fight if the tax was not relieved. They were guided by Fergus, son of Nemed; Beothach, son of Iarbonel, son of Nemed; and Erglann, son of Beoan, son of Starn, son of Nemed, with his two brothers, Manntán and Iarthacht. Thirty thousand by sea and thirty thousand by land were the Nemedians who participated in the expedition, as well as the plebs who were brought with them to increase the ranks of the gathering.

Settled in front of the beaches of Tor Inís, the Nemedians sent Alma "One Tooth" to the tower to ask Conand mac Febair for a report that would allow them to pay the tribute at the end of three years. However, Conand was indignant at the message and Alma returned to report that he had made no profit from that trip. The Nemedians persuaded him to come back to ask Conand for a one-year postponement: to illustrate their poverty and the impossibility of putting together the onerous annual tax, adding the promise of a complete remission at the end of the granted deadline. If he did not get the respite, he would proclaim war. The Nemedians preferred to fall all together: men, women, and children, rather than still suffer great misery.

"I grant you," Conand replied, "on condition that you do not part until the set deadline. If you don't pay the tribute at that time, my Fomorians and I want you to gather in one place so that we can destroy you all!"

11. The Attack on Conand's Tower

The Nemedians accepted the conditions. Meanwhile, they sent messengers to Scythia to ask for help from their former compatriots. Smol mac Esmol reigned in Scythia, whose daughter Relbeo was the mother of Fergus Lethderg and Alma.

As soon as they learned of the situation in which the sons of Nemed were, they put out to sea a huge fleet that immediately set sail for Ériu. The expedition included not only talented warriors but also powerful druids of both sexes, plus dangerous animals such as foxes and wolves. The fleet anchored near Tor Inís and Conand mac Febair was ordered to grant freedom to the Nemedian people; otherwise, war would have been waged. The messengers sent to Conand returned, reporting that the leader of the Fomorians was ready to fight.

However, Princess Relbeo, who had joined the ranks, with her druidic arts changed her appearance into that of a concubine of Conand and, penetrating the tower, mingled with the lovers of the Fomorian leader and thus could spy on Conand's plans.

On her advice, the Nemedians built a high solid wall around Conand's Tower, then unleashed poisonous animals against the Fomorians. The rush of those strange and dangerous animals opened a series of breaches in each quarter and in their wake came the Nemedians.

Conand, who considered it an ignominy to not confront his enemies face to face, threw himself out with his squadrons. He thought it was easier to do battle in the open field than to wait for wolves and pigs to enter the tower through the shattered walls.

When the attackers saw them come out, they tied up the poisonous beasts and, leaving a guard to watch them, proceeded to battle. Fergus Lethderg moved to personally engage the mighty Conand. He could not refuse: The battle was fierce but in the end, the Fomorian leader was killed.

The siege lasted for a long time as the druids of both sides opposed spell to spell. Many valiant warriors fell on both sides, but in the end, with a desperate effort, the Nemedians got the better of their enemies. They surrounded and massacred all the Fomorians; not one of them managed to escape.

After being looted, Conand's Tower was set on fire and the Fomorian women and children perished in the stake.

12. The Rescue of the Fomorians

As Conand's Tower burned, the Nemedians celebrated their victory and shared the spoils among themselves. Then, behold, sixty Fomorian ships appeared on the sea. Morc mac Dela, who had run to Africa to ask for help from the people of his people, commanded her and now, albeit belatedly, came to support Conand mac Febair. Morc learned with pain of Conand's death and moved against the Nemedians, determined to avenge him.

Though tired, the Nemedians rushed to battle, determined to no longer tolerate the presence of the Fomorians on Ériu's soil. The two fleets met on the sea and the men began to fight fiercely. The battle turned into a horrible carnage and the fury of the contenders was so great that they did not even notice the gigantic tidal wave that overwhelmed them from all sides. However, even if they had seen it, it would have made no difference; they all fought with such enthusiasm that no one could break away from the opponent. Thus it was that the wave overwhelmed the two fleets and all perished. Only one Nemedian vessel with thirty people on board was saved from the cataclysm.

It was the year 3066 after the Creation of the World, that is, 2132 years before the birth of Christ.

13. The Fate of the Nemedians

For two hundred and sixteen years the Nemedians had remained in Ériu, from their arrival to the destruction of Conand's Tower. The thirty surviving Nemedians divided Ériu into three parts, each under the sovereignty of a captain. At Beothach, son of Iarbonel, son of Nemed, he touched the third from Tor Inís to the Bóann River. To Semion the "Spotted," son of Starn, son of Nemed, the third from Bóann to Belach Conglais. To Britain Mael, son of Fergus Lethderg, son of Nemed, the third from Belach Conglais to Tor Inís.

However, life wasn't easy for the few who survived. Epidemics wiped them out. As if that were not enough, the Fomorians had returned and all lived in terror of their revenge.

Fergus Lethderg and twenty-four of his sons died of poisoning. The one who prepared the mortal drink for them was Dreco ingen Chalchmáel, poetess and druid. The mountain on which they perished took the name of *Nemthen* (the mount Nephin), "Mighty Poison."

Between the epidemics and the Fomorian threat, the lives of the Nemedians in Ériu had become untenable. So it was that they decided to leave the island of Ériu and resume the sea routes. Some of the Nemedians, however, did not want to leave their homes and preferred to stay in Ériu rather than attempt the adventure in other countries. Beothach, son of Iarbonel, son of Nemed, remained to guide them, assisted by ten warriors who were chosen to remain on the island. Unfortunately, Beothach died from one of the frequent epidemics that raged on the island.

In the meantime, those who had decided to leave were busy building the ships. The preparations for the departure lasted seven years. Having prepared a fleet, the Nemedians split into three parts, each group under the orders of a chief. The ships set sail from the shores of Ériu, and once they set sail, the fleet split into three parts. Each flotilla took a different direction. Between ships, vessels, and small boats, it is said there were a total of one hundred and thirty boats.

Semion Brecc, son of Erglan, son of Beoan, son of Starn, son of Nemed, turned his bows south and brought his group of men back to Greece, unaware that they were facing a destiny of slavery.

Iobath, son of Beothach, son of Iarbonel, son of Nemed, turned his prow to the north and went north. It is not known for sure which islands he found in the cold boreal seas. Some say that his descendants settled in a land called "Beozia," where they cultivated the druidic arts and gave birth to a great people of wizards and warriors.

The third group instead turned the bow to the east. Erglann, Manntán, and Iarthacht, the three sons of Beoan, son of Starn, turned their bows east and headed for Dobar and Iardobar, in the north of Alba (Scotland).

Their posterity settled in those lands until the Picts in turn arrived in Alba from Ériu, forcing them to leave the country. The same group included Britain Mael, son of Fergus Lethderg, who landed farther south, in the land that took the name of Britannia from him. From him descended the Britons, who populated that country and were still there in Roman times, until Hengist and Horsa, the two sons of Guictglis, king of the Saxons, came to subdue them, pushing them back to the western shores. An ancient poet sings:

Generous son of Fergus Lethderg,

all Britons, victory with great fame,

from him without exception they descended.

And other poets confirm with these verses:

Britain Mael, son of the warrior,

noble offspring came from him,

son of Lithderg from Lecmág

from which the Britons in the world descend.

Those few of the Nemedians who had remained in Ériu soon returned to suffer under the yoke of the Fomorians. It was a long and sad slavery, which ended only when the people of Fir Bolg arrived in Ériu to free them.

14. Those Who Return

It will be remembered that the Nemedians had built the two royal fortresses of Rath Chindeich and Rath Chimbaith not for them, but for their distant descendants, who would bring the institution of royalty to Ériu. It is also said that of the twelve cleared plains, only one-third was destined for themselves; the remaining two-thirds were for each group of descendants whose arrival was prepared.

And indeed, from the three small groups of fugitives who had left Ériu, as many strong and proud peoples would descend. Of these peoples, two were destined to return to Ériu to invade and colonize it once again.

From the group of Semion Brecc, son of Erglan, son of Beoan, son of Starn, son of Nemed, who had returned to Greece, descended a strong and proud posterity, the people of Fir Bolg. They returned to Ériu to conquer it. The descendants of Ibáth, who had settled in the northern regions of the world, became a people of valiant warriors and wise druids. The Túatha Dé Dánann, in turn, were destined to return to Ériu to snatch it from the Fir Bolg and to close the war with the Fomorians once and for all.

The Fir Bolg: The Third Invasion

Descendants of the Nemedians, the Fir Bolg come to Ériu to escape from slavery and misery. Their rulers are absolutely the first to reign on the soil of Ériu.

1. Descendants of the Nemedians in Greece

As we have seen, the few survivors among the Nemedians, after being decimated in the war against the Fomorians, had split into various groups and relied on the sea. One of these groups, led by Semion Brecc, son of Erglan, son of Beoan, son of Starn, son of Nemed, had returned to the original land of Greece. They hoped to be welcomed with fraternal friendship by those people who, after all, belonged to their own blood.

However, in those lands, the descendants of Semion had multiplied to become thousands, so much so that the Greeks were afraid of them and reduced them to slavery, forcing them to dig the land and dirt it, then transport the soil in leather bags and spread it on the rocky heights up to level plains of clover.

Anger and sadness increased in the souls of the descendants of Semion, and hatred was born toward the Greeks, who had reduced them to slavery. And so, exhausted and saddened by this condition, they finally decided to escape the intolerable servile yoke. Five thousand gathered together and took the leather sacks they used to carry the land, and with them they built fragile *currach*. Aboard those fragile boats they set out to sea. Others say they stole the fleet of the king of the Greeks.

Their ancestors had fled the noble island of Ériu. They decided to return there to live as free men.

2. *The Three Arms of the Fir Bolg*

The leaders who organized the escape of the slaves from Greece were five brothers: Slaine, Rudraige, Gann, Genann, and Sengann.

They were the five sons of Dela, son of Loch, son of Ortecht, son of Tribuad, son of Oturp, son of Goisten, son of Uirthecht, son of Semion Brecc, son of Erglan, son of Beoan, son of Starn, son of Nemed.

At their side were their wives: Fuad, wife of Slaine; Etar, wife of Gann; Anust, wife of Sengann; Cnucha, wife of Genann; and Liber, wife of Rudraige.

Five thousand men and women moved under the orders of the five brothers. One thousand and one hundred and thirty boats, large and small, set sail on Wednesday, bound for the west.

Slaine, who served as judge among his brothers, spoke thus:

It is time for effort, commitment and we must be alert.

The sea is raging and gray with foam.

Each of our graceful boats

it leaves behind intolerable wrongs.

Unheard of is the tyranny of the Greeks.

We must try to achieve

the valleys of Ériu, rich in salmon.

They sailed in the Torrian Sea until, after a year and three days, they rounded Spain. Then, heading north, in seven days, driven by a south-east wind, they saw the island of Ériu in the distance.

The wind picked up and became stronger. The waves hit the small fleet and broke it into three groups, which drifted away from each other. Thus, three distinct ranks were formed, which were later called Gailioin, Fir Domnann, and Fir Bolg. It is equally correct, however, to call them generically Fir Bolg, the "Men of Bags," because they all came by sea in the sacks they had used to transport the soil.

The ranks of the Gailioin, "Armed with a spear," got this name because its men defended themselves with darts or spears (gaileón). It was the first of the three groups to touch the banks of Ériu. Led by Slaine, they disembarked in Laigin, on Saturday, in the place that in honor of their captain was named Inber Slaine.

The Fir Domnann, the "Men who dig the earth," were so called because their task in Greece had been to dig wells to take the earth. Led by Gann and Sengann, this second host landed three days after that of the Gailioin, on Tuesday, in Irrus Domnainn, in northwest Connacht.

The Fir Bolg, the "Men of Bags," were so called because their task, in Greece, had been to transport the earth in leather sacks (bólg). This third group, led by Genann and Rudraige, landed three days after that of the Fir Domnann, on Friday, at Tracht Rudraige, in the Ulaid.

After disembarking over a period of seven days and in three different bays, the three ranks set off toward the center of Ériu and gathered at Uisnech Meath, at the central point of the island.

It was the year 3266 after the Creation of the World, 1932 years before the birth of Christ, and Ériu was again trampled by the feet of men after being uninhabited for over two hundred years.

3. Eriu Divided in Five Parts

Finding themselves in Uisnech Meath, in the central place where all the provinces of Ériu meet, the five captains of the Fir Bolg said to each other: "We thank the gods for having returned to you, Ériu. May the country be divided equally among us."

The five brothers divided Ériu among themselves and each of them took a fifth.

Slaine took the fifth of the Laigin. Gann took the fifth of the eastern Mumu. Sengann took the fifth of the western Mumu. Genann had for himself the fifth of the Connacht. Rudraige had the fifth of the Ulaid.

Thus, it was that Ériu was divided for the first time into five "fifths," which met on the hill of Uisnech Meath, in the precise center of the island. This division into five parts was perpetuated over time and became, with some variations, the traditional division into five provinces of the island of Ériu.

4. The Kings of the Fir Bolg

The Fir Bolg were the first to create social and political institutions in Ériu. They introduced the custom of royalty, with an elected ruler in place of the warrior leaders of yore. The Fir Bolg kings were the first and oldest rulers of Ériu. They established their palace in Líath Drum, the "Gray Hill" of the Meath, in the place that would one day be called Temáir.

When they first chose their ruler, the five captains of the Fir Bolg gathered in Uisnech Meath, in the central point of Ériu, and elected Slaine, who was the youngest of the five, but certainly the wisest and certainly not the one of less value. Slaine mac Dela was the very first Supreme King of Ériu.

Slaine reigned for a year and then died in Ding Ríg. He was the first of his people to be buried in the soil of Ériu.

He was succeeded by his brother Rudraige, who reigned for two years, then died near the *Brú na Bóinne*.

He was succeeded by Gann and Genann, who reigned jointly for four years. They died of disease, along with two hundred other people, in Fremainn Meath.

Sengann then ascended to the throne and reigned for five years. He was killed by Fiacha, son of Starn, son of Rudraige.

Fiacha reigned for five years, then was killed by Rinnal, son of Genann.

Rinnal, son of Genann, likewise reigned for five years, then was killed in turn by Fodbgen, son of Sengann.

After four years of reign, Fodbgen was killed in the plain of Mág Muirthemne by Eochaid, son of Erc, son of Rinnal, son of Genann, who assumed the kingship of Ériu.

Eochaid, son of Erc, was an exemplary monarch. During his ten-year reign, there was no rain but only dew. In his day, lying was banished by Ériu, and he was the first to establish the rule of justice. His wife was Tailtiu, daughter of King Mágmór of Spain. However, he was also the last king of the Fir Bolg.

Thirty-six years alone did the Fir Bolg's dominion over Ériu last. In fact, the arrival of the mysterious and powerful Túatha Dé Dánann was already being prepared.

CAP 5:

THE TÚATHA DÉ DANANN

The Túatha Dé Danann: The Tribes of the Gods of Danaan

From another line of the Nemedians arise the Túatha Dé Danann, a people of semi-divine beings, versed in war and druidic arts, who are preparing to reach Ériu in their turn.

1. The Túatha Dé Danann

The fourth invasion that came from the sea to occupy Ériu was that of the Túatha Dé Danann, the "tribes of the gods of Danann." They say that the Túatha Dé Danann derived this name from their three young men, sons of a certain Danann, so skilled and wise in the druidic arts that they were called "three of the gods of Danann." From these, the Túatha Dé Danann took their name.

Others say that the Túatha Dé Danann were so-called as three classes made up their social body: the noble leaders who led the tribes [*túatha*]; the wise druids, experts in pagan arts, assimilated to real divinities [*dée*]; and the talented artisans who practiced creative and artistic activities [*dána*].

And, indeed, the men of the Túatha De Danann excelled in everything: They were formidable warriors, peerless artisans, and druids who were expert in every doctrine. They may not have been gods, but the ignorant people ended up mistaking them for such. Or perhaps they were truly gods and Christian copyists transformed them into a host of heroes of antiquity, endowed with great abilities and almost divine powers.

2. The Origin of the Túatha Dé Danann

After the destruction of Tor Inís, the Nemedians had taken to the sea, leaving the island of Ériu.

Semion Brecc had led his group of survivors to the original land of Greece, without imagining that a destiny of slavery awaited them; from them, however, those Fir Bolg would descend who would later reign over Ériu.

The three sons of Beoan, together with Britain Mael, had led their party to Alba and Britain, and they had given birth to the proud people of the Britons. Beothach, son of Iarbonel, had instead remained in Ériu together with his group. When he died, however, his son Iobath decided to abandon the island. In turn, and sometimes the prows to the north, he led his little retinue into the distant boreal seas.

It appears that Iobath died on the journey and it was his son, Bath, who assumed command of the group. Some say that in the far north there is an island called Beozia and that it was in that boreal land that the people led by Iobath and Bath landed after a long voyage. Settling on the northern islands of the world, the Nemedian exiles there learned occult science, magic, druidic arts, witchcraft, and magical skills until, in those arts, they surpassed all the scholars of foreign lands.

Four were the four cities in which they obtained their education: Falias, Gorias, Finias, and Murias.

In these four cities resided four wise druids: Morfessa in Falias, Esras in Gorias, Uscias in Finias, and Semias in Murias. And it was from these that the Nemedian exiles learned the occult sciences and secret doctrines. From these came the Túatha Dé Danann, the "tribes of the gods of Danann."

3. The War with the Philistines

Others say that the northward migration took place much later and that Iobath and Bath instead led their ranks of exiles to Greece, settling near the territory of Athens. In fact, Beozia is the name of a region located not far from Athens, in Achaia.

It is also possible that the Túatha Dé Danann came to Greece from the northern islands of the world. On this point, the sources are not very clear.

At that time it happened that the Philistine fleet, coming from Syria, landed in the territory of Achaia and attacked the Athenians. A series of bloody battles broke out between the Philistines and the Athenians, in which the Athenians had the worst. Many of the strongest warriors of Athens were killed, so that they soon found themselves outnumbered by the fierce and ferocious Philistines.

The Athenians then turned to the Túatha Dé Danann, whose druids were experts in the pagan arts. They began to form diabolical spirits that blew into the bodies of the corpses that had fallen on the battlefield, and they rose from the sleep of death and returned to consolidate the broken ranks of the Athenian armies.

The Philistines, astonished to see those they had killed the day before take to the field again the next day, informed their druids of the incident. The oldest of them advised the warriors to observe the battlefield well and to plant stone pegs in the necks of the slain. In this way, if it was through the intervention of necromantic arts that the fallen came back to life, the bodies would immediately be putrefied; but on the contrary, if they were truly raised from the dead by divine will, the corpses would no longer suffer decay and corruption.

The next day, the Philistines again went to battle and, after the victory, carefully inspected the battlefield. When they found a corpse that seemed to have come back to life, they stuck a hazelnut peg in the back of its head, and as the old druid had said, the body of the slain suddenly turned into a heap of worms.

As a result, the strength of the Athenians was humiliated and the Philistines took over. Remembering how the Túatha De Danann had lined up against them, they decided to take revenge and attack them.

As soon as the Túatha Dé Danann learned of the Philistines' intentions, they fled back to the sea and turned their bows to the north.

4. Into Lochlan and Alba

Fleeing Greece, the Túatha Dé Danann first arrived in the country of Lochlann [Norway], where the Fomorians had their kingdom. The Túatha Dé Danann were well received by the people of Lochlann, as there were among them experts in many disciplines and skilled in all arts and techniques. They allied themselves with the Fomorians and there were also marriages between the two peoples.

Some sources claim that the four cities of Falias, Gorias, Finias, and Murias were located in Lochlann and that the Túatha Dé Danann here taught the young people of this country the arts and techniques they were familiar with. However, it is more likely that those cities were located on the northern islands of the world and that the Túatha Dé Danann had left them before returning to Greece.

Be that as it may, after staying for some time in Lochlann, the Túatha Dé Danann decided to go out to sea once again. Their ruler at that time was Nuada Airgetlam. He led the Túatha Dé in the north of Alba [Scotland], which at that time was also controlled by the Fomorians. Here, they remained for seven years, settling between the towns of Dobar and Iardobar.

When their people had become numerous, the Túatha Dé Danann decided to invade Ériu against the Fir Bolg, judging that the island belonged to them by hereditary right.

5. Kings, Heroes, and Artisans of the Túatha Dé Danann

The king of the Túatha Dé Danann was, at that time, Nuada Airgetlam. A mighty warrior, Nuada possessed the Claíomh Solais, a sword destined to give victory to whoever wielded it. It was he who led his people in the migration from Lochlann to Alba and from Alba to Ériu. However, the spiritual leader of the Túatha Dé Danann was Eochaid Ollathair, called the Dagda Mor.

He was the repository of druidic wisdom. To him belonged the Coire Ansic, a magical cauldron that provided food without ever running out. The Dagda Mor also had a herd of pigs, of which one was always alive and another always ready to be cooked, while its trees were always full of fruit. He also possessed a club that, when struck, could kill as well as resurrect whoever he had killed. It was so heavy that it was dragged on wheels and left a trace deep enough to be used as a border moat for a province.

Furthermore, the Dagda Mor possessed a magical harp to which he had taught wonderful music, but which could be played only if he was the one who touched its strings.

Then there was the champion Ogma, brother of the Dagda. Beautiful in the features of his face, he was the inventor of the Ogham alphabet, consisting of a series of lines arranged differently along a vertical edge.

There were Brian, Iuchar, and Iucharba, the three sons of Delbaeth, son of Ogma. Their mother was Danann, also a daughter of Delbaeth, who had generated them by joining incestuously with her father.

163

These three were so skilled in the druidic and pagan arts, and had attained such excellence in them, that their people not only called them "the three gods of Danann" but did not disdain to take their own name from these three: Dé Danann, the "tribes of the gods of Danann." Then there was Eochaid Bress, another brother of the Dagda, destined to become king of the Túatha Dé Danann, but without any glory, because due to bad governance he would have risked bringing his people to ruin.

There was also Manannan mac Lir, the knight of the crested sea. He drove his chariot over the waves in the same way that men drive their chariots on earth. In fact, his mare, Enbarr, ran a lot on land or sea, and whoever rode her was never thrown from the saddle and killed. Manannan also owned pigs which, killed every day, returned to live the following day. The men of the Túatha Dé Danann feasted on these pigs. His currach, which was called *Sguaba Tuinne*, had the advantage of arriving alone at its destination. His sword was called *Fragarach*, and none of those injured by it had managed to survive. Manannan's wife was the blonde Fann daughter of Aed Abrat, whose beauty was legendary even among Danann women.

Then there was Dian Cecht, the healer of the Túatha Dé Danann. His sons Miach, Octriuil, and Airmed were all talented doctors and healers, having inherited the art from their father.

Then there was Lugh, although at the time of the departure of the Túatha Dé Danann from Alba he had not yet revealed himself. He was also called Samildanach, "He who is skilled in all the arts," as he was an expert in the art of the poet, the druid, the physician, the blacksmith, and the carpenter. He was also a great warrior: He would be given the invincible spear, the Spear of Lugh.

And there was still Brígit, who some say was another daughter of the Dagda. She was an expert in poetry, divination, medical art, and metallurgy. However, she was above all the lady of knowledge, the inspiration of poets and seers. She was the first to modulate a whistle to call each other in the middle of the night.

Then there was a triad of peerless artisans. Of these, Goibniu was an unparalleled blacksmith: He supplied weapons to the Túatha Dé Danann and prepared their banquets. Credne Cerd was a very skilled coppersmith, the greatest among the artisans of copper and bronze. And Luchtaine mac Luachaid was a great carpenter. The skill of these three was so great that in battles they continually forged new weapons for the warriors to replace the blunt ones.

Then there was Coirpre the poet and three satirists, whose names were Cridenbel, Bruinne, and Casmaol.

And there was still Morrigan, with her sisters Badb Chatha and Macha.

Fierce, bloodthirsty, relentless, the Morrigan descended into battle and determined who should win and who should defeat; he fed on severed heads and pierced bodies. In the fray, she took many forms, but the most common was that of a crow. In this aspect, she fluttered over the armies, so that they could no longer distinguish friends from enemies. However, even if her character was usually frightening, Morrigan could also take on bewitching features: She sometimes seduced warriors, especially in critical moments, on the eve of battles. Another name of the Morrigan was Anu, in honor of which two hills in the Múmu were called the "the breasts of Anu."

Finally, Dínann and Beuchuill were the two witches of the Túatha Dé Danann. They and their sisters Aircdan and *Be Theite* were the four daughters of Flidais.

6. Geneaology of the Túatha Dé Danann

The most direct ancestor of the Túatha De Danann was named Tait.

This is his genealogy: Tait, son of Tabarn, son of Enna, son of Baath, son of Iobath, son of Beothach, son of Iarbonel Faid, son of Nemed. Two children of Tait are remembered: Allui and Alda. Allui's children were Ordam and Innui. Son of Alda, Edleo. It is from Ordam, Innui, and Edleo that the Danann tribes descended.

Nuada, king of the Túatha Dé Danann at the time of their arrival in Ériu, belonged to Ordam's lineage. This is his genealogy: Nuada, son of Echtach, son of Etarlam, son of Ordam, son of Allui, son of Tait.

Nuada had many children, among whom we remember Caicher, Etarlam, and Lugaid. Caichér was Uillenn's father. Etarlam was the father of Ernmas, mother of the three war goddesses, Morrigan, Badb Chatha, and Macha, who some say are three names for the same woman.

Coirpre the poet also belonged to Ordam's lineage. This is his genealogy: Coirpre, son of Tuar, son of Tuirell, son of Cai Conaichenn, son of Ordam, son of Allui, son of Tait.

Let us now see the offspring of Innui, son of Allaui, son of Tait.

Eochaid Ollathair called the Dagda Mor, the champion Ogma, Allot, Eochaid Bress, and Delbáeth were the five sons of Elatha, son of Delbáeth, son of Neit, son of Innui, son of Allui, son of Tait.

The Dagda Mor was, in turn, the father of Aengus, Aed, Cermait, and Mídir. Some say that Brigit was also a daughter of the Dagda.

Cermait, son of the Dagda, had three sons, who would one day reign jointly over Ériu. They were called Mac Cuill, Mac Greine, and Mac Cecht, the Son of the Hazel, the Son of the Sun, and the Son of the Plow.

Ogma, brother of the Dagda, was the father of Delbeeth. He was, in turn, the father of Fiacha, Ollam, Innui, Elchmar, Brian, Iuchar, and Iucharba. Mother of the last three was Danann, who was also a daughter of Delbaeth himself. Ollam had Ái for his son.

Fiacha, son of Delbaeth, son of Ogma was the father of Ériu, Banba, and Fodla, who would one day be the three queens of the Túatha Dé Danann, wives of the three sons of Cermat Mílbel. All three would give their name to the island of Ériu. Ernmas, daughter of Etarlam, son of Nuada was the mother of these three.

Allot, brother of the Dagda, was the father of Orbsen, better known as Manannan mac Lir, the knight of the crested sea.

The other brother of the Dagda, Eochaid Bress, was the father of Rúadán and Duach Dall. Duach Dall was the father of Eochaid Garb, who in turn was father of the noble Bodb Derg and Náma. The latter was the father of Caichér and Nechtan.

Delbaeth, the last of the Dagda Mor brothers, was the father of Boann. She was the wife of Elchmar but she had fathered, with the Dagda, the son Aengus.

Dian Cecht the healer was son of Esarg, son of Neit, son of Innui, son of Allui. He had several children, including Cian, Cú, and Céithen, and then Miach, Octriuil, and Airmed, who were themselves skilled healers, and again Étan the poet. Coirpre, son of Etan, was also a poet. Another poet was Abean, son of Bec-Felmas, son of Cú, son of Dian Cecht; this Abean was the poet of Lugh.

Lugh was the son of Cian, son of Dian Cecht. His mother was Ethniu, daughter of Balor.

Finally, we now see the lineage of Edleo, son of Alda. The only known member of this tribe is En, son of Bel-En, son of Satharn, son of Edleo, son of Alda, son of Tait.

7. The Alliance With the Fomorians

By the time the Túatha Dé Danann were stationed in Lochlann, they had formed an alliance with the Fomorians, which was even closer when they passed into Alba. In this time between the two lineages, there had been several marriages, from which a mixed lineage was born. It is not clear in what times and modalities the Danann family tree was intertwined with the Fomorians; perhaps already in the time of Net, son of Innui, son of Allui, son of Tait.

This Neit had two wives, Nemain and Fea, with whom he had three children: Dot, Esarg, and Delbaeth. Son of Dot was Balor, whom we will find again as head of the Fomorian army during the war against the Túatha Dé Danann. Son of Delbaeth was Elatha, who would reveal that he was a king of the Fomorians.

On the other hand, Esarg's descendants include Dian Cecht and his sons, whose belonging to the Danann people cannot be doubted.

So, we have Balor and Elatha, descendants of Neit, who not only were Fomorian chiefs of Nemedian blood but also had Danann lineage. Elatha was, in fact, the father of some of the noblest Danann chiefs, including the Dagda Mor, Ogma, and Eochaid Bress.

But if the belonging of the Dagda and Ogma to the Túatha Dé Danann cannot be doubted, some texts say instead that Bress (the son Elatha had from a Danann woman, Eri) was accepted among the Túatha Dé as an adopted son. Despite this uncertain position, Bress was elected king of the Túatha Dé Danann; but when he was overthrown due to his bad governance, he returned to his father Elatha and convinced him to lead the Fomorians in the war against the Túatha Dé Danann. We will examine these facts later.

Even Lugh did not have a very clear position: His father was Cian delle Túatha Dé Danann and his mother Ethniu, daughter of the Fomorian Balor. However, Lugh's fidelity would always go to his father's people, for he would be the main architect of the victory of the Túatha Dé Danann over the Fomorians.

8. The Four Treasures of the Túatha Dé Danann

In all their movements, from the northern islands of the world to Greece, from Greece to Lochlann, and from here to Alba and finally to Ériu, the Túatha Dé Danann had not neglected to carry their four treasures, which were respectively a stone, a spear, a sword, and a cauldron.

From Falias they had brought the Lía Fáil, the "stone of destiny," which would be placed in Temair. This stone used to cry out as it was stepped on by a legitimate king who was about to assume the supreme kingship of Ériu.

From Gorias they had brought the Lúin of Celtchar, the "Lugh's spear," which was later assigned to Lugh. A battle was never won against this spear, nor against whoever held it in his hand.

From Finias was brought the Claíomh Solais, the "sword of light," belonging to Nuada. It was invincible when pulled from the scabbard.

From Murias was brought the Coire Ansic, the "cauldron of the good god," belonging to the Dagda Mor, whose content was such that no company, however numerous, went away unsatisfied.

The Advent of the Túatha Dé Danann: The Fourth Invasion

We temporarily leave the Lebor Gabála Érenn chronicle to enter into more detailed texts. The Túatha Dé Danann and the Fir Bolg meet with mutual suspicion on Ériu's soil.

   1. *The Arrival of the Túatha Dé Danann*

The Túatha Dé Danann landed in secret in *Corco Belgatan*, near the place where *Connemara* then arose, on the Monday of Beltane [1

May] of the year 3303 from the creation of the world, or 1895 years before the birth of Christ. When they landed, they burned the boats so that none of them could go back. Their hearts were happy because they had reached the land of their ancestors.

The smoke from the burning ships invaded the air and land around the Túatha Dé Danann and the sun was obscured for three days and three nights. Protected by that thick darkness, the Túatha Dé Danann advanced to Mag Rein, where they settled. That is why it would later be said that they had come directly from heaven into Mag Rein, descending on clouds of smoke.

2. The Dream of Eochaid mac Eirc

At that time, Eochaid mac Eirc was king of the Fir Bolg; his wife was Queen Tailtiu, daughter of Mag Mór, king of Spain. They dwelt in the place which was called Líath Druim, the "Gray Hill," but which would one day be *Temair*, the Hill of Tara, the seat of the Supreme Kings of Ériu. The night the Túatha Dé Danann landed in Ériu, Eochaid happened to have a strange dream. Puzzled, he related the vision to his druid Cesarn.

- I saw a flock of black birds coming out of the ocean. They swarmed over us and fought with the people of Ériu. They confused and destroyed us. However, one of us struck the noblest of those birds and tore off a wing. Oh, wise Cesarn, what is the meaning of my dream? "The times that are preparing for us are bad times," replied the druid. "A people of warriors comes from the sea, a thousand heroes cover the ocean. Mottled boats swoop down on us. A people skilled in the magical arts announces infinite types of death for us. Evil spirits will betray you and harm you, and eventually get the better of you.

3. Sreng to the Camp of the Invaders

Upon hearing of the landing of the Túatha Dé Danann, the Fir Bolg sent men to Connacht to find out who these invaders were. The spies returned to Temair and reported seeing a crowd of proud heroes, well-armed and fearsome, good at music and dance. Then the Fir Bolg were afraid because the newcomers surpassed all the people of the world in any art. King Eochaid heard the advice of his trusted advisors, and they replied, "It will be an advantage to know something about them. Who are they and what do they intend to do? Where do they want to settle down? Let Sreng, son of Sengann, come and visit them, as he is certainly not afraid to ask questions."

Sreng son of Sengann, son of Dela, was one of the best champions of the Fir Bolg. He took his enormous burnished red shield, the two large-handled spears, the deadly sword, the four-pointed helmet, and the iron mace. Thus harnessed, he left Temair and went to Mag Rein to parley with the newcomers.

4. The Meeting Between Champions

When the sentries of the Túatha De Danann saw such a champion approaching, they immediately sent Eochaid Bress, son of Elatha to meet him. With his shield, his sword, and his two spears, Bress left the camp and stepped forward. The two men approached, keeping an eye on each other, without saying a word, and each was struck by the other's stature and weapons. When they were close enough to talk to each other, they stopped, and having lowered their shields to the ground, they huddled behind them, observing each other across the boundary line.

Bress was the first to speak, and when Sreng heard that the other spoke his own language, he felt less uncomfortable. So, they drew closer, and each said his name, which was his lineage and which were his ancestors.

Then Sreng said, "When you mentioned your ancestor Nemed, your words made my flesh and my tongue glad. I greet you as a brother. We are both descended from Semion Brecc, son of Erglann. Moderate your pride and let our hearts come together. Tell your king that your people and mine are brothers, descendants of one noble lineage. If we clash, many will be mowed down cruelly and it will certainly not be a pastime that will entertain us."

"Take off your shield and let me see you," Bress said. "May I relate your appearance to the Túatha De Danann?"

"All right," Sreng said. "It was only for fear of your sharp spears that I placed my shield between us."

So he pushed aside his shield and Bress remarked, "Your spears are strange and menacing. I'd like to look at them better."

Sreng untied the bindings of his spears and passed them to Bress, who weighed them in his hands and saw that they were strong, balanced, and sharp in cut, although they had no points. Bress said, "I've never seen spears like this. With a wide tip, heavy and sharp blades. Unfortunate is the one who gets hit. Their blows are powerful and their use causes serious wounds. Tremendous is the horror they inspire. What do you call them?"

"We call them *craisech*," Sreng replied. "They pierce shields and smash skulls and bon. Their blows cause death or wounds that never heal."

"Powerful weapons," Bress said. "They mean wounded bodies, gushing blood, broken bones and shattered shields, scars and infirmities. They bring disabilities and death. Those who use them have fratricidal fury in their hearts. It will be better if we come to an agreement before the sacred soil of Ériu is soaked with the blood of our brothers."

So, the two champions started to argue. "Where were you last night?" Bress asked.

"I was in the heart of Ériu, in the Enclosure of the Kings, in Temair. I was with Eochaid mac Eirc, the Supreme King of Ériu, and the leaders of the Fir Bolg. Where were you?"

"In the crowded camp of Mag Rein, with our king Nuada and the champions of the Túatha Dé Danann. We came from the north immersed in a magical fog. We sailed in the sky to the island of Ériu."

"I have traveled a long way to come here and now I must return to report what I have discovered," Sreng concluded. "Tell me what intentions animate your people."

"He's fine," Bress said. "This is one of the two sharp spears I have brought with me. We call it *sleg*. Bring it and show it to your people, so that they can see which weapons they will have to fight against."

Sreng nodded and, in exchange, left Bress one of his craisech, so that he could show it to the Túatha Dé Danann.

"Tell the Fir Bolg," Bress finally said, "that if they give us half of Ériu, we will occupy it peacefully. However, if it doesn't, then there will be battle."

"As for me, I'd rather give up half of Ériu than taste the edge of your weapons," Sreng said. "However, I will report your words to my king Eochaid and to the assembly of Temair. Farewell, valiant warrior. We met in distrust, we part in peace. And whatever happens, you and I will remain brothers."

5. The Reation of the Fir Bolg

For many days, Sreng mac Sengann walked through the forests and valleys of Ériu, until he came to the hill of Temair. King Eochaid mac Eirc and the entire assembly of Fir Bolg leaders awaited him here.

Immediately, the Fir Bolg asked him, "What news do you bring us?" Sreng told them about the Túatha De Danann, and said, "Their warriors are sturdy men, virile, bloodthirsty, and strong in battle. Their shields are solid, their blades very sharp. It will be hard to fight them. Better to give them half of Ériu and make them happy."

175

"No!" shouted the Fir Bolg. "We will never make such a concession. If we show ourselves too tolerant, those foreigners will end up taking all of Ériu."

6. The Preparation for War

As soon as Bress returned to the camp of the Túatha Dé Danann, he reported of his encounter with Sreng: "A good hero, with great and wonderful weapons. He is tough and ready to fight, with no fear whatsoever." Hearing these words, the Túatha Dé Danann understood that the Fir Bolg would not willingly give up half their land, and that there would probably be a battle. Then they left the place where they were and settled in a better one, in the far western reaches of Connacht. They camped on the plain of Mag Nia, with their backs protected by the mountain of Sliab Belgatain, not far from the place where they had landed.

"This is a good place to build a fortress," they said. "It is difficult to reach, safe and impregnable. From here we could wage our war." And they began to build palisades and dig ditches.

7. The Druidic Attack

While the Túatha Dé Danann were still erecting the fortifications at Mag Nía, their three war goddesses, the Badb Chatha, Macha, and the Mórrigan, went to Temair, where the Fir Bolg were concocting their plans. With their arts, druids brought fog and clouds over the Fir Bolg and unleashed a terrible rain of fire and then a shower of vermilion blood on the warriors' heads. For three days and three nights, the Fir Bolg had no respite, nor could they see and hear each other. The three druids of the Fir Bolg, called Cesarn, Gnathach, and Ingnathach, took three precious days to break that spell, and it took that time for the Túatha Dé Danann to complete their fortifications.

8. The Meeting Between the Army

The Fir Bolg gathered their men at a meeting point. Heroes came from all over Ériu, and all together amounted to twelve fianna. Then the armies set out and took sides at the eastern end of Mag Nia. The seven fianna of the Túatha Dé Danann awaited them at the western end of the plain.

When the two armies were facing each other, Nuada mac Echtach, the Danann king, sent his poets to repeat to the Fir Bolg the same offer made previously, that is, that he would be satisfied to take that half of the island that had been given to him. King Eochaid mac Eirc ordered the poets to hear the answer from the very voice of his leaders gathered there, who scornfully rejected the proposal. "So," said the Danann poets. "Will we have to fight?"

"Yes, but the battle will be postponed," the Fir Bolg replied. "We must prepare because our armor is dented, our helmets are chipped, and our swords are not sharp. We want to have time to strengthen spears and shields, make helmets sparkle, sharpen swords, and build spears like your slegs. As for you, it will also be your intention to make spears like our craisech."

And so they agreed to postpone the preparations for a quarter of a year.

9. The Valley of the Mound of Encounter

While the two ranks awaited the day of the fight, the young Ruad, with twenty-seven young men, went west to the end of the plain, to play a game of *iománaíocht* with the Túatha Dé Danann. An equal number of young Danann took the field and an energetic and expert game began. The Fir Bolg, who had scored only one *cúl* during the game, were seized by a sudden surge of anger.

The speed and vigor of the Danann team could not do much against the brutality of Ruad and his men: In the encounter, flesh was torn and bones broken. Thus, the meeting ended with the defeat of the young people of Túatha Dé Danann. The Fir Bolg left the best Danann players dead or seriously injured.

This event left bitterness and discontent in the hearts of the Túatha Dé Danann, who were even more determined to have revenge in the fight. The bodies were buried on that field, and a mound was raised in memory of the meeting. Since then, that place has been named *Glenn Cairn Aillem*, the "Valley of the Mound of Encounter."

The First Battle of Mag Tuired: The Defeat of Fir Bolg

In Mag Tuired, in the "Plain of the pillars," the Túatha Dé Danann fight their first great battle. It is a fratricidal confrontation, as the Fir Bolg are also of Nemedian descent, and therefore all the more painful.

1. *Before the Battle*

On the eve of the battle, Eochaid mac Eirc, Supreme King of the Fir Bolg, called his poet Fathach and said to him, "Go west, and ask the Túatha Dé Danann how we should fight our battles. Will it be a matter of one day or several days?"

Fathach was welcomed by Nuada mac Echtach, king of the Túatha Dé Danann, and by his advisers: Eochaid Ollathair, known as the Dagda Mor, and Eochaid Bress, son of Elatha.

"What we propose," they replied, "is one fight a day, but they will have to face exactly the same number of warriors on both sides. Let it go on until all of you or us have been killed."

Eochaid grudgingly accepted that condition, as the Fir Bolg had numerical superiority. However, at that time it was customary for the challenger to choose the weapons and the methods of combat, and he had to comply with the decision of the Túatha Dé Danann.

Then Eochaid sent for Fintan, the strategist of the Fir Bolg, who was most wise in matters of war. On the advice of these, the Fir Bolg erected a large *ráth* which was later called "Fence of the packs" because of the packs of dogs that ate the bodies of the fallen in combat, or even "Fence of the pools of blood," for of the vermilion blood in which the wounded lay.

Nearby, the Fir Bolg dug a "healing well," in which the healers put special medicinal herbs. Anyone who was immersed in it would have their wounds miraculously healed.

The Túatha Dé Danann also built a ráth, which was called the "Enclosure of the assaults," and there they dug their "well of healing."

When these works were completed, the weapons ready, and the strategies established, the Fir Bolg went to ask the Túatha Dé Danann if they were ready for battle.

"It is up to you to decide how we will fight tomorrow," they told the Túatha Dé Danann.

"We will line up in the center of the Mag Nía plain with four fíanna each," the Túatha Dé Danann replied.

2. Mag Tuired, the Plain of the Pillars

By the time the day of the great battle came, summer had begun six weeks earlier. The armies rose at dawn and the early morning sun glinted on the blades of swords and spears. In compact ranks, the armies advanced through Mag Nía. As the ranks advanced, Fathach, the poet of the Fir Bolg, set up a stone pillar in the middle of the plain, in memory of that day, and from the top of that pillar began to report the event. He praised the valor of the warriors, recalling past victories and exhorting them to new glorious feats in the impending conflict.

But when the resplendent ranks had passed by him, Fathach stood motionless on his pillar, looking into the distance. From there, full of anguish, the poet wept with great sadness, and shouted:

"With what glory, with what bearing the hosts advance! Their power is gathered in the plain of Mag Nía. However, the army of the Túatha De Danann advance against the finely crafted swords of my brothers. The bloodthirsty Badb Chatha will thank them for the corpses scattered where the armies now advance proudly. Tomorrow, those who survive will weep for the heads of their comrades, brothers, sons, and fathers, whom the enemies will have taken out as war prey." And he added sadly, "And many and many years after this battle has been lost or won, pillars of stone will remain to commemorate the victory of the champions and the death of the heroes. Where the grass now grows, hundreds of pillars will rise, and Mag Nía will be known as the 'Plain of Pillars' [*Mag Tuired*]."

The pillar that Fathach erected was the first of its kind to be erected on a plain, and was named Cairthi Fáthaig. In that place, the first battle of Mag Tuired began.

3. The First Day of Battle

The Fir Bolg army and the Túatha Dé Danann army clashed in the center of the Mag Tuired plain. The Dagda Mór led the Danann ranks, while the young champion Cirb mac Buain led the Fir Bolg army. The battle lasted all day, in a great din of death. The shield straps snapped off, the swords fell off the hilts, and the nails shot from the spear points. The first to fall in that battle was Edleo mac Alda, the first of the Túatha Dé Danaan to die on the soil of Ériu. Who killed him was Nercon. However, soon many other heroes followed him into death.

The Dagda Mór advanced from the west, through the ranks of the Fir Bolg, making itself around the desert. On the other hand, the young Cirb fought with equal prowess, and around him the desert was also forming. In the evening, a large number of heroes lay stretched out on the ground. The Túatha Dé Danann were driven back and withdrew. The Fir Bolg did not pursue them, but returned to their *ráth*.

Each warrior brought a stone and a head to the king, with which they raised a large mound. King Eochaid addressed his victorious warriors: "May this monument mark our victory forever! May all men look at this monument and remember forever the names of those who fought in this battle, the names of the Fir Bolg, of the heroes who fought and won!"

That night, the druids and healers from both sides brought healing herbs to sprinkle in the water of the "wells of healing." The water of these wells was thick and green, and the wounded who were immersed in them came out healed.

The corpses were buried, and mounds and pillars were raised above them.

4. One vs Three

The next morning, before the second day of fighting began, King Eochaid left the ráth unescorted and came to a well to perform his morning ablutions.

While he was there, he raised his head and distinguished on the top of a nearby hill three warriors of the Túatha De Danann, who had seen him in turn and were now descending, determined to take his life. The king tried to negotiate, but the three enemy warriors did not want to give him quarter. Suddenly, a young man from the Fir Bolg appeared, engaging the three Danann warriors in fierce combat and killing them all. However, soon after, the young man died from his injuries. The Fir Bolg, who came in search of their ruler, buried the hero who had so bravely defended him and, each carrying a stone in his hand, erected a monumental *carn*.

Since then, the hill where the fighting took place has been called "Hill of the three" [*Tulach an trír*], while the mound erected in memory of the brave warrior was named "Mound of the one man" [*Carn an éinfhir*].

5. The Second Day of Battle

It was again strong and well-tempered armies that later returned to confront each other, coming from the west and the east in the middle of the Mag Tuired plain. The Túatha Dé Danann were led by a new group of leaders, including Ogma, Mídir, Bodb Derg, and Dian Cecht the healer. The Fir Bolg were led by Mella, Esc, Ferb, and Febar, sons of Slaine Finn, son of King Eochaid.

The clash was terrible, fierce. Swords broke on shattered bones and warriors' cries mingled with screams of pain. Despite the valor of the Túatha Dé Danann, the outcome of the battle turned once again in favor of the Fir Bolg. Among these was Slaine, son of King Eochaid, who made his way through the Danann ranks, breaking shields and prying off heads. A Danann chief, Nemed mac Badrai, tried to oppose him but was killed. His tomb would be marked with a pillar called the "Stone of Nemed" [*Lía Nemid*].

After that, Slaine pursued Calchu's two sons and their companions, who had escaped the left wing of the Danann army toward the edge of *Loch Mesca*, and killed them at the edge of the lake. Seventeen stones were placed on the ground to commemorate their deaths.

It seemed that the Fir Bolg must have the upper hand on this second day of battle as well, but then Bress, son of Elatha, the champion of the Túatha Dé Danann, led his fían through the enemy ranks and no man remained standing before his fury. Thus, when night fell, the Fir Bolg were driven across the battlefield, although each still carried a head and stone for King Eochaid.

"Are you the losers today?" asked the king. "Yes," Cirb said. "But the winners will not be able to take advantage of it."

6. The Third Day of Battle

On the third day, as they set out for battle, the warriors of the Túatha Dé Danann looked at each other, saying, "Who will be leading us?"

"It will be me," said the Dagda Mor. "Because you have a true divinity in me."

He proceeded with his sons and brothers to the ranks of the Fir Bolg. These were advancing from the opposite direction and led by Sreng mac Sengann. Again, the battle resumed. Many hand-to-hand battles raged between the most renowned warriors of both sides. The helmets were shattered, the metal-rimmed shields were dented, the long spears were chipped, and the bronze-green-edged swords were dipped in blood. The Dagda tore the men to pieces on this side, while Cirb did the same on the other. Each of them felt the blows that the other brought in the fight. Eventually, the two heroes met and began hitting each other, swinging furiously with their strong swords. When it was sunset, Cirb fell.

Then the Fir Bolg were driven back to their ráth. That night, it was the warriors of the Túatha Dé Danann who returned to their camp, each with a stone and a head. Among these was the head of Cirb. This was buried behind the rath and a mound called "Cirb's Head Mound" [*Carn cinn Cirb*] was placed on it.

On that sad night, Fintan the sage came in Mumu, to join the Fir Bolg. His thirteen sons, thirteen lugubrious warriors, came to the Supreme King Eochaid and formed a guardhouse. All had already been tested in battle, and each had been wounded several times. Therefore, they were the most reliable soldiers in the world.

7. The Fourth Day of Battle

The fight on the fourth day was a flamboyant upheaval, bright with color and blood. The throng of the fight was oppressive and furious, moving back and forth with ups and downs. The druids stood atop the pillars, casting spells, while the poets took note of the greatest feats and turned them into ballads.

The kings of both sides participated in that battle: Nuada mac Echtach on one side and Eochaid mac Eirc on the other. The first was surrounded by a body of Scythian warriors, the second by the thirteen sons of Fintan. Their sons followed them: Lugaid, son of Nuada, and Slaine, son of Eochaid. At their side were champions: Bress mac Elatha with Nuada, and Sreng mac Sengann with Eochaid. They were all great warriors, and at their feet were death and blood.

All this saw Fathach from his column, as he looked east and west. "Certainly, the Fir Bolg will lose many brothers," he shouted. "Many will be the heads that will roll and the beheaded bodies on the plain. I will no longer believe in their strength, as long as I remain in the stormy Ériu! I am Fáthach the poet and I am in great pain. Now that the Fir Bolg are caving in, I surrender to the fast advancing disaster!" Furies, monsters, and witches who announced doom screamed aloud, and their voices echoed through the rocks, over waterfalls, and in the hollows of the earth. It was like the rattle of the last day of life, when all men will leave this world. Some heroes still paced the battlefield, delivering furious blows. At their sight, the armies stopped and swayed, and then splashed away like boiling water from a pot.

8. The Cut-Off Arm of the King

In the fury of the clash, it happened that Sreng mac Sengann and his companions launched themselves against the Scythian soldiers who protected Nuada. After defeating them, Sreng himself engaged the king of Túatha Dé Danann in combat. Sreng struck Nuada with a shower of slashes from his sword. Nuada defended himself with his shield and responded with his blade. Thirty blows were given and received, until Sreng, with a great sweep of the sword, smashed the edge of Nuada's shield. The blade fell on the king's right arm and severed it from his shoulder. Nuada's arm fell into the dust, but soon the Dagda came to cover the king. The leaders of the Túatha Dé Danann took the king and carried him away from the camp, while the blood that gushed from the wound flooded their backs, which arched under the weight.

9. The Massacre

After King Nuada was wounded, Bress charged the Fir Bolg with great fury but was shot down at the hands of King Eochaid himself. Although some say that he was killed, this cannot be true, as Bress later succeeded Nuada as king of the Túatha Dé Danann.

In any case, the Dagda, Ogma, Alda, and Delmag launched themselves upon King Eochaid but were temporarily repulsed by Mella, Esc, Ferb, and Febar, the four sons of Slaine, who all fell in the fight. The place where they were buried is called "Sepulchres of the sons of Slaine" [*Leaca mac Sláinge*].

On the other side, the four sons of Gann charged the lines of the Túatha Dé Danann, but were killed by Goibniu the blacksmith, Luchtaine the carpenter, and Dian Cecht the healer. Their monument was called "Mound of the sons of Gann" [*Dum mac Gainn*]. Then the three sons of Ordan, the druid of the Fir Bolg, tried to break the line of the Túatha Dé Danann, but they were killed by Cian, Cu, and Cethen, the three *Clanna Cáinte*. The place where they were buried is called "Mound of the druid" [*Dum na nDruad*].

Shortly thereafter, the ranks of the Túatha Dé Danann advanced, led by Brian, Iuchar, and Iucharba, the three *Clanna Tuirell*, and charged the Fir Bolg. They supported their assault on Carpre, son of Den, and the sons of Buan, who were killed. The place where they were buried was named "Tombs of the sons of Buan" [*Leachta Mac Buain*], while Carpre's tomb is not far away.

10. The Dead of King Eochaid mac Eirc

The Supreme King of Ériu, Eochaid mac Eirc, fought in the center of the line, performing wonders of valor, when he was suddenly seized by a terrible thirst. Then he called his son Slaine and champion Sreng, and ordered them to keep the enemies at bay while he went in search of a source to quench his heat. The two champions stood in defense of the king, while Eochaid left with an escort of one hundred soldiers. Immediately, Lugaid, son of Nuada, launched himself against Sreng and Slaine in an attempt to reach the king. In the course of that fight, both Lugaid and Slaine, the sons of the two kings, died. On the site where the hero Danann was buried, a pillar was later erected, called the "Stone of Lugaid" [*Lía Lugaide*].

Meanwhile, the druids of the Túatha Dé Danann, realizing that King Eochaid was tormented by a burning thirst, used their spells to dry up all the springs, rivers, and lakes of the surroundings. Thus, Eochaid, desperate for a source, arrived at the beach of *Trácht Éthaile*. Herem his host was surprised by a detachment of three times fifty Danann warriors, led by the brothers Cisarb, Luam, and Luachra, the sons of Nemed mac Badrai.

The two ranks faced off in a fight, in which the three brothers attacked King Eochaid and struck him with all their weapons, so that the foam of the sea turned red with the blood of the Supreme King. Thus died Eochaid mac Eirc, the last king of the Fir Bolg. His warriors buried him where he fell and raised a huge pile of stones over his grave, which took the name of " Eochy's Cairn " [*Carn Eochaid*].

His three young assailants also died from their wounds and were buried not far away, along the shore of the lake. Their funeral monument was called "Sepulcher of the sons of Nemed" [*Leaca mac Nemid*].

11. The Tale of The Dagda Mor

When the black shadow of the night covered the fury and atrocities of the fourth day of battle, King Nuada spoke from where he had been laid down. "Tell me, how did the battle go?"

"I will tell you, noble Nuada," replied the Dagda. "I will report the disasters and atrocities. Our warriors have fallen in the face of the violence of the Fir Bolg. Our losses are so high that we can hardly count them. Our champion, Bress mac Elatha, made a glorious slaughter among the enemies, killing three times fifty.

"But then Sreng mac Sengann stepped in and engaged you in a fierce fight. It seemed you could resist him, fiery Nuada, but Sreng overcame your defenses and severed your right arm! At that sight, we were disheartened, and many died, good men, warriors covered with blood-red wounds. Among these fell your father Echtach, the valiant Ernmas, Fíachra, Etargal, and Tuirill, son of Ogma. Eochaid, Supreme King of Ériu, has also done great deeds against us. However, then the king was seized by a great thirst and, to satisfy it, he went to wander on the beach of Trácht Éthaile. Nemed mac Badrai's three sons surprised him on the silent sands and killed him. Lugaid, your son, is dead, and Slaine, son of Eochaid, is also dead. After these events, it was Sreng who dominated the fight. As night fell, the warriors kept running back and forth across the battlefield. They staggered, wounded, yet no one turned and fled. We were very tired on both sides, and so we stopped killing each other and stood aside to pause and think."

12. Sreng's Lament

That night, the Fir Bolg were sad, hurt, and full of bitter resentment. A hundred thousand had fallen, and a hundred thousand lay in the plain of Mag Tuired. Those who survived buried friends and relatives. Mounds were prepared for the bravest men, stones for the warriors, simple graves for the soldiers, hills for the heroes. The entire plain of Mag Tuired was filled with pillars, as Fathach had prophesied. After that, the Fir Bolg met in council. Of twelve fianna, only three hundred warriors remained. The decision to make was whether they should abandon Ériu or go into battle again. The three hundred decided to fight with the Túatha Dé Danann to the end, but Sreng mac Sengann opposed: "Resistance means destruction and death!"

It was a wonderful and terrible battle
and we fought with courage and resolve.
There was the clash of hard swords,
the clash of lances of noble warriors,
the studs of the shields fell apart.
But now full of pain and blood are the plains of Ériu,
and disaster met us in the woods.
Too many valiant warriors have fallen.

And he concluded, "We offer a peaceful solution to our enemies, before suffering other pains and troubles!"

But the Fir Bolg warriors refused to listen to Sreng's wise words and voted for battle. The three hundred went back to grabbing their shields and swords and spears, and prepared for a final fight.

13. The Duel Between Sreng and Nuada

The next day, the fifth day of battle, the decimated Fir Bolg armies made a final raid across the Mag Tuired plain. It was a studied and ferocious charge. Their swords were thick as bristles and they cut their way in a blaze of fury, overcoming all resistance. They threw themselves fiercely against the ráth of the Túatha Dé Danann and broke down its doors. The Fir Bolg swarmed into the enemy camp, and the Danann warriors were caught unprepared for their fury. Thus it was that Sreng mac Sengann, who had carried out the final attack against his will, challenged King Nuada mac Echtach to finish the fight they had waged the previous day. Nuada, though weak and suffering from the mutilation of his arm, went to meet Sreng with a firm and proud step, and said:

"If you want to fight me, you will have to tie your right arm to your side, because, as you can see, I have lost mine."

"If you've lost your arm," Sreng retorted, "there's no obligation to fight again, because our first fight was on equal terms. There was only one fight between us and it ended."

With this magnanimous gesture, Sreng spared Nuada from death and defeat. The first battle of Mag Tuired was thus over.

14. The Destiny of the Fir Bolg

The Túatha Dé Danann met in council and it was decided to stipulate a pact of peace and friendship between the two peoples. "Let Sreng and his three hundred men choose from the five provinces of Ériu which one they want to live in," said Nuada and Bress. "Let's stop this carnage." Sreng chose Connacht, and the survivors of the Fir Bolg went to settle there. Many heroes would have stood out in their lineage, including Ferdiad, who clashed with Cú Chulainn, and Erc mac Cairpri, who brought him death.

Others say that the Fir Bolg who survived the battle left Ériu to the invaders and took refuge with the Fomorians, settling in the islands of Aran and Islay, and in Isle of Man and Rathlin island, where their leaders built impressive fortifications, some of which can still be admired today.

15. The New Supreme King of Ériu

Thus it was that the Túatha Dé Danann took possession of Ériu and prepared to establish their kingdom there. They went to the "Gray Hill" [*Líath Druim*] in Meath, the place that would one day be Temair, the fortress from which the Supreme Kings of the Fir Bolg had reigned until that day on the green island. The Túatha Dé Danann came to settle their sovereign. King Eochaid mac Eirc had died, but his wife, Tailtiu, daughter of Mag Mór king of Spain, still lived. The Túatha Dé Danann welcomed her among them and gave her a new husband, Eochaid Garb, son of Duach Dall, son of Bress.

However, it was not Nuada mac Echtaich who settled in Temair. He had lost his right arm in combat and, according to Danann laws, a ruler must be perfectly intact in body and limbs. So, he was deposed and it was Eochaid Bress who succeeded him. Bress was the first Supreme King of Ériu of the Danann lineage.

Actually, Bress was Supreme King for only seven years. Then, some say, he died from drinking while he was still hot, during a hunt for Sliab Gam. Others tell an even more exciting story of him, which we will now see.

Amy Hughes

The Kingdom of Bress: A Bad King

The Túatha Dé Danann dominate Ériu, but King Nuada, having lost his arm, must give way to a new ruler. He is the charming Eochaid Bress, the one whom the Danann women chose to reign in Temair.

1. *The Birth of Bress*

The story of Bress's conception takes us back to the time when the Túatha Dé Danann still lived in Lochlann, before they left for Ériu to snatch it from the Fir Bolg. One day, one of the Danann women, Eri, daughter of Delbaeth, was looking at the land and the sea from Máeth Scéni's house when she saw a silver boat appear on the waves. On board the boat was a handsome man with shoulder-length golden hair, dressed in a robe and tunic interwoven with gold thread. On his chest, he wore a golden brooch made splendid by a precious stone and five gold rings around his neck. He carried two bronze-tipped silver spears and a gold-hilted sword with silver interlacing and gold studs. The waves carried the boat to shore and the man said to Eri, "Is this the right time for our union?"

"I'm not at all committed to you," the woman replied.

"Come without obligation," the man replied.

Although she had already refused many suitors, Eri could not refuse the advances of that charming man, and lay with him, but wept disconsolately as he rose to take his leave.

"Why are you crying?" he asked her.

"I don't know who came to me," she said.

"You will not ignore it: Elatha, son of Delbaeth, king of the Fomorians, has come to you," he said. And he added, "From our meeting, you will have a son and he will not be given a name but Eochaid Bress, the Beautiful. And every beautiful thing that will be seen in Ériu, be it plain or fortress or beer or torch or woman or man or horse, will be compared to this son and one will then say: 'It is a *bress*.'"

Elatha gave her a ring, enjoining her to never to part with it by selling it or giving it away, except for a man whose finger it would fit. Then the man went off the way he had come and the woman returned to her house.

Eri gave birth to the child she had conceived so amazingly and this was named as Elatha had said: Eochaid Bress. After a week, Bress was as big as a baby of two. He continued to grow at double the rate until he had reached the stature of a boy of fourteen. In a short time, he grew tall as handsome and strong as Elatha had prophesied.

2. Enthronement of Bress

King Nuada had won the first battle of Mag Tuired but unfortunately, in the course of it, he had lost an arm, which Sreng mac Sengann had cut off cleanly. This mutilation cost him the throne, as physical defects were considered incompatible with sovereignty. The healer Dian Cecht replaced his severed arm with a silver prosthesis capable of repeating all the movements of a real arm, but this was not enough to restore sovereignty. Nuada was nicknamed *Aircetlám*, "Silver Arm." A dispute then arose between the men of the

Túatha De Danann and their wives as to who should become king. They wanted the king to become the handsome Bress, their adopted son, and asserted that by entrusting the kingdom to him they would strengthen the alliance with the Fomorians. Bress was still a boy when, due to that controversy, the Túatha Dé Danann granted him sovereignty over Ériu. Bress offered seven hostages among his mother's relatives so that, should her inability make it necessary, sovereignty could be restored.

In the year 3304 from the Creation of the World, or 1894 years before the birth of Christ, Bress settled in the palace of Temair, as Supreme King of Ériu, the first of the Túatha Dé Danann.

3. The Satired Dagda Mor

The young King Bress had received a piece of land as a gift from his mother. There, he wanted the Dagda Mór to do the earthworks for the construction of his fortress. However, the Dagda was soon tired of the work. Inside the *ráth*, he used to meet an indolent blind man. His name was Cridenbel and he spoke with an open heart. Cridenbel thought his rations small and the Dagda's large, so he said, "If you have honor, Dagda, give me the best three pieces of your food ration." The Dagda gave them to him every night. The pieces for the satirist were big: Each was the size of a pig. However, those pieces were also a third of the Dagda's ration, and because of this, his health deteriorated. One day, while the Dagda was at work on the ráth, he saw his son Aengus coming toward him.

"Health to you, Dagda!" said Aengus.

"And you too," replied the Dagda.

"Why do you look so sick?" Aengus asked him.

"There is a reason. Every evening, Cridenbel the satirist asks for the best three pieces of my ration."

Then Aengus reached into his bag and took out three gold coins. "I have a tip for you. Put these three coins in the three pieces you give Cridenbel every night."

The Dagda did as Aengus advised him. When Cridenbel asked him for the three best pieces on the plate, the Dagda gave him the ones with the gold coins. Cridenbel ate the portions, but the gold got into his belly and the satirist died.

4. Bress Gives a False Judgement

Bress was told that the Dagda Mor had killed Cridenbel with a poisonous herb and, judging on that basis, sentenced the Dagda to death.

But he said to him, "What you say, oh king of the warriors of Ériu, is not the 'truth of the ruler' because, while I was at work, Cridenbel continued to bother me. He said to me, 'Give me the best three pieces of your portion, Dagda; my food is bad this evening.' I would have died if three gold coins I found today had not helped me: I put them in my ration and then I gave them to Cridenbel, as gold was the best thing in front of me. Therefore the gold is in Cridenbel's womb and he is dead."

"The thing is clear," Bress said. "Have the satirist's belly open to see if there is gold inside. If it is not found, you will die. If it is found, you will save your life."

The satirist's belly was ripped open and the three gold coins were found in his stomach. The Dagda was saved.

5. The Reward of the Dagda Mor

The next morning, the Dagda Mor returned to his work. Aengus approached him and said, "You will soon have finished your work. Ask for no other compensation except that Ériu's herds be brought to you. From among them, choose a dark heifer with a black coat, docile and vigorous." The Dagda finished building the ráth and Bress asked him what he wanted as a reward for his toil. He answered the Dagda: "I ask that all of Ériu's cattle be gathered on one plain."

The king did as the Dagda had asked, and the Dagda chose the heifer that Aengus had pointed out to him. To Bress, it seemed foolish. He had thought that the Dagda would ask for something more.

6. Malgovernment of Bress

When Bress had assumed sovereignty, he allowed three kings of the Fomorians—Elatha mac Delbáeth, Indech mac Dé Domnainn, and Tethra—to impose tribute on Ériu, and from then on there was no more smoke from a roof that was not subject to their tribute. So, Bress imposed heavy taxes and appropriated the treasures and even the food of his people. The Túatha Dé Danann, a people of his maternal relatives, resented him because at Bress's house their knives did not get dirty with grease and their breath never smelled of beer. In the Bress house, there was no entertainment; there were no poets, bards, satirists, harpists, bagpipers, or buffoons to amuse them. Their athletes no longer competed, nor were their champions seen testing their skills in front of the king. The champions had also been subjected to a service: While the Dagda was building the fortress for Bress, Ogma's job was to bring firewood to the fortress. Every day, he transported a bundle from the islands of Mod Bay, and because he was weak from lack of food, the sea tore off two-thirds of his load. Thus, he brought only a third and supplied people every other day.

7. The End of the Kingdom of Bress

Bress had reigned for seven years when, one day, a poet, Coirpre, came to court and asked the king for hospitality. Bress made him sit in a miserable and cramped house, in which there was no fire, no furniture, and no bed. On a saucer, he was offered only three tiny dried loaves. When he awoke the next morning, Coirpre did not say a single word of thanks. Instead, he said:

Without ready food on a plate
without milk to feed the calves
homeless against the dark of the night
without prize the storytellers:
such be the fate of Bress.

"For Bress, there is no more prosperity," he concluded.

This was the first satire ever uttered in Ériu and from that day, good luck was no longer at Bress's side. Then the leaders of the Danann tribes went to talk to their adopted son Bress and appealed to the guarantees given. Bress recognized that the kingdom should have been surrendered, and from that moment he was not considered fit to reign. However, Bress asked to be allowed to stay for another seven years.

"You can," the Danann assembly declared. "But the guarantors themselves up to that time will ensure that we enjoy all the goods that have been given to you: the houses, the lands, the gold and silver, the cows and food reserves, and moreover that all are in the meantime free from taxes and duties."

"You will get what you ask for," Bress said.

8. Bress Goes to the Fomorians

If Bress had asked for this seven-year delay, it was to rally the Fomorian warriors and forcibly impose his dominion over the Túatha Dé Danann. For this, he went to his mother, Eri, and begged her to tell him what his lineage was. She told him about how she had been seduced by Elatha mac Delbaeth and about the ring he had given her, which she now fitted perfectly on Bress's finger.

Placing the ring of Elatha, Bress in the middle, he embarked with his mother and his entourage for the country of the Fomorians. They entered those enchanted places and came to a beautiful valley where many groups of men were gathered. They reached the most beautiful group and were asked who they were. They replied that they were people of Ériu. The Fomorians challenged Bress to various friendly fights, because at that time it was customary, when a group of men went to the gathering of another group, to compete in competitive games. They ran a race with dogs and horses, and in either case, the Danann dogs and horses were faster than the

Fomorian ones. Then they were asked if they had anyone skilled at swordplay, and only Bress himself was found. However, when he put his hand to the hilt, Elatha recognized the ring that Bress wore on his finger and asked who that warrior was. Eri answered for him, telling the king that Bress was her son. She told him the whole story.

Elatha was worried and asked Bress, "What need brought you out of the kingdom you ruled?"

Bress replied, "Nothing else has brought me but my injustice. I stripped the Túatha Dé Danann of goods, treasures, and their own food. Never before have taxes or duties been imposed on them."

"It's bad," Elatha said then. "Their prosperity would be better than crushing them; better for you to get requests than curses. Why did you come?"

"I came to ask you about the warriors," Bress said. "I want to take that land back by force."

"You have no right to take back with an unjust action what you have not been able to keep rightly," Elatha told him. And he advised him to turn to Indech mac De Domnainn, king of the Fomorians, and to his champion, Balor, to hear what advice and help they would give him.

Hearing Bress's request, they decided to forcefully impose dominion and taxes on the Túatha Dé Danann, gathered all the forces from Lochlainn westward to Ériu, forming a single bridge of boats to Ériu. Never had an army arrived in Ériu more terrible and frightening than that of the Fomorians. The men who came from Lochlann and those who came from the *Insí Gall* competed in that expedition.

The Healing of Nuada: The Arm and the Throne

Unexpectedly, after the expulsion of Bress, it is the old king Nuada who resumes the leadership of the Túatha Dé Danann. A highly skilled young healer restored his lost arm.

   1. *The Healing of Nuada: First Version*

When Nuada lost his arm, the healer Dian Cecht had made a silver one with a movable hand and fingers and attached it to him. This is the reason why Nuada had received the nickname of *Aircetlám*, "silver arm."

One day, Miach and Ochtriullach, two talented healers, came to the palace of Nuada. Now it happened that the guardian of the palace, who had only one eye, going beyond the walls of Temair, saw the two young men arrive on the embankment. He asked them who they were. Knowing that they were doctors, he wanted to test them, asking them to put an eye back on him in place of what he had lost. Miach and Ochtriullach replied that they could replace his eye with that of a cat, and the keeper agreed to the transplant. In this way, the guardian took advantage and disadvantage at the same time: When he wanted to rest or sleep, his eye opened to the squeak of mice or the flight of birds or the rustle of bushes; on the other hand, when he had to guard the ranks at the assembly, just then the cat's eye wanted to rest.

Having passed the test, the two healers were allowed to enter the palace. They found Nuada sighing pitifully, examining his silver arm.

"I hear the sigh of a warrior," said Miach.

"Maybe it's a champion's sigh for a beetle blackening his side," Ochtriullach added.

Miach approached Nuada and took off his silver arm. Immediately, a scarab emerged from the wound and fled all over the fortress. The men rushed and killed it. Miach then looked for another arm of equal length and thickness. Everyone was asked and the only one that suited him was the arm of the swineherd Modan. So a man was sent to cut off the swineherd's arm to bring to Miach.

"Do you prefer to put the arm of the swineherd, or do you want to go and look for herbs that make the meat grow around?" Miach asked Ochtriullach.

The latter chose to stare at the swineherd's arm and Miach set off in search of herbs. When he brought them back, the limb was fixed without any defects.

2. The Healing of Nuada: Second Version

He had three sons, Dian Cecht, like him talented doctors and healers. Two males, Miach and Ochtriullach, and a female, Airmed. Now, it didn't seem a good thing to Miach that his father Dian Cecht had treated Nuada's arm by replacing it with an artificial one. So, he went to look for the severed arm and as soon as he had it he said,

"Joint with joint and tendon with tendon!" The arm healed in nine days and nine nights.

For the first three days, he put it against his side and it was covered in skin. For the second three days, he held it against his chest. For the third three days, he covered it with white tufts of reeds after they had been blackened by the fire. Finally, he reattached Nuada's arm, which was soon as whole as it was before.

3. The Death of Miach

That treatment did not seem good to Dian Cecht, who struck his son's head with a sword, cutting the skin to the flesh. However, Miach healed by his own arts. Then Dian Cecht hit him again, cutting the flesh to the bone. The boy recovered by the same means. Dian Cecht struck for the third time, reaching the membrane of the brain. The boy recovered again. Then Dian Cecht struck again, cutting the brain in two and Miach died.

At this point, Dian Cecht said that no doctor could heal him from such a stroke.

When Miach was buried, three hundred and sixty-five herbs grew on his grave, according to the number of joints and tendons. Then came Airmed, Miach's sister. She opened her mantle and divided those herbs according to their properties. However, Dian Cecht went to her and mixed up the herbs, so that since then no one knows their healing properties.

4. Nuada King Again

After the flight of Bress, the Túatha Dé Danann found themselves without a ruler. However, now that Nuada's body had returned to being whole and perfect, there was no longer any reason why he could not resume the kingship. Thus it was that the former king returned to Temair and was restored to his dignity as sovereign.

In the year 3311 from the Creation of the World, or 1887 years before the birth of Christ, Nuada Airgetlam settled in the palace of Temair, as Supreme King of Ériu.

The Birth of Lugh: Prisioner on the Tower of Glass

Ancient sources state that Lugh was the son of Cian of Túatha Dé Danann and of Ethniu, daughter of Balor, leader of the Fomorians. However, to know the details of his conception and birth, one must refer to the folk tales collected by the hands of the Irish narrators of the nineteenth century.

1. Genealogy of Balor

At that time, among the Fomorians, there was a mighty and terrible leader. His name was Balor of mighty blows, son of Dot, son of Neit, and he ruled over *Insí Gall* [the Hebridean islands].

Balor's grandfather was Neit, son of Innui, son of Allui, son of Tait (who was the progenitor of the Túatha Dé Danann).

This Neit (let's go back to his genealogy for a moment) was the father of three children: Delbaeth, Esarg, and Dot.

Delbaeth was the father of Elatha, who in turn was the father of many Danann champions, including Dagda Mor, Ogma, and Bress. Esarg was the father of Dian Cecht, the healer. Neit was the father of Dot, father of Balor.

Balor's wife was Cethlenn with crooked teeth, with whom he had a beautiful daughter, Ethniu. This is precisely the story of Ethniu, daughter of Balor and of Cian, son of Dian Cecht.

From their love was born Lugh, champion of the Túatha Dé Danann during the second battle of Mág Tuired and, later, their ruler. The story of the conception and birth of Lugh is unknown to the most authoritative sources. It does not appear in the ancient genealogies, nor is it treated in epic poetry. If we know it today, although in a form that is not always consistent with the ancient chronicles of Ériu, it is thanks to the tenacious memory of the Irish people, who handed it down in many versions, from father to son, allowing it to not be lost.

2. How Balor Had His Wicked Eye

It is said that when Balor was still a child, he would go and spy through a hole in the roof in the house of his father Dot's druid. The druid was preparing some magical concoction and the steam rising from the cauldron, passing through the smoke hole, reached Balor in the eye.

From that day on, Balor had the singular power to kill anyone who looked with that eye. Thus, in battles, four men opened his eyelid with a handle that had been attached to it, and a single glance of the evil eye swept away the entire enemy army.

Therefore, Balor was also called "Evil Eye."

3. The Prophecy

Now, a druid gave Balor a disturbing prophecy: He told him that he would be killed by his own grandson. At that time, Balor's little daughter, Ethniu, was just born. To escape the terrible fate, Balor had her locked up in a large glass tower, on the island of Tór Inis, and placed twelve nurses next to her, whom he ordered to prevent her from looking at any man, or even just coming to knowledge of the existence of beings of a sex other than her own.

Ethniu grew up alone in her tower and became a beautiful young girl. Throughout her life, she never saw male individuals. However, she happened to see men from afar sailing on the sea aboard their curaig. Thus it was that, in the course of the night, she began to dream of a beautiful young man and, unwittingly, fell in love with that unknown creature. In vain, she asked her twelve nurses who or what was the being she saw in her dream, but the women, according to the orders received, did not answer her questions.

4. Balor's Palace

According to a tale handed down by the people of Ériu, one day Balor turned to Goibniu, the incomparable craftsman of the Túatha Dé Danann, to build an immense palace for him. So Goibniu and his son left Ériu and went to Tór Inis, where the tower of Conand mac Febair had risen in the time of the Nemedians. Once on that icy island, Goibniu and his son set to work. They erected such a splendid building that Balor decided that the two artisans would not leave his kingdom alive, lest they could build an equally beautiful palace elsewhere. So, while Goibniu and his son were at work on top of the roof, Balor ordered all the stairs and scaffolding around the palace to be removed. The two craftsmen were stuck at the top of the building so that they would starve to death.

As soon as they realized the unfair maneuver, Goibniu and his son began to demolish the roof, so Balor was forced to let them down. However, even though Goibniu and his son were saved, Balor still refused to let them return to Ériu. Not only that, he ordered the two craftsmen to repair the damage they had caused to the roof.

"I can't fix the roof without some special tools I left at home," Goibniu replied. "But if you, Balor, let me go back to Ériu to pick them up, I could finish the work.

Balor did not escape the fact that Goibniu was attempting a ruse. "You and your son will never go back to Ériu," he declared. "My son will be the one to go in your place to get the necessary tools. Tell him where to go and where to look."

"All right," Goibniu said, addressing Balor's son. "Listen, boy. Put yourself out to sea and turn the bow toward Ériu. Once you disembark, you will find a road. Walk it. You will come to a house that has a sheaf of wheat in front of the door. Entering that house, you will find a one-handed woman and a one-eyed child. Ask the woman. She will tell you where the tools are."

Balor's son did as he was told. He disembarked in Ériu and, after following the indicated route, easily located a house that had a sheaf of wheat in front of the door. He entered and found a one-handed woman and a one-eyed child. The woman was waiting for him, as she had previously agreed with Goibniu what to do in case Balor prevented the craftsman and his son from returning home. So the woman said to him:

"The tools you are looking for are at the bottom of that chest. However, they are so deep that to get them you will have to go into the chest and carry them up on your own."

Balor's son obeyed, but as soon as he entered the chest, the woman closed the lid, imprisoning him. She then sent a message to Balor telling him that she would not release the boy until Goibniu and his son returned home with the right compensation. Balor was forced to consent to the request. However, before the two artisans left the island, Balor asked Goibniu who could repair the palace on their behalf. The latter replied that, after him, there was no better architect in Ériu than a certain Gabidien.

5. *The Wonderful Cow*

Back in Ériu, Goibniu sent Gabidien to Tór Inis, advising him to accept, as the only compensation for his work, the gray cow of Balor, which with a single milking was able to fill twenty barrels. Gabidien made the proposal and Balor accepted it. Once the work was finished, Balor gave the cow to Gabidien but he was careful to not give him the magical halter, without which there was no way to hold the cow and prevent it from returning to its previous owner.

Gabidien returned to Ériu with the wonderful cow, which turned out to be a bad investment. That cow gave Gabidien so much trouble, with her constant escapes and raids, that he was forced to hire samples to keep an eye on her during the day and bring her home during the night. The agreement with them was that Gabidien would forge a sword for each champion but that, if the cow were lost, the champion who guarded it would pay with his life.

It happened that one of the cow keepers, Cian, son of Dian Cecht, let it slip away. Desperate, Cian followed in the animal's footsteps to the sea, after which the cow seemed to disappear into the waves.

Poor Cian was already tearing his hair out of despair when he saw a currach coming from the sea, aboard which a man rowed vigorously. This man was none other than Manannan mac Lir, the knight of the crested sea, who approached the shore and asked Cian what had happened. Cian explained it to him.

"What would you give to him who took you to the place where the gray cow is?" asked Manannan.

"I have nothing to give," said Can.

"I only ask you," said Manannan, "half of what you can get before returning here."

Cian gladly agreed and Manannan made him get on the currach. In the blink of an eye, the two arrived in Tór Inis. The fortress of Dún Baloir rose from the rocks above them. "When you have to go back to Ériu," said the knight of the crested sea to Cian, "just turn your thoughts to me, and I will return to take you with my currach."

6. Cian and Ethniu

As Cian soon discovered, the kingdom of Balor was a cold and dark place. Here there was no fire and people ate only raw meat. Because this diet did not suit Cian, he lit a fire and began to cook food. From a distance, Balor saw that flickering flame. He approached and was so enthusiastic that he appointed Cian stoker and cook.

Time passed and Cian was able to explore the island. Once he saw Balor go to Tór Mór, the great tower that rose from the top of the cliff. Intrigued, he waited for Balor to come out, after which he himself approached the tower. Because he knew a spell that could release every lock, he managed to enter the palace, easily opening all the locked doors and closing them behind him. Entering a large, cold hall, Cian found nothing better than to light a fire. The glow of the flames attracted the attention of a girl. It was Ethniu, Balor's daughter, who recognized Cian as the boy she had known in her dreams and with whom she had secretly fallen in love. Cian also fell in love with the beautiful girl. Since then, whenever he could, Cian sneaked into Tór Mór to be next to Ethniu. This went on for a long time until the girl realized she was pregnant. Later, she gave birth to a baby boy. She entrusted him to Cian to take him away.

7. The Request of Manannan

And so it was that Cian went to the seashore, taking with him the child and the gray cow attached to the halter. It was enough for him to think of Manannan mac Lir that the knight of the crested sea, as he had assured him, appeared on his currach. Cian boarded the boat with the child and the cow.

But the maneuver did not escape Balor, who ran on the cliff and, with a mighty spell, raised a terrible storm. Manannan, whose druidic powers were even greater, calmed the raging waters. Then Balor transformed the sea into an expanse of flames. Manannan threw a stone into it and the flames were extinguished. Back safely in Ériu, Manannan asked Cian to honor his promise.

"I got nothing in Tór Inis but a child," Cian replied. "I cannot cut it in two. It will be good if you take it whole."

"That's exactly what I wanted," said Manannan. "When he grows up, there won't be a champion like him."

8. The Prophecy Is Completed

Manannan mac Lir later gave the child a name, calling him Dal-Duana, the "blindly obstinate." It is said that many years later the young man was on the seashore. Suddenly, a ship passed by, on which there was a man. Without caring who the stranger was, the boy took a dart from his pocket and threw it, killing him. That man was Balor, who, in accordance with the prophecy, was thus killed by his own grandson. However, ancient sources tell a different version of Balor's death. According to these sources, that young man, who was none other than Lugh, champion of the Túatha Dé Danann, and later their king, killed Balor in combat, during the second battle of Mag Tuired. However, this is what we will see in the next sections.

9. The Youth of Lugh

These are the stories that people tell about the birth of Lugh, even if in these stories the boy's name is never made explicit. Written sources agree that Lugh's father was Cian, son of Dian Cecht, while Ethniu, daughter of Balor, was his mother. However, these sources do not reveal the background of his birth. They inform us that little Lugh was brought to the house of Dúach Dall and entrusted to Tailtiu, daughter of the king of Spain. She, it will be remembered, had been the wife of Eochaid mac Eirc, the last king of the Fir Bolg. After the first battle of Mag Tuired, the men of the Túatha Dé Danann had welcomed her with them and had given her Eochaid Garb, son of Duach Dall, as a husband.

Tailtiu was, thus, Lugh's adoptive mother, and she raised him with love, as if he were her own. When Lugh was of the right age, he was sent to Temair, where he made a valuable contribution to the war that the Túatha Dé Danann were preparing against the Fomorians.

Other sources, equally authoritative, affirm instead that Lugh's godfather was Manannan mac Lir, who educated him as a great champion and always protected him. Still others say that the young Lugh worked as a helper in the forge of Gabidien, in which he was able to practice numerous techniques until he surpassed anyone else in skill and craftsmanship.

The Arrival of Lugh: The Samildanach at the Gates of Temair

Nuada Airgetlam is again Supreme King of Ériu. The Túatha Dé Danann are reunited at the court of Temair when a young man of bewildering abilities approaches the gates of the fortress.

   1. Lugh at the Gates of Temair

After the escape of Bress, Nuada Airgetlam, now restored to his rank as Supreme King of Ériu, held the Feast of Temair. He himself presided over the banquet when a beautiful young man arrived at the gates of the fortress. There were two guardians in Temair: Gamal mac Ficail and Camall mac Ríagaill. While the latter was on guard, he saw an unknown company approaching. A handsome and haughty young warrior with royal insignia was at the head of that group.

The guardian asked, "Who are you?"

The young man replied, "Here is Lugh, son of Cian, son of Dian Cecht, and of Ethniu, daughter of Balor. I am the adopted son of Tailtiu, daughter of Mag mor, king of Espáin, and of Eochaid Garb, son of Duach Dall."

"What art do you practice?" asked the guardian. "No one enters Temair if he does not possess an art."

"You can ask me," Lugh said. "I am a carpenter."

"We don't need you. We already have a carpenter. It is Luchtaine mac Luachaid."

"You can ask me. I am a blacksmith."

"We don't need you. We already have a blacksmith. It is Colum."

"You can ask me. I am a champion."

"We don't need you. We already have a champion. He is Ogma, son of Etain."

"You can ask me. I am a harpist."

"We don't need you. We already have a harpist. It is Abcán mac Bicelmois."

"You can ask me. I am a hero."

"We don't need you. We already have a hero. It is Bresal Etarlam."

"You can ask me. I am a magician."

"We don't need you. We already have wizards. Numerous are among us the druids and men who have powers."

"You can ask me. I am a doctor."

"We don't need you. We have Dian Cecht as a doctor."

"You can ask me. I am a cupbearer."

"We don't need you. We already have cupbearers. Delt and Drúcht and Daithe, Tae and Talom and Trog, Glé and Glan and Glési."

"You can ask me. I am a good bronze craftsman."

"We don't need you. We already have a bronze craftsman. It's Credne Cerd."

And Luhg said, "Then ask the king if he has only one man who has all these arts in himself. If so, I will not enter Temair."

The guardian went to the palace and reported everything to the king. "A man came to the door. His name is *Samildanach*, '[The person who] unites many arts,' and all the arts that help your people he possesses. He is the man of each and all arts."

2. The Three Challenges of Lugh

Then Lugh was put to the test in front of the *fidchell* board (a board game used by the aristocratic class, similar to chess). He won all the games.

All this was then reported to Nuada. "Let him in," said the man, "because never before has a man like him come to this fortress." The guardian let Lugh pass. He entered the fortress and sat on the "Sage's Seat" [*Suide Súad*] because he was wise in every art.

Then Ogma got up and challenged him to throw a huge paving stone that could hardly have been moved by eighty pairs of oxen. Ogma made the first throw by throwing it out of the building, into Temair's fence. Lugh picked it up and, relaunching it, dropped it back into the building, exactly in its place, then repaired the damage that had been done to the building by doing so.

"Play the harp for us," the warriors told him. Thus, Lugh sounded the melody of sleep on the first evening, and the king and his warriors fell asleep and slept from that evening until the same time the next day. Then the melody of weeping sounded, and everyone was moved and wept. Finally, the melody of joy sounded, and everyone was filled with joy. Laughter filled the fortress.

3. Lugh Elected Temporary King

When Nuada experienced Lugh's great abilities, he realized that the young man could free them from the threat posed by the Fomorians. The Túatha Dé Danann held council regarding Lugh, and Nuada decided to cede the kingship to him for as long as necessary to resolve the threat posed by the Fomorians. So, Lugh went up to the seat of the Supreme King and the king rose before him until thirteen days had passed.

4. The Whisper of the Men of the Goddess

The morning after his temporary enthronement, Lugh met with Eochaid Ollathair, called the Dagda Mor, and Ogma, and Goibniu and Dian Cecht were summoned with them. A whole year they remained in that secret meeting, discussing the measures to be taken against the danger represented by the Fomorians, so that place then took the name of "Whisper of the men of the goddess" [*Amrún Fer nDéa*].

Then they summoned the druids of Ériu, the doctors, the charioteers, the blacksmiths, the givers of hospitality, and the judges, and with them, all secret talks were held.

The magician Mathgen said that he would enchant the mountains of Ériu to make them tremble under the Fomorians by bending their tops toward the ground. The twelve main hills of Ériu would fight alongside the Túatha Dé Danann:

Slíabh Liag, Denna Ulad and Bennai Boirche, Brí Ruri and Slíab Bládmai and Slíab Snechtai, Slíab Mis and Blaí-slíab, Nemthenn and Slíab Maccu Belgodon, Segais and Chruachán Aigli. The actual name are:

Slieve League (Donegal), Morne Mountains (Down), Slieve Bloom (Laois), Slieve Snaght (Donegal), Slieve Mish (Kerry or Antrim), Nephin Mountains (Mayo), Curlew Hills (Sligo), Croagh Patrick (Mayo).

The cupbearers said that they would bring the twelve main lakes of Ériu to the Fomorians, but that the thirsty Fomorians would find no water there. These are the lakes: Dercloch, Loch Luimnig, Loch n-Orbsen, Loch Rí, Loch Mescdae, Loch Cúan, Loch Laig, Loch n-Echach, Loch Febail, Loch Dechet, Loch Ríoach, and Már-loch.

The current names of these lakes are: Lough Dergh, the widening of the River Shannon beyond Limerick, Lough Corrib, Lough Ree, Lough Mask, Strangford Lough, Belfast Lough, Lough Neagh, Lough Gara, Loughrea, and the northern branch of Lough Ree.

Then the Fomorians would turn to the twelve great rivers of Ériu: the Búas, the Bóann, the Banna, the Nem, the Laí, the Sinann, the Múaid, the Sligech, the Samaír, the Finn, the Ruirtech, and the Siúir; but all the rivers would have withdrawn from them and the Fomorians would not have been able to find a single drop. However, the Túatha Dé Danann would be guaranteed a drink even if they remained in battle for seven years.

The rivers are: Bush, Boyne, Bann, Blackwater, Lee, Shannon, Moy, Sligo, Erne, Finn, Liffey, and Suir.

The druid Figol then said, "I will make three showers of fire fall on the faces of the enemies; I will take away from them two-thirds of their valor, their skill, and strength; I will force urine into their bodies and horses' bodies. Each breath that Ériu's men take will increase their valor, skill, and strength. Even if they stay in battle for seven years, they will never be tired."

At this point, the Dagda Mor laughed. "The powers you claim to possess, I can exercise alone."

"You are therefore the good god [*dag-dáe*]!" they all said. And for this reason, Eochaid Ollathair was given the name of Dagda ever since.

Then the council was dissolved and the participants decided to meet after three years on the same day. Thus, the arrangements for the battle were decided, Lugh, Ogma, and the Dagda went to the three great Danann artisans: Goibniu, Credne, and Luchta, who gave them battle equipment. Then, for seven years preparations were made and weapons were manufactured.

Amy Hughes

Return From Tir Tairngiri: The Battle of Mag Mor An Oenaig

During the seven years of truce established between the Túatha Dé Danann and the Fomorians, the digression of the Aided chloinne Tuirill takes place, where Lugh, more radiant than ever, enters the scene at the head of a fairy host...

1. The Arrival of Lugh from Tir Tairngiri

In the time of King Nuada Aircetlam, the Fomorians demanded a heavy tribute: a tax on the cupboard, one on the millstone, one on the brickwork, and a tax calculated in the measure of one ounce of gold per nose of each individual of the Túatha Dé Danann, to be paid for on the hill of Uisnech Meath, which was then called "hill of Balor," west of Temair. The Fomorians extorted their tribute every year and cut off the nose of the man who didn't pay. On the day when the heavy tribute was to be paid, King Nuada called the assembly of the Túatha Dé Danann on the hill of Balor. They had recently gathered when they saw an army deploy to the east and come across the plain. The young warrior who went ahead seemed to have great authority over each other. Similar to the setting sun was the splendor of his face and so bright that it could not even be looked at.

It was Lugh, who came from Tír Tairngiri, the "land of promise," at the head of his ranks. With him came the sons of Manannan mac Lir. Lugh rode Aonbarr, Manannán's mare, as fast as the naked, cold spring wind. Under his hooves, the sea was like the earth, and his power was such that whoever mounted him was never thrown from the saddle and killed. Lugh then had on the armor of Manannan, and on his head the Cennbarr helmet, which had a precious stone set behind and two stones in front. Under the helmet, his face shone like the sun on a summer day. He also had, on his left side, the Fregartach, the sword of Manannan. None of those who had been wounded had ever managed to survive and those who saw it unsheathed in battle did not even retain the strength of a woman in labor.

2. The Rebellion Begins

The host led by Lugh reached the assembly of the Túatha Dé Danann. The newcomer and King Nuada had just exchanged greetings when they saw a group of rough and hostile-looking men approaching. They were the nine times nine messengers of the Fomorians who came to collect the annual tribute.

Here are the names of the four darkest and cruelest: Eine, Ethfaith, Coron, and Compar. Upon their arrival, the king and all the men of the Túatha De Danann stood up. The tyranny of those tax collectors was such that, out of fear, none of the Túatha Dé Danann dared to exercise authority, not even to punish their son or adopted son. Lugh asked Nuada, "Why did you stand up before this uncivilized host and not do it for us?"

"We are forced to do this," replied the king of Ériu. "If even a one-month-old baby remained seated in their presence, they would consider it reason enough to kill him."

"My word, I feel like killing them!" said Lugh.

"Your gesture would be against us," warned the king of Ériu. "We would get nothing but death and destruction."

"You have been subjected to such abuses for too long!" Lugh retorted.

He led his squad against the Fomorian tax collectors and massacred them. He killed nine men eight times; the nine remaining men he left alive under the protection of the king of Ériu.

"I would kill you," Lugh said, "if I didn't prefer you to report the news to your bosses yourself. If I sent my messengers, they might be subjected to some affront."

3. The Fomorians Attack

The surviving messengers arrived in Lochlann, the land of the Fomorians, and told their leaders what had happened: How a noble-looking man had come to Ériu and how he had killed all the debt collectors except themselves. "And the reason he spared us," they concluded, "is that we brought you the news."

"Do you know who this could be?" asked Balor, lord of the Fomorians.

"I know!" his wife Cethlenn intervened. "He is the son of our daughter, and it is for us a sign and a prediction that, with his arrival, we will no longer have any power in Ériu."

Then the nobles of the Fomorian tribes gathered in assembly: Eb and Senchab, nephews of Net, Sotal Salmor, Lúath Leborcham and Tinne Mór Trísgatal, Loisginn Lomglúinech, Lúath Linech, the druid Lobas, Líathbar mac Lobais, philosophers, fortune-tellers, and scholars; Balor himself, his twelve white-lipped sons, and Balor's wife Cethlenn. Then Bress, son of Balor, said, "I will go to Ériu at the head of seven massive Fomorian squadrons. Prepare the ships for me: Embark the provisions. I will battle Lugh and bring his severed head back to you!"

"That's the right thing to do!" they all agreed.

"Get my ships ready," Bress said. "And load them with food and provisions."

They equipped the ships in great haste and stowed them with food and drink in abundance. Lúath Linech and Lúath Leborcham, who of all were the fastest, were sent to gather an army for Bress.

And when all the Fomorian warriors were gathered in one place, the men prepared their armor and valuable weapons. Then Bress and the army under his command embarked for Ériu. As the ships set sail from the port, Balor shouted, "Battle Lugh Ildánach and cut off his head! Then chain that island they call Ériu to the stern of your ships. Let deep water take its place. Drag it north of Lochlann, and may none of the Túatha De Danann follow it up here!"

They brought out from the port the ships and the fast vessels loaded with pitch, incense, and myrrh. They set their sails and struck a single violent stroke of the oars, and the ships leaped over the immense, liquid expanse of the oceans, over the humid and high reliefs of the deepest sea. They did not slow down until they landed in the port of Ess Dara, in Connacht.

Part of the Fomorian army entered western Connacht and began to devastate it. At that time the local king of the province was Bodb Derg, son of Dagda Mor.

4. The Refusal of Nuada

When the news reached Temair, Lugh was in the company of Nuada Aircetlam, king of Ériu. Thus, they learned that the Fomorian tribes had landed at Ess Dara, where Dara Derg, druid of the Fomorians, had fallen by the hand of the same Lugh. As he learned the news, at the conjunction of day and night, Lugh prepared the Aonbarr, the mare of Manannan mac Lir. Then he went to report to Nuada how the Fomorians, having arrived in Ess Dara, plundered the territory of Bodb Derg. "I would like you to help me take up battle against them," Lugh said to the king.

"I will not give you my help," Nuada replied. "I will not avenge an action that was not directed against me."

Not content with that answer, Lugh mounted his horse and rode away from Temair, galloping west to meet the invading armies.

5. Lugh Meets His Father

Lugh had not strayed far from Temair when he saw three well-equipped warriors approaching. They were the three sons of Dian Cecht: Cu, Cethen, and his father, Cian. "Why do you get up so early in the morning?" they asked him after greeting him.

"I have an important reason," Lugh replied. "Foreigners came to Ériu and stripped Bodb Derg, son of the Dagda. What help will you give me?"

"You will have the protection of a hundred warriors from each of us."

"It's a good help," Lugh said. "But I would like much more: That you do everything to gather the men of the *síde* from wherever they are."

Then the three sons of Dian Cecht separated to do what was asked of them and Lugh went on his way. He didn't know that he had seen his father for the last time.

6. This Morning, the Sun Rises from the West

After taking leave of his father, Lugh continued to ride west, toward the hills of Gairech and Ilgairech, fording the Sínnan River at Áth Luain. He crossed Roscommon (*Bearna na hÉdargana*), then proceeded to Magh Luirg and Carlow Mountain (*Corr Slíab na Seagsa*). Beyond the point of Sén Slíab, he reached Mag Mór an Óenaig, the "Great plain of the assembly," where the Fomorians had built a field. Then Bress got up and said, "It seems strange to me that the sun rises this morning from the west and not from the east as on other days."

"It would be better if it were!" replied the druids. "That glow is the radiance of Lugh's face!"

Lugh approached the Fomorians and greeted them.

"Why are you greeting us?" they asked him.

"A serious reason for you, because if half are of your lineage, my other half belongs to the Túatha Dé Danann. So give me back the cattle looted from the men of Ériu!"

A voice from the enemy army replied, "May you not enjoy a lucky morning if you take only one cow away from here, whether it be sterile or dairy!"

Then Lugh cast a spell on the stolen cattle and each dairy cow returned to the house it belonged to. He left them only the barren cows, so that the Fomorians would not leave the territory before they were defeated by the warriors of the síde.

7. The Battle of Mag Mor An Oenaig

Lugh encamped not far from the Fomorian camp and waited for three days until the síde men came to his aid and sat around him. Finally, Bodb Derg showed up accompanied by twenty-nine hundred men and asked:

"What reason does the battle delay?"

"We were expecting you," Lugh said. Then Lugh put on the breastplate of Manannan and put on his head the *Cennbarr* helmet, the reflection of which gave his face the radiance of the sun. He took a dark blue shield bearing the scarab's mark and encircled the protective sword, beautiful and sharp, at his left side; yet he armed himself with two large-stemmed spears, whose tips had been dipped in the blood of poisonous snakes. The commanders of the men of Ériu stood around him, each in his place. They raised bundles of spears on their heads and made very solid barriers of shields around them. Then, approaching Mag Mor an Oenaig, they asked the Fomorians to fight.

The hosts hurled themselves against each other, deadly and hissing spears. After they had broken them, the warriors drew the climbing swords from the dark-edged scabbards and began to strike each other with ardor. Forests of flames rose above the heads of the contenders, originating from the blows of the warriors and the poison of their weapons. Lugh glimpsed the battle line in which Bress was, and rushed under him violently, striking the champions around him until he had taken down a hundred warriors of his escort. It was then that Bress asked Lugh to spare him. "If you grant me life, I will bring all the Fomóire tribes to you to fight a decisive battle in Mag Tuired. I will give you the sun and the moon, the sea and the earth as a guarantee that I will come to war, provided that the lineage of the Fomorians is still with me."

With these assurances, Lugh saved his life. Then it was the turn of the druids to ask for mercy. So, Bress and the druids returned to Lochlann to prepare for the final battle.

The Fate of Delbaeth's Children: The Vengeance of Lugh

The killing of Cian by the three sons of Delbaeth, and the vengeance of Lugh. These facts take place on the eve of the second battle of Mag Tuired, the narration of which will be resumed in the next section.

1. *The Killing of Cian*

Separated from Lugh, the three sons of Dian Cecht ran to seek help against the Fomorians. Cu and Cethen went south, while Cian went north, stopping at Mag Muirthemne plain. He had just entered it and was crossing it when he saw in front of him three young armed men. They were Brian, Iuchar, and Iucharba, the three sons of Delbaeth mac Ogma, known as Tuirell. Their mother was Danann, daughter of Delbaeth herself, who was therefore also their sister. So great was the skill and valor of Delbaeth's three sons, so vast was their experience in the druidic arts, that they were reputed to be gods and called Trí Dé Danann, the "three gods of Danann." From them, the Túatha Dé Danann themselves had not disdained the name by which they were known: the "tribes of the gods of Danann."

Now, the three sons of Dian Cecht and the three sons of Delbaeth loathed each other and brought hatred to each other to the point that, no matter where they met, they would not have avoided a deadly contest, which only the strongest would survive.

"If my brothers were here, we would fight fiercely," Cian considered. "But since they are not with me, the best advice is to withdraw." Seeing a herd of pigs nearby, he struck himself with the druidic wand, took on the appearance of a pig, and began to scrape the earth like other animals. Brian, son of Delbaeth, said, "Brothers, did you see the warrior who was crossing the plain a little while ago?"

"We saw it," confirmed Iuchar and Iucharba, "but we don't know what took him away."

"Unwise is he who, in times of war, does not diligently observe uncovered places," Brian reproached them. "I know why that warrior disappeared: He hit himself with the druidic wand and took on the appearance of a pig. Now he's in that herd over there, and he scrapes the ground as other animals do, but he's not our friend."

"This is a danger to us!" said the other two. "The pigs belong to some of the Túatha Dé Danann. Also, even if we killed them all, the druid beast could still make it in his beard and escape us."

"What's the use of learning the teachings in the four cities of knowledge (Falias, Gorias, Finias, and Murias)," said Brian, "if you can't tell a druid animal from a natural one?"

And he promptly struck his brothers with his druidic wand and turned them into two agile and slender dogs who immediately rushed to the druid pig's trail. The pigs fled and the druid was isolated from the others. He saw a hazel bush and headed in that direction, but just as he was about to throw himself into it, Brian threw the spear at him and pierced him. Then the pig squeaked loudly and said, "It was a wicked act to hit me, since you recognized me."

"I think you have a human voice," Brian said.

"In fact, I am a man: Cian, son of Dian Cecht. Spare me!

Iuchar and Iucharba said they were willing to grant Cian the grace of life, but Brian refused, saying, "I will not give you grace! Indeed, I swear on the spirits of the air that even if life returned to you seven times, I would tear it away from you seven times!"

"If so, satisfy my request," said Cian. "Let me get back to my true form."

"Go ahead," said Brian. "I find it easier to kill a man than a pig."

Cian resumed his original appearance and said, "Please have mercy on me."

"I won't have any!" Brian said.

"Well, whatever happens, I have outwitted you," said Cian. "If you had killed me in the form of a pig, you would have had to pay a fine only for the value of a pig. But if you kill me in human form, there will never be a higher price of honor than you will have to pay for my death. As for the weapons with which I will be killed, they themselves will report the crime to my son."

"It's not the weapons that finish you off, it's the stones we pick up from the ground," Brian hissed.

And the three brothers left their weapons and began to hurl the stones which they picked up from the ground at him. They stoned him violently and ferociously until Cian was left with a shapeless heap of lifeless flesh. Then they buried his body, but the earth refused to accept that burden and threw it back to the surface. Six times the sons of Delbaeth tried to bury the corpse and always the ground refused it. Only when they buried it the seventh time did the ground end up receiving it. Then the three sons of Delbaeth left Mag Muirthemne and went to join the ranks of Lugh to fight the Fomorians.

2. The Pain of Lugh

After the victorious fight of Mag Mor An Oenaig, Lugh went to look for his father, Cian. Not finding him, he asked his brothers, Cu and Cethenm if they had seen him. They said no. Lugh wondered if his father had not been killed by the Fomorians in the course of the battle, but Cu and Cethen denied that this had happened.

"Yet my father doesn't live," Lugh declared. "Well, I swear that my mouth will not touch food or drink until I know what fate he has met." He left, accompanied by the army, and searched the area where he had seen his father for the last time. From there he followed in his footsteps to Mag Muirthemne. When he arrived at the point where Cian had been killed by the sons of Delbaeth, it was the earth itself that spoke to Lugh, saying, "Your father found himself here in grave trouble, when the sons of Delbaeth saw him. He was forced to look like a pig, but they killed him in his true guise."

Cian's body was found and exhumed, and was torn with wounds. "It is an enemy's death that the sons of Delbaeth have given him," said Lugh. He kissed his father's broken limbs three times and added,

"This crime tears me apart. My pain is such that my ears hear nothing, my eyes see nothing, and there is not a single beat of life left in my heart. I am sorry to not have been present at the moment when the crime took place. It is a nefarious deed that men of the Túatha De Danann have betrayed each other. They will take a long time to repair the damage caused, and they will be destroyed." Cían's body was again placed in the pit and a tombstone was raised over it. A stele was placed, on which his name was engraved in Ogham letters. "It is from Cían that this mound will be called, even if his limbs are in tatters," said Lugh. And while the funeral lamentations were sung around, he, too, raised a song of anguish:

- *My heart broke in my chest*
since Cian the hero is no longer alive.
For the sons of Delbáeth it is not false news;
all will suffer in anguish.

And he added, "This action will only cause harm to the Túatha Dé Danann. Pain and misfortune will fall on the people of Ériu and fratricide will be perpetrated for a long time in this land." Then he turned to his people and said, "Go to the king of Ériu and the Túatha Dé Danann, but don't spread the news before I do it myself."

3. Lugh Asks to Speak

Then Lugh returned to the fortress of Temair. The assembly of the Túatha Dé Danann was held in the Banqueting Hall. Nobley and with honor, Lugh took his place alongside King Nuada. He looked around and saw Delbaeth's children. Of all, they were the men judged to be the best in dexterity and agility, the most handsome and most honored among those in that assembly. They were also the ones who had fought hardest against the Fomorians.

Lugh ordered the chain to be shaken, asking to speak, and everyone prepared to hear him. He said to the assembly, "Whom do you turn your attention to, men of the Túatha De Danann?"

"To you, really!" he was answered.

"I have a question for you," Lugh said. "What revenge would each of you exercise on the one who killed your father?" Those words were followed by a profound silence. King Nuada was the first to arouse himself and said:

"It is certainly not your father who was killed!

"It really is. And some of those I see in this room know better than I how his life was taken."

Then the king of Eriu said, "For the one who killed my father, I would certainly not reserve the death of a day, but I would tear away one limb a day, until it fell before me."

Everyone present spoke the same way, and Delbaeth's sons like everyone else. And Lugh said, "This same declaration also comes from those who killed my father, as all the men of the Túatha Dé Danann are here. So, let them pay me a reparation. If they do not, I will not violate the law of the king of Ériu or his right of asylum. However, the killers do not attempt to leave the Banqueting Hall until they have reached an understanding with me."

"If I had killed your father, I would be happy if you accepted the price of the repair (*éiric*)," Nuada said doubtfully.

Delbaeth's sons understood that Lugh was speaking to them. Iuchar and Iucharba proposed to admit the crime, as they knew well that Lugh would not dissolve the assembly until he had obtained their confession; but Brian feared that Lugh would later refuse the redress he had promised.

So Brian stood up and said, "You speak to the sons of Delbaeth, Lugh, for you suppose we killed your father, Cian. Well, it wasn't us, but we will give you reparation as if we had committed the crime."

"Even if you don't believe it, I will still accept that you pay me the price of the repair," Lugh replied. "And I tell you this: If you think it is too much for you, you will be given a part of it."

"We hear the demand from your own lips."

"That's what the reparation I demand will be," Lugh said. "You will get me three apples, a pig's skin, a spear, a chariot and two horses, seven pigs, a puppy, a roast-spit, and three screams on a hill. This is the price I ask. If it is exorbitant for you, you will immediately be given a part of it; if you think it's not too high, then pay for it."

Brian was perplexed for a moment. "It is not a heavy price, nor would a hundred times higher be heavy. However, from the smallness of the fine, I suspect you have some sinister design in store for us."

"It doesn't seem to me that what I ask of you is a small thing," said Lugh. "In any case, I will give you the guarantee of the Túatha Dé Danann that I will not expect more and that I will be loyal to you. Therefore, give me equal guarantees."

"Our people should be enough for you. We are no small thing," replied Delbaeth's children.

"That's not enough for me," said Lugh. "It often happens that reparation is promised in the presence of all and then you try to back out."

Then the sons of Delbaeth appointed Nuada, king of Ériu, Bodb Derg, son of the Dagda, and all the noble danann as guarantors who would pay the price of reparation required by Lugh.

"And now I'll let you know the true price of the repair," Lugh said.

4. The Price of Reparation

Before the assembly, Lugh explained to the sons of Delbaeth: "The three apples I am asking for are the three apples in the Hesperides (Isberne) garden, east of the world. No other apples will satisfy me other than those, because they are the most beautiful in the world. They are the color of pure gold, and the head of a one-month-old baby is no bigger than any fruit.

"They have the taste of honey. Those who eat even a single bite of them heal wounds and heal diseases and, no matter how much you eat, they never end. You are good champions, but I don't think you have the ability (which I don't mind) to snatch them from the people who possess them, because it was predicted that three young warriors would come from the west to take them by force.

"The skin I ask of you is that of the pig belonging to Tuis, the king of Greece. The nature of the animal was such that every sore it touched was healed and, when it crossed a river, the water changed into wine.

"The druids revealed that these virtues did not reside in the pig but in its skin; for this, he was skinned and from that moment the Greeks jealously preserve the remains. That skin has thaumaturgical powers: It can heal any wound and disease, even if the man is dying, and the water that is filtered there after nine days becomes wine. I think it will not be easy for you to have that skin from the Greeks, willingly or strong.

"The spear has the name *Arédbair* and belongs to Pisear, king of Persia. He chooses the target himself and allows it to accomplish the greatest feats. Its tip is kept in a cauldron filled with water so that the ground on which it rests does not burn and the spear does not penetrate it to the point that it can no longer be pulled out. It won't be easy for you to get it.

"The horses and the chariot I ask of you belong to Dobar, king of Sicily. Their nature is such that they run in the same way on both land and sea. There are no faster and more powerful horses in the world and there is no chariot that is equal to it in form and strength. The horses, however much they can be killed, return intact the next morning, as long as care is taken to not scatter or break the bones.

Nor is there a better wagon for structure and solidity. It won't be easy for you to have them.

"The seven pigs belong to Ésal, king of the Pillars of Gold. Even if you kill them every night, the next day they are more alive than before. Anyone who tastes a single bite knows neither disease nor infirmity.

"The puppy I am asking of you is a dog belonging to the king of Iruad. Its name is Fáilinis and it can catch any animal it sees. All the beasts of the world fall to their death just looking at it. It's hard to get!

"The roast spit is one of those that the women of the afterlife (*Inis Cennfinne*) possess.

"And finally, the three screams you have to shout must ring out on the Midchain hill north of Lochlann. Midchain and its children are bound by a ritual injunction (geis) that they must not allow anyone to shout from that height. My father Cian received his war training with him. Even if I forgave you his death, he would never forgive you! When all your exploits are successful, my vengeance will take place on you there.

"Here is the price of the repair I ask you," concluded Lugh.

5. The Advice of Delbaeth

Silence and amazement fell on Brian, Iuchar, and Iucharba. The three brothers went with their heads down to Dun Tuirell, the fortress of their father, Delbaeth mac Ogma, complaining of the sad fate that awaited them. "This is bad news," Delbaeth said. "By seeking payment for the price of repair, you will bring misfortune and death upon you. However, if Lugh wanted it, you could also succeed in your enterprise, at the cost of enormous effort. Yet no man would be able to pay such a price of reparation without druidic help. So, go to Lugh and ask him to borrow the *Aonbarr*, the mare of Manannan mac Lir.

"If he truly expects you to pay him the fee, he will give it to you; otherwise, he will tell you that it does not belong to him and that he cannot grant what has been loaned to him. In that case, you will ask him for the *Scúabtuinne*, the currach of Manannan. He will give it to you because a ritual injunction forbids him to refuse a second request. The boat will be more useful to you than the horse!"

Delbaeth's sons presented themselves to Lugh, greeted him, and declared that, without his help, they would not be able to pay him the price of reparation. So, they asked him to borrow the *Aonbarr*, Manannan mac Lir's mare.

"It doesn't belong to me," was Lugh's dry reply. "I will not loan what was loaned to me."

"Then give us the Scuabtuinne, Manannan mac Lir's boat," said Brian.

"I'll grant it. It's in Bru na Bóinne," said Lugh.

The three brothers returned to Dun Tuirell and told their father that they had obtained the boat.

"Getting it won't help you much," Delbaeth observed. "Although he is anxious to get what he needs for the battle of Mag Tuired, Lugh would be much happier if you succumbed in the course of the quest."

On those words the brothers left, leaving their father sad.

6. The Lament Before Departure

Delbaeth's sons went to the port where the currach was located. Their sister, Ethniu, accompanied them. As soon as he boarded the boat, Brian complained about the limited space. "Besides me, there is hardly room for another person!"

"A ritual injunction forbids complaining about this boat, dear brothers," Ethniu warned them. And with death in her heart, she raised this song:

Evil deed you have done,

noble and beautiful host.

Lugh's father you killed him, and it's bad.

The three brothers answered:

Ethniu, don't talk like this:

alive is our love, daring the deeds.

A hundred times better to be killed

than to suffer the death of the idle and the cowardly.

And Ethniu:

Look for the towns and islands of the sea

until you reach the beaches of the Red Sea.

Your exile from Ériu,

there is no more painful event.

After these heartbreaking words, the three warriors pushed the currach away from the beautiful, rugged shores of Ériu.

7. The Golden Apples of the Garden of Isberne

"Which route will we take first?" Iuchar and Iucharba asked themselves.

"We will go in search of apples, as it is the first request that has been addressed to us," Brian replied. "Therefore, we ask you, Scuabtuinne, boat of Manannan: Go to the Garden of Isberne."

Immediately, the currach took the run on the crests of the green-sided waves, the shortest way in the ocean, until, finally, it reached a port and a shelter on the shores of the Isberne islands.

"How do you think we should approach the garden?" Brian then asked. "The warriors of the country and the king's champions are on guard, led by the sovereign himself."

"What should we do but attack?" the brothers answered. "If we are the strongest, we will take the apples away. Otherwise, we will fall into the enterprise. It is not up to us to escape the dangers that loom over our heads without finding death somewhere."

"Instead of being remembered for our folly, it would be desirable that we proclaim our foresight and sing it again after our death,"

Brian said. "In my opinion, the best advice is to enter the garden in the form of hawks. The guardians can only oppose small arms. Our agility and dexterity will ensure that spears and arrows miss the targets. When the guardians have run out of bullets, we will drop on the apples and take away one of each. If I can, I will catch two myself: one in the claws and another in the beak."

Agreeing to this, Brian beat himself and his brothers with the druid rod and all three mutated into hawks of incomparable beauty. When the guardians of the garden spotted them, they hurled a furious shower of darts and poison-tipped spears at them. As planned, the three hawks kept themselves alert until the guardians ran out of bullets. Then they boldly went down on the apples. As he said, Brian took two away; the brothers one each.

The news of the theft immediately reached the ears of the king of the Isbérne islands, who had three beautiful and very wise daughters. Having assumed the appearance of three griffons with sharp claws, they launched themselves into the sea in pursuit of the three hawks. Before and behind their flight, fiery rays shot up.

"We are in a tight spot," said Iuchar and Iucharba. "If we do not find help, we will soon be burned by the rays of fire."

"I'll give you my help if I can," Brian said. He struck himself and the brothers with the druidic wand and all three turned into swans. Immediately, they plunged into the water as the griffins passed overhead. When there was no more danger, the three swans resurfaced and resumed their human aspect. After that, Delbaeth's sons reached the currach.

8. The Pig Skin of King Tuis

Determined to have, by love and by force, the skin of the pig of the king of Greece, the sons of Delbaeth landed on the shores of Greece and headed for the court of King Tuis. "In what form will we present ourselves?" Brian asked.

"Where else but ours?" the brothers said.

"I don't think it has to be that way," Brian replied. "We would rather go under the aspect of Ériu's poets and men of art: We will obtain greater honor and reputation among the noble people of Greece."

The two brothers accepted that proposal with skepticism, as they had no poem at hand and would not have been able to compose one. However, they wrapped the poets' ribbon in their hair and presented themselves at the palace doors. When the guardian asked who they were, they replied that they were Irish poets and that they came with a poem for King Tuis. The king immediately ordered them to be introduced into the court, pleased that poets had come from so far in search of a protector.

The sons of Delbaeth were granted the most generous of hospitality and the three brothers immediately gave themselves over to drinking and joy. When, finally, the royal poets rose to sing their own compositions, Brian told the brothers to sing a poem for the king.

"We don't have any," Iuchar and Iucharba replied. "You can ask us only the art practiced up to now: to tear by force what we want, or to succumb to the opponents."

"Not the best way to compose a poem," Brian said. He stood up and, gaining attention and silence, sang:

King Tuis, I do not hide your glory,
I praise you like the oak above kings.
The skin of a pig, booty without contrast,
is the fee that I request from you.
In the war of the neighbor against the ear,
the neighbor's beautiful ear will be against him;
he who gives us the gift of wealth,
not for this he will have the bareest court.

The storm of the winds and the rough sea
to oppose, I am a sharp sword;
the skin of a pig, booty without contrast
it is the fee I ask for, Tuis.

"A good poem," King Tuis said cautiously. "But I didn't understand a single word that made sense.

"I'll tell you what it means," Brian said then. "As the oak excels among the trees of the forest, so you, King Tuis, dominate the kings of the earth in generosity, valor, and nobility. These are the qualities that I praise in you, and as a gift for my panegyric, I ask for nothing but the pigskin that is in your possession.

"As *os* and *cluas* are, in Gaelic, two names to indicate the ear, so, for that pigskin, if you do not give it to me willingly and without contrast, it will be you and I against each other's ear. 'Other.' Here is the meaning of my poem."

"A poem that I would surely praise if it did not mention my pig's skin," said the king. "You are foolish, man of poetry! I would not give that skin to poets, or artists, or princes, or even the most sublime kings of the earth, unless they tore it from me by force! But since I am not without generosity, I will give you three times the red gold that that same skin can contain."

"I knew my request would not be easily granted, but I also knew that I would receive a good reward," Brian said. "However, I will take only the red gold which will be measured in my presence, diligently and as is appropriate." The royal stewards were sent to the treasury together with the strangers so that they could measure the compensation in person. "Fill your skin twice for my brothers first," Brian said. "The last scrupulous measure will be for me, who composed the poem."

But as soon as the skin was unfolded, Brian grabbed it with his left hand. With his right, he drew his sword and lowered it on the man closest to him, splitting him in two. Taking possession of the skin, Brian wrapped it around his body. Then the three sons of Delbaeth fled the court, shooting down all those who tried to stop them. No Greek escaped their swords: All nobles and warriors were killed or maimed. King Tuis threw himself against them and engaged Brian in a heroic and fierce fight, but he succumbed to the poisoned sword of Brian.

Meanwhile, Iuchar and Iucharba fought valiantly, carrying out a carnage among the Greek troops, until they had practically exterminated them. When they were left alone in the now empty court, Delbaeth's sons laid down their weapons and used the magical virtue of pigskin to heal terrible wounds. Delbaeth's sons stayed for three days and three nights in the Greek court, where they could recover from the fatigue of that fight, and had in their arms, and as bedmates, the most beautiful women in Greece.

9. The Lance of the King of Persia

Then, Iuchar and Iucharba asked Brian where they should go. "To Pisear, king of Persia, to request the spear from him," was the reply. They reached the currach and left the blue water beaches of Greece, satisfied that they had already obtained the apples and pigskin. They did not stop until they reached the shores of Persia. "In what form will we present ourselves to the king's court?" Brian asked.

"In what other place if not in what is proper to us?" The brothers said.

"Doesn't seem like the right choice," Brian replied. "We go rather under the aspect of poets, as we did with the king of Greece." The brothers approved of the counsel, given the success it had given them the previous time. Again, they gathered their hair in the ribbon of poets and presented themselves at the gates of the royal fortress. They told the guardian that they were poets who came from the distant land of Ériu with a poem for the king. They were let in. The king and the nobles of the Persian court welcomed them and seated them with great honors right around the king. When the poets got up to sing their compositions, Brian told the brothers to get up and recite a poem. "Do not ask us for an art that we do not possess," answered Iuchar and Iucharba. "If you want, we will practice what we are experts in, which is to fight and exchange mighty blows!"

"It would be a very singular exercise in poetry!" Brian commented. "Since I own the poem, then I will recite for the king." And he sang these lines:

Little fame has any other spear with King Pisear

in the battles in which he annihilates his enemies.

Pisear does not suffer oppression

from those to whom he inflicts wounds.

The yew, the most beautiful of trees,

he is called king without contrast.

May his splendid stem

penetrate the deadly wounds.

"A good poem," commented King Pisear, "but I do not understand what the mention of my spear, Ériu's poet, means."

"I'd like it as a reward," Brian said.

"You don't have much brain to make such a request of me," said the king. "Know that the people of this court have never given greater honors in exchange for a poem, and it is already fortunate that they did not have you put to death immediately!"

At those words, Brian remembered the apple he had in his hand. He threw it against the king's forehead, making his brain come out the back of his neck. Then he drew his sword and hurled himself on those around him. The brothers did not neglect to do the same and began to give him a hand with ardor and courage, until they had carried out a massacre, decimating the nobles, the courtiers, and the ranks of the royal palace. That night, having healed the wounds with the pigskin of King Tuis, they were able to dispose of the women and princesses of the court. Finally, they found the lance, called *Arédbair*. It had the blade plunged into a cauldron of water; otherwise, the ground on which it rested would have burned due to the heat given off by its tip and the spear would have penetrated the earth.

10. The Wagon and the Horses of the King of Sicily

Upon leaving Persia, Delbaeth's sons wondered which direction to go.

"We will go to Dobar, king of the island of Sicily," Brian said. "It is he who owns the two steeds and the chariot requested by Lugh." They embarked, carrying the launch with them. Alto was the spirit of the three champions, after the feats they had accomplished. They came to the court on the island of Sicily.

"In what aspect will we present ourselves?" Brian asked.

"Under which if not the one that belongs to us?" the brothers said.

"This is not the way we should do it," Brian said. "We will assume the remains of Ériu's mercenaries to enter the service of the sovereign. Perhaps we will learn where the horses and the chariot are kept." Having agreed to do so, the sons of Delbaeth reached the clearing in front of the royal fortress, and the king of Sicily, the princes, and the nobles went to meet them in procession. After receiving the homage from the newcomers, King Dobar asked them who they were.

"We are mercenaries of Ériu," was the reply. "We earn money from the kings of the earth." The king asked the three brothers if they were willing to stay with him and it was in this way that they made an agreement with the king. However, after spending fifteen days and a month in the fortress, they still hadn't seen the king's horses and chariot. Then Brian said to his brothers, "Let us take the weapons and travel equipment, and present ourselves to the king, declaring ourselves ready to leave the country, to abandon this part of the world, if he does not show us the chariot and horses."

They went to the sovereign, who wanted to know the reason for their traveling outfit.

"You will know, noble king," Brian said. "We mercenaries of Ériu are guardians and advisers to princes who possess precious treasures, repositories of the secrets, advice, and plans of those we serve. Now, since we came to your court, you haven't treated us this way. We know you own the two best steeds and the most beautiful chariot in the world, yet we haven't seen them."

"It is a pity that you made it a point of departure," said the sovereign. "I would have shown them to you from day one if I had known you wanted to see them. However, since you ask me now, I will show them to you, for mercenaries who were dearer to me never came to my court."

He then sent for the horses and had them hitched to the cart. Towed by them, his ride was as light and fast as the cold spring wind, the same on land and sea. Brian watched the animals carefully, then stopped the chariot and, grabbing the charioteer by the ankle, threw him against a rock, killing him. Immediately, he jumped into the chariot, struck King Dobar with a slash, and broke his heart in his chest. Then, with his brothers, he faced the people of the fortress, killing everyone who came within range.

11. The Pigs of the Kings of the Golden Columns

Fleeing from the kingdom of Sicily, Iuchar and Iucharba asked what was the next destination.

Brian replied, "From Esal, the king of Golden Columns, to ask him for the seven pigs that Lugh ordered us to bring him." They left for the village of Esal by the direct route, without encountering obstacles.

However, they found the people of the country on alert and the ports closely guarded, for fear of the sons of Delbaeth, as news of their fatal deeds had spread all over the world. Esal, king of the Golden Columns, went to meet them at the edge of the port and asked, in a reproachful tone, whether it was true that the most powerful rulers in the world had fallen by their hands in the countries they had gone to. Brian did not deny the truth, heedless of the punishment the king might have inflicted on them.

"What prompted you to do it?" King Esal asked.

Brian then explained to him that the reason lay in the killing of a man and the unfair sentence that had been imposed on them. He told of their adventures and what had happened to the sovereigns who had denied them what was requested and to the hosts who defended them.

"Why did you come to our country?" asked the king again.

"For your pigs," Brian said. "They are part of the repair price that has been imposed on us."

"And how do you intend to take them?"

"We'll accept them gratefully, if we get them willingly," Brian said. "Otherwise I will fight you and your people. Then you would succumb and we would take the pigs away in spite of you."

'If that's what you came for," the king considered, "it would be a mistake to fight you."

After deliberating in assembly with his advisers, King Esal decided to spontaneously grant the pigs to the sons of Delbaeth, as until then no one had been able to resist the strength of the three brothers.

The sons of Delbaeth, therefore, expressed their gratitude and gratitude to Esal, amazed to receive the animals so easily. That night, King Esal led them to the royal fortress. The three brothers were served with exquisite food, drink, and soft beds, as they could not wish for. The next day, when they got up, they went to the king, who gave them the pigs.

"It was wise to have given them to us," Brian said. "Other than this, no other part of the compensation was obtained in any other way than by fighting."

"What path will you take now, sons of Delbaeth?" Esal asked.

"We will go to the land of Iruad to look for the little dog Fáilinis."

"Then consent to my request," Esal said again. "Let me come with you to the ruler of Iruad. He has my daughter as his wife and I would like to induce him to give you the dog without battle and without conflict."

"It suits us," the brothers declared.

12. The Dog of the King of Iruad

The royal boat was set up and no adventure is reported of their journey until they reached the beautiful beaches of Iruad, the land of the cold north. The ranks and armies of the town guarded the ports and inlets and, when they spotted them, raised loud cries of alarm.

But King Esal went ashore peacefully and, going to his son-in-law, told him from beginning to end the adventures of the sons of Delbaeth. "Why did you bring them to my country?" the sovereign finally asked.

"Because of your puppy," Esal replied. "It is part of the repair price that has been imposed on them."

"It was a bad idea to come with them for this purpose. No divinity has granted any warrior in the world the right to take over my bitch Failinis, either peacefully or by force."

"That's not how you should act," King Esal warned him. "Those three young men have already brought down many kings. It is preferable to surrender the bitch without giving battle."

They were words thrown to the wind. Esal returned to tell the sons of Delbaeth that the king's answer had been negative. The three brothers immediately took up arms and fiercely challenged the armies of Iruad to battle. The ranks faced each other, and the fighting turned fierce and violent. Delbaeth's sons began to strike the warriors of Iruad, maiming and killing a large number of them.

In the heat of the fray, Iuchar and Iucharba found themselves on one side, Brian on the other. However, where Brian passed, he opened rifts in the enemy ranks. He and the king of Iruad found themselves face to face and began to inflict mighty and ferocious blows, engaging in a bloody, poisonous, and relentless fight.

It was Brian who got the better of his opponent. The king of Iruad was dragged, bound, among the ranks to the feet of King Esal.

"Here's your son-in-law," Brian told him. "I swear by my valiant weapons that it would have been easier for me to kill him three times than to bring him here alive once."

The little dog Failinis was given to the sons of Delbaeth. Once the pact was made, the king was untied and the sons of Delbaeth, after taking leave of Esal, having healed the wounds received with the magical pigskin, left happy and satisfied onboard the currach.

13. Return to Ériu

As Lugh was informed that the sons of Delbaeth had obtained everything that would be useful to them in the battle of Mag Tuired, he placed a druidic enchantment on them so that they would forget that they had not conquered all the required items, and at the same time instilled in them the ardent desire to return to Ériu. Thus, Brian, Iuchar, and Iucharba returned to their homeland, forgetting the missing part. At that time Lugh was in the company of King Nuada in Howth (*Benn Etair*), where an assembly was being held.

Informed of the arrival of Delbaeth's sons, Lugh secretly left the gathering and went to Temair. He closed the gates of the fortress behind him and put on Manannan's armor and equipment. Meanwhile, the sons of Delbaeth presented themselves to the king, who welcomed them along with the nobles of the Túatha Dé Danann and asked if they had the price of repair with them.

"We have it," the three brothers replied. "Where is Lugh so that we can deliver it to him?"

"He was here just now," said the king.

He was looked for everywhere but no one found him.

"I know where he is," Brian said. "It was revealed to him that we had arrived and that we had the treasures with us, and he went to Temáir to avoid us."

Then messengers were sent to him, to whom Lugh replied that he would not come and that the price of repair was to be remitted to the king of Ériu. After the king had taken over the apples, the pigskin, the spear, the cart with the horses, the seven pigs, and the dog, they all went to Temair. Lugh went out into the clearing and received them in his turn.

"A man has never been killed, and never will be, who has not paid the required compensation in full," he said. "There is, however, a part that cannot be overlooked, and that is what is missing from the completion of the price of repair. Where is the roast-spit? What about the three cries on the hill that you have not yet uttered?"

When the three sons of Delbaeth heard those words, they were struck with astonishment and discouragement. That same night, they left the assembly and went to Dún Tuirell. They told their father, to whom they relayed their adventures and how Lugh had treated them. Then Delbaeth too was gripped by grief and sadness.

In forcing Delbaeth's sons to return to Ériu before the search was over, Lugh was cunning. He forced the three brothers to leave their treasures in Temair, specifically the pigskin, capable of healing any wound, before embarking on their latest and most risky undertaking.

At dawn the next day, the three brothers once again reached their boat, accompanied by their sister, Ethniu. Seeing them leave, she groaned with a heart full of sadness.

14. The Island of Beautiful Heads

Delbeth's sons, therefore, set out to fetch the spit of the women of Inis Cennfinne, the "island with beautiful heads." For a quarter of a year, the sons of Delbaeth sailed on the stormy waves of the green sea, without finding this island or a place where anyone could give news. Then Brian put on a diving suit, wore on his head a helmet of transparent crystal, and dived into the depths of the sea. He wandered for fifteen days on the bottom of the salty sea in search of that land, which he ended up tracking down.

Upon entering the city, Brian saw a group of beautiful women engaged in sewing or embroidery. Among the various things next to them was the roast spit. Brian stole it and was about to escape through the doors when the women burst out laughing.

"A very daring action, warrior!" they mocked him. "Even if you had your brothers with you, the least courageous of the hundred and fifty women here would have allowed you to take the spit away. However, go ahead and get one, as, fearless and brave, you dared to take it even though we were all here!"

Then Brian walked over to where he had left the currach. Iuchar and Iucharba, thinking that he had been away too long, were already considering lifting the anchor and hoisting the sails when they saw him coming toward them on the crest of the waves and rejoiced wholeheartedly.

15. Three Shouts at the Top of a Hill

The three brothers finally went to Lochlann, where they would pay the last part of the price of repair that had been imposed on them. There were still three shouts to go from the top of Midchain hill.

When they reached the top of the hill, the guardian of the place moved toward them. It was Midchain, who had been Cían's master of arms and would certainly not forgive his killers.

Brian rushed forward as soon as he saw him and the assault of the two champions was like the fury of two bears, or the tearing of two lions. Midchain was overwhelmed. As soon as he fell, his sons—Corc, Conn, and Aod—came to fight against the sons of Delbaeth.

The fight was magnificent in the grandeur of the blows, the strength of the soul, and the range of valor. Midchain's three sons sank spears into the bodies of Delbaeth's sons; however, neither the anguish, nor the weakness of the end, prevented the wounded from passing through their adversaries in their turn. Midchain's three sons also fell into the languor of death.

"How are you, my beloved brothers?" Brian asked.

"We are dead," Iuchar and Iucharba replied.

"Standing!" Brian ordered. "I hear the signs of death approaching. We must let out the three cries required from the top of this hill!"

"We are not able," said Iuchar and Iucharba.

Then Brian stood up and, although he, too, was losing blood in abundance, he lifted a brother with each hand. The three shouts rang out from the top of the hill.

16. The Lament of Delbaeth's Sons

Having fulfilled the last obligation, Brian carried the brothers to the currach, which took to the sea alone. "I see the promontory of

Benn Etair, and Dún Tuirell, our father's fortress, and Temáir of the Supreme Kings of Ériu," Brian shouted.

"If only we could see them, we would be healthy again," said Iuchar and Iucharba. "For the sake of your generosity, brother, raise our heads on your chest so that we can contemplate Ériu. After that, it will be the same to receive life and death." And they sang this song:

Receive our heads on your chest, Brian,
You, generous red-armed son of Delbaeth,
torch of valor without betrayal,
so that we can contemplate the land of Ériu.
Get on the chest and shoulders
these heads of ours, virile champion,
because we see on the water from afar
Uisnech Meath, Óenach Tailten, and Temáir.

Áth Clíath and sweet Bóann with you,
Fremann, Tlachta before Temáir,
the plain of the Meath, dewy Mag mBreg,
and the peaks next to the beautiful Óenach Tailten meadow.

If we saw Benn Étair from afar
and Dún Tuirell to the north,
welcome the end that would follow
even death of torments.

And Brian replied:

Alas, brave sons of Delbaeth!
Birds would go through the wounds in my hips;
But not the torn hips make me suffer,
as much as knowing that you are equally fallen.

And Iuchar and Iucharba said:

We prefer death to seize us,
Brian mac Delbaeth who never ran away,
rather than seeing you wounded and hurt,
without a doctor who can heal you.
"Because there is no one to heal the wounds,
neither Miach, nor OrMiach and not even Dían Cécht.
Alas, Brian, who never wanted to betray,
misfortune to have delivered the pigskin to Lugh!

17. The Rejection of Lugh

The currach landed at Benn Étair and from there the sons of Delbaeth reached Dún Tuirell, their father's fortress.

"Go to Temair, dear father," they said. "Go talk to Lugh, give him the spit and ask him in friendship for the enchanted hide of the pig that will help us."

And Brian sang this song:
Get away from us, Delbaeth!
Go speak to Lugh the victorious,

catch him still in his sleep, in the south;

ask him in friendship for the enchanted skin!

And Tuirell replied:

For all the treasures of the world, of the north and south,

as much as I asked the victorious Lugh,

I would not get it, it is certain,

than your grave and burial.

And Brian:

For flesh and blood, you are close

to Lugh, son of Cian, son of just Dian Cecht.

Don't make us violence for violence,

even if we killed his father!

Beloved father, free and noble,

don't be late in your journey,

you would never find us again, if you were,

alive before your eyes.

Delbaeth, therefore, went to Temair to find Lugh. He handed him the roast-spit and asked for the pigskin that would heal his children, but Lugh refused. And so Delbaeth returned to his children empty-handed.

"Take me with you," Brian said. "Maybe so I can have it.

Brian went to Lugh and begged him to grant him the pigskin. However, Lugh replied scornfully that he would not hand it over to them all over the earth, unless he was certain that death would come to them anyway, and this to repay them for their crime.

18. The Tragic Destiny of Delbaeth's Sons

Then Brian went back to Iuchar and Iucharba and lay down beside them. Life escaped from his body and those of his brothers. Their father, Delbaeth, composed this song for them:

My heart is oppressed for you,
handsome heroes from great battles;
after your ardor and great deeds,
better for me that you were alive.
I am Tuirell, devoid of strength
on your graves, proud warriors;
as long as the boats go out to sea,
I will compose neither poem nor song.

And at those words, he fell on the bodies of his children, expiring. All four were buried together and, thus, Lugh's revenge was accomplished. This is the story of the tragic fate of Delbaeth's children.

The Adventure of Dagda Mor: Meeting at the Wading

After the seven years of truce, the Fomóire land in Ériu. The Dagda Mor, lord of wisdom and druidic art, is sent to parliament, whose figure suddenly reveals grotesque and paradoxical elements.

1. The Woman of the Unshin River

Six of the seven years of truce had already passed and there was now only a year left for the great battle that would decide who would have sovereignty over Ériu: the Túatha Dé Danann or the Fomorians. The Dagda Mor went to Glenn Edin, in the north of the island, where he had a home. He had, in fact, arranged to meet a woman there on Samhain's day.

Arriving in Corann, Connacht, he found the woman bathing in the *Unshin* River. She kept one foot in Alloch Echae, on the southern bank, and the other in Loscuinn, on the northern bank. Nine braids hung from her head. The Dagda spoke to her and the two joined in love. That place has since been known as the "couple's bed" [*Line na Lánomnou*].

That woman was the Morrigan, daughter of Ernmas.

The Morrigan revealed to the Dagda that the Fomorians would land at Mag Ceidne. She told him that she would call Ériu's people of arts (*áes dána*) to meet with her at the ford of Unshin, where she would leave her instructions for the next battle. And finally, she added that she would go to the *Scétne* to annihilate the king of the Fomorians, Indech mac Dé Domnann: She would deprive him of the blood and the glands of his value.

Later, in fact, as she had said, Morrigan held out her bloody hands to the fighters who were waiting at the ford of the Unshin. Since then, that place would have been called "ford of destruction" [*Áth Admillte*], as the destruction of King Indech was planned there. It was then that Ériu's aes dána uttered enchantments against the Fomorian hosts.

This was a week before Samhain. Then the Morrigan and the Dagda Mor separated, and on the eve of Samhain, all of Ériu's men gathered once more. Six times thirty thousand was their number.

2. The Dagda Mor Goes to the Fomorians

When the last of the seven years of truce also ended, the Fomorians landed in Ériu, in Mag Ceidne, just as the Morrigan had prophesied. Samhain's day was now near. Then Lugh sent the Dagda Mor to spy on the moves of the Fomorians and to slow their advance so that the warriors of the Túatha Dé Danann could gather for battle.

The Dagda went to the enemy camp and asked for a postponement. He got what he asked for. Then, to make fun of him, the Fomorians cooked him oatmeal, knowing full well that he was greedy. They filled the king's cauldron, five fists deep, with forty times twenty barrels of fresh milk and an equivalent quantity of flour and fat. Then they threw goats, sheep, and pigs in it and boiled them with the soup. Finally, they poured the contents of the cauldron into a large hole in the ground.

Then Indech mac Dé Domnann, the king of the Fomorians, invited the Dagda to eat that porridge and told him he would be put to death if he didn't finish it all. He should have eaten his fill so that he could not use satire against the Fomorians.

So the Dagda took his ladle, which was so big that it could hold a man and a woman in the hollow, and ate until he was finished. The Dagda said, "The broth is good, if its aroma is good." And when he put the ladle in his mouth, which contained half of a salty pork and a quarter of lard, he declared, "As the old wise men say, the pieces do not spoil!"

After completely draining the hole, he ran his fingers across the bottom and scratched whatever was left between the dirt and gravel. When he finished eating, he fell asleep. His belly was bigger than the central cauldron of a house, and the Fomorians laughed at him.

The Dagda then went to Tráig Eaba, but it was not easy for him to move due to how swollen his belly was. His clothing was indecent: a short cloak that barely covered his elbows and a grayish tunic that reached the protrusion of his ass and left his penis uncovered. On the feet, horse leather shoes with fur on the outside. He dragged behind his club, mounted on wheels, which could be moved only by eight men, tracing a furrow so deep that it could serve as a border ditch for an entire province. For this reason, that groove was called the "groove of the Dagda stick" [Slicht Loirge an Dagdai].

3. The Dagda and Indech's Daughter

Along the way, the Dagda Mór was confronted by a beautiful young girl, pleasant in shape, with long hair gathered in beautiful braids. His desire ran to her, but he was helpless because of his belly, and the young woman began to mock him. They fought and she slammed him so hard that the Dagda sank to his butt.

The Dagda stared at her angrily, "What is your intention, girl?"

"This is my intention," replied the young woman. "To force you to carry me on your back to the house of my father, Indech mac De Domnann." And it hit him so hard that the furrow around the Dagda was filled with the excrement of his own belly. Then she satirized him three times to force him to carry her on his back. However, the Dagda said that a *geis* weighed on him and forbade him to carry anyone who did not call him by his real name.

"So, what's your name?" asked the girl.

"Fer Benn," he replied.

"This name is exaggerated!" the young woman laughed. "Get up and carry me on your back, Fer Benn!"

"That's not just my name," the Dagda retorted.

"Well, what's your name?"

"Fer Benn Brúach."

"Get up and carry me on your back, Fer Benn Brúach!"

"That's not my name alone," the Dagda said again.

"Tell me your full name, then!" the girl urged.

The Dagda then gave her his very long name, convinced that the young woman would never have been able to repeat it in full, but she repeated it without making a single mistake:

"Get up and carry me on your back, Fer Benn Brúach Brogaill Broumide Cerbad Caic Rolaig Builc Labair Cerrce By Brig Ollathair Boith Athgen mBethai Brigtere Tri Carboid Roth Rimaire Ríog Scotbe Obthe Olaithbe! Get up and take me away from here!"

The Dagda had to agree to the request. "I will, but stop mocking me, girl!"

"It won't be difficult," she said.

Before exiting the hole, the Dagda finished emptying his belly. Indech's daughter had to wait until he was finished. Then he got up and started to take the girl on his back. In doing so, he placed three stones in his belt, which fell one by one (but others say that it was his testicles that fell). The girl jumped on him and in doing so the curls of her pubis were uncovered. Then the Dagda was seized by a sudden passion. They were in Trácht Eboile, and there is still a trace of where they lay.

Indech's daughter then said to the Dagda, "You will not go into battle. You will not go there because I will be a stone at the mouth of every ford you have to cross.

"You will not hold me back," said the Dagda. "I will tread heavily on every stone, and on every stone the trace of my heel will remain forever.

"That may be so, but the stones will be turned upside down so that you cannot see them. You will not be able to overcome me, because I will call the children of Tethra, and in every ford, in every step you cross, I will be a gigantic oak."

"I will overtake you," the Dagda replied. "And on every oak, the mark of my axe will remain forever."

Then the young woman said, "Here, let the Fomorians advance across the country, for all the Danann warriors have now gathered for battle." And she added that she would turn his magical arts against his own people. With his enchantments, he would hold back the Fomorians and with his druid rod, he would face the ninth of every enemy host.

The Second Battle of Mag Tuired: The Defeat of the Fomorians

Mag Tuired, not far from where they had previously defeated the Fir Bolg, the Túatha Dé Danann, led by Lugh, must now face the threat of the Fomorians. Their freedom and Ériu's supreme royalty are at stake.

1. The Threat of Indech

The Fomorians marched to *Scetne*, while the men of the Túatha Dé Danann were in *Mag Aurfolaig*. The two ranks were about to clash in battle. "Ériu's men want to fight us?" Bress mac Elatha asked Indech mac Dé Domnann.

"I'll be the one to fight them," Indech replied. "And I give you my word that their bones will fall apart if they don't accept our terms and pay us the tribute.

2. Lugh Prepares the Armies for Battle

The Túatha De Danann held high respect for Lugh, and feared an early death for the hero of many talents; therefore, they had decided not to let him go and fight. For this purpose, they had left nine guardians to watch over him: Tollusdam, Echdam, Eru, Rechtaid Finn, Fosad, Feidlimid, Ibar, Scibar, and Minn.

Lugh prepared Ériu's army for the next battle and arranged the spells with which wizards and druids would upset the enemy ranks. Those who had the highest rank among the Túatha De Danann had gathered around him. Lugh asked each one what contribution he would make to help the fate of the battle.

"It's not difficult," said Goibniu, the blacksmith. "Even if Ériu's men remain in battle for seven years, every blunt spear and every broken sword will be replaced in a single day. No spearhead forged by my hand will miss the target; no flesh pierced by that spear will ever taste life again, and this is much more than Dolb, the Fomorian blacksmith, is capable of."

"It's not difficult," said Credne, the bronze craftsman. "I will provide nails for the spears, hilts for the swords, and bosses and harnesses for the shields."

"It's not difficult," said Luchta, the carpenter. "I will provide Ériu's men with the shields and spear shafts they will need."

"It's not difficult," said Dian Cecht, the healer. "I will treat any injured within a day, so that he is ready to fight for the next morning. As long as he hasn't cut off his head, pierced his brain, or severed his spine."

"It's not difficult," said Ogma, the champion. "I will fight the king of the Fomorians, repel nine of his allies three times, and defeat a third of the enemy army in the name of Ériu's men."

"It's not difficult," Morrigan said. "I am resolute. I will pursue whoever has been sighted, and I will kill and annihilate those who can be caught."

"It's not difficult," the sorcerers said. "We will see the soles of the feet of the Fomorians when our magical arts have brought them down. They could easily be killed after we deprive them of two-thirds of their strength by forcing urine into them."

"It's not difficult," the cupbearers said. "We will give the Fomorians an unquenchable thirst, but we will hide from them every lake and river of Ériu, so that they will not be able to quench the heat in any way."

"It's not difficult," said the druids. "We will pour bursts of fire on the faces of the Fomorians, so that they cannot look up and our warriors can use their strength to kill them."

"It's not difficult," said Coirpre, the satirist. "I will cast curses against the Fomorians, satirize them, and deprive them of their honor. By the strength of my art, they will no longer be able to oppose the warriors of Ériu."

"It's not difficult," said Beuchuill and Dínann, the two witches of the Túatha Dé Danann. "We will cast a spell on trees, stones, and clods of earth, so that the Fomorians see in them armies and flee in terror and trembling.

"As for me, it's not difficult," the Dagda Mor said last. "I will join Ériu's men, both striking and annihilating with druid magic. Where both sides collide, on the battlefield of Mag Tuired, the bones of the enemies under my mace will be like hailstones under the hooves of a herd of horses.

In this way Lugh, addressing the Túatha Dé Danann, spoke with each of his own art and infused such strength that each of them found in himself the courage of a king or prince.

3. The Second Battle of Mag Tuired Begin

On Samhain's day, the armies of the Túatha Dé Danann and the Fomorians deployed in the plain of Mag Tuired, the site chosen for the great battle. In that same plain, thirty years earlier, the Túatha Dé Danann had fought against the Fir Bolg and had defeated them, taking from them the royalty of Ériu.

For this reason, the antique dealers distinguish a first battle of Mag Tuired, fought by the Túatha Dé Danann against the Fir Bolg, and a second battle of Mag Tuired, fought against the Fomorians. Others refer to the two battles as the Battle of Mag Tuired Theas, in the south, and the Battle of Mag Tuired Thuaid, in the north, respectively. As these verses say:

Thirty years, it is known,
from the battle of Mag Tuired South
at the battle of Mag Tuired North,
into which Balor fell from the great hosts.

4. Spells and Deeds of Valor of the Túatha Dé Danann

Thus began the battle between the two hosts, and at the beginning neither kings nor princes took part, but equally strong and proud warriors. The clashes were repeated every day, and a certain perplexity began to creep among the Fomorians. Their broken weapons remained in the field as they were, and the men given up for dead showed no sign of life the next day. However, this was not the case with the Túatha Dé Danann: The next day, their weapons were even more powerful than before, and those who had been wounded or killed went down into battle alive and well again.

This is because Goibniu the blacksmith, in his forge, forged swords and spears and javelins with only three blows. At the same time, Luchta the carpenter made the shafts of the spears with three blows of the ax, of which the third was the finishing one that allowed the shaft to enter the joint of the spear.

When the shafts were placed to the side of the forge, Luchta threw the shafts into the joints of the spears and there was no longer any need to fix them again. Then Credne the coppersmith, with three blows, made the nails and threw them into the joints of the spears and it was no longer necessary to strike them again, as they remained well stuck.

As for the dead and wounded, Dian Cecht and his three sons, Miach, Octriuil, and Airmed, provided. (Here, there seems to be a small inconsistency; according to what the text of the *Cath Maige Tuired* had previously reported, Miach had already been killed by his father, Dian Cecht, after Núada's recovery.)

A magical spring was found in Achad Able, west of Mag Tuired and east of Loch Arboch: It was the source of Slaine. Dian Cecht had put in it every grass that grew in Ériu, so that the source was also called Loch Luibe, "Lake of herbs." In those waters, Dian Cecht and his three sons immersed mortally wounded men, reciting druidic spells and formulas on them. The dead and the wounded emerged from the source not only perfectly intact but also endowed with such ardor that it made them much more agile in combat than they had ever been before.

5. The Death of Ruadan

The situation loomed unfavorably for the Fomorians, and they chose a man who spied on the field and habits of the Túatha De Danann. They sent Ruadan, son of Bress and of Brigit, daughter of the Dagda. The Fomorians believed the young man was less conspicuous, having Danann blood.

Ruadan went and told the Fomorians of the wonders wrought by the blacksmith, the carpenter, and the bronzesmith, and also spoke of the four healers who were waiting at the Slaine spring.

Then the Fomorians sent him back to kill one of the most important men, Goibniu the blacksmith.

Ruadan went back to the danann camp and asked Goibniu to give him a spearhead. Then he asked Credne for nails and Luchta for a rod. Everything he asked for was given to him. There was a woman who sharpened her weapons: Cron, mother of Fianlach. It was she who ground Rúadán's spear. And because it was she, a mother, who handed him the weapon, the beam of weavers has since been called "mother's spear" in Gaelic.

After he was given the spear, Ruadan turned and hurled it at Goibniu. However, Goibniu pulled it out and aimed it at the young man, piercing him. Ruadan died in the presence of his father at the Fomorian assembly. Then his mother, Brigit, came and cried, mourning the death of her son. It is said that this was the first funeral lament that was ever heard in Ériu.

Goibniu then bathed in the Slaine spring and came out healed.

6. The Octriallach Cairn

Among the Fomorians was a warrior, Octriallach, son of Indech. He told the Fomorian warriors to go and get stones in the Drobesa river, one for each, and to throw them into the source of Slaine, so that, from that moment, it was no longer possible to bring the dead back to life. So they did: Each man put a stone in the spring, the spring was drained, and the so-called "Mound of Octriallach" [*Carn Octríallaig*] was formed.

Carn Ochtriallaig is a cairn located northwest of Mag Tuired, today near Heapstown (Heapstown Carn).

7. The Great Battle

When the time came to clash in the final battle, the Fomorians emerged from their camp and formed strong and indestructible ranks.

Among them, no chief or worthy man was without a chain mail on his skin, a helmet on his head, a spear in his right hand, a sharp sword at his belt, and a shield on his shoulder. Attacking the Fomorians that day was like "hitting your head against a rock," like "putting your hand into the snake's nest," like "putting your face in the fire."

Here are the kings and leaders of the Fomorian army: Balor, son of Dot, son of Neit, Bress, son of Elatha, Tuirie Tortbuillech, son of Lobas, Goll and Irgoll, Loscennlom, son of Lomglúinech, Indech mac Dé Domnann, Octriallach, son of Indech, Omna and Bagnai, and Elatha, son of Delbaeth, son of Neit.

Across the field, the Túatha Dé Danann moved and went to clash in battle. However, just as the battle was about to begin, Lugh escaped his nine guardians and it was he who found himself, in a battle chariot, at the head of the Danann army.

Lugh encouraged Ériu's men to fight bravely to not be enslaved. It would have been better for them to die by defending their land than to once again be subject to paying tribute to the Fomorians. Standing on one foot and keeping one eye open, he circled the Danann warriors, singing a long spell. The ranks threw themselves against each other, shouting frighteningly; then they clashed and a furious melee began in which warriors hit each other. Deafening was the noise of the multitude of warriors and champions who with shields and swords and their own bodies parried the blows of spears and swords of others. Deafening was the din all over the battlefield: the cries of the combatants, the clash of shields, the crack of swords and ivory-hilted blades, the shaking and resounding of quivers, the darting and hissing of spears.

Many strong men fell into the stillness of death. Great was the massacre and many were those who lay in the pits. Pride and shame stood side by side. There was anger, there was fury. Blood flowed abundantly on the white skin of the young warriors, mutilated by the hands of stronger men when they exposed themselves to danger for fear of appearing cowardly.

As they hit each other, the tips of the toes and hands almost touched; and by the stickiness of the blood under their feet, the warriors kept slipping and falling. Their heads were torn off while they were on the ground. They engaged in a chaotic, tearing, terrible, bloody battle: The tips of the spears were red in the hands of the enemies.

8. The Sword of Tethra

During the fighting, Ogma the champion found Orna, the sword of Tethra, king of the Fomorians. Ogma took the sword out of its sheath and cleaned it. Then the sword recounted the deeds it had accomplished: In those days, in fact, it was the property of the swords to tell the actions that had been undertaken thanks to them. For this, the swords were entitled to the tribute to be cleaned after they were removed from the scabbard. Since then, spells have been preserved in swords.

9. The Harp of the Dagda Mor

In the course of the battle, Lugh, the Dagda Mor, and Ogma had to chase the Fomorians, as they had kidnapped Uaithne, the harpist of the Dagda, and his harp, in which the god had enclosed the music so that it would play only if he was the one to touch it. That harp had two names: *Daur Dá Bláo*, "oak of the two blossoms," and *Cóir Cethar Chuir*, "with four angled music."

Finally, the three broke into the enemy banquet hall, where Bress and his father Elatha were. The harp was hanging on the wall, and the Dagda called it:

Come on, Daur Dá Bláo!

Come on, Cóir Cethar Chuir!

Come, summer! Come, winter!

Voice of harps, bellows, and bagpipes!

The harp immediately broke off the wall and went to the Dagda, killing nine men. As soon as the Dagda had the harp in his hand, he played the three arias by which the harpist is distinguished: the melody to move, the melody to cheer up, and the melody to sleep. He played the melody to move, and the women wept; the aria blew to cheer and the women and boys laughed; the air blew to sleep and the warriors fell asleep. Thus the three were able to escape unharmed to the Fomorians, who wanted to kill them.

On the way back, the Dagda took away the heifer he had demanded of Bress as a reward for his work. The heifer bellowed to summon the calf, and all of Ériu's cattle, which the Fomorians had taken as tribute, followed her to pasture. Thus, the people of Ériu got their herds back.

10. The Death of Nuada

During the battle, Nuada Aircetlam, king of Túatha Dé Danann, and Macha, daughter of Ernmas, fell. It was Balor, son of Dot, son of Neit who gave them death.

The satirist Casmaol fell by the hand of Octriallach, son of Indech.

11. Lugh Against Balor

Lugh met his grandfather, Balor, in the fury of the fray. Balor only opened his evil eye on the battlefield. Such was the destructive power of his eye: All the warriors Balor stared at, even if they were thousands, lost all their strength and offered no resistance to the enemy.

Lugh advanced toward Balor, determined to avenge Nuada's death, and began to cast a long spell against him. Then Balor said to the men of his entourage, "Open my evil eye, boys, so that I can see this charlatan who is talking to me." Four men lifted his eyelid with a shiny handle that was attached to it. At that moment, Lugh threw a stone with his sling and hit him in the terrible eye. This went through his head and came out of the back of his neck. The evil gaze of the eye thus turned against the Fomorian army, paralyzing it.

Balor's body fell on his own army and three times nine Fomorian warriors died under his weight.

In this way, the prophecy was fulfilled that Balor was destined to die at the hands of his daughter's son; and it was Lugh, son of Ethniu, daughter of Balor who gave him death.

12. The Head of Balor

When Lugh decapitated Balor, the severed head flew off and hit Indech mac Dé Domnann's chest. A gush of blood splashed on the lips of the king of the Fomorians.

Indech then called his *filí*, Loch Lethglas, the "Half-green," who was green all over, from the ground to the top of his head, and asked him whatever hit him so hard. Loch Lethglas gave him a long reply in *retoiric*, in which he told him that he could not recognize Balor's killer. Then Lugh looked up at him and the two accused each other of having uttered wrong prophecies.

13. Fomorians' Defeat

The moment was favorable for the Túatha Dé Danann. The Morrigan, daughter of Ernmas, urged the warriors of Ériu to fight with pride and ardor. She gave a long song in retoiric which began with the words:

Arise, O king, to fight! ...

The battle became a total defeat for the Fomorians, who were driven back to the sea by the Túatha Dé Danann. Champion Ogma faced Indech mac Dé Domnann, king of the Fomorians, and both fell in the fight.

Deprived of their king, the Fomorians surrendered.

14. The Count of the Fallen

When the battle ended and the Fomorians fell into the hands of the Túatha Dé Danann, Lugh wanted to negotiate with the survivors. First, the *filí* Loch Lethglas asked him for the grace of life.

"Fulfill my three wishes," Lugh told him.

"They will be satisfied." Loch nodded. "I will forever eliminate from Ériu the need to be on guard against the Fomorians, and in any difficult case, the judgment that your mouth will give will resolve the matter forever." Thus, Loch was spared and, by the grace that was bestowed upon him, gave a name to each of the nine chariots of Lugh, its drivers, its whips, and its horses. Lugh was satisfied but, before letting him go, he asked Loch how many were killed.

"I don't know the number of ordinary people and servants," Loch replied. "But as for the number of Fomorians, nobles and lords and champions and sons of supreme kings and kings, I know this: three plus three times twenty, plus fifty times hundred men, plus twenty times hundred men, plus three times fifty, plus nine times five, plus four times twenty per thousand, plus eight plus eight times twenty, plus seven plus four times twenty, plus six plus four times twenty, plus five plus eight times twenty, plus two, plus forty, including Neit's nephew Balor with ninety men. This is the number of those killed among the great kings and noble Fomorians who fell in battle.

"As for the number of common people, poor people, servants, and men of every trade who came together with the great army (because every lord and king of the Fomorians had come to battle with his entourage, and therefore all fell, both free men and their non-free servants), I have taken into account only a part of the servants of kings.

"And as regards the men who fought paired and the reserves, these warriors, who did not reach the heart of the battle but who died there, will not be counted, just as we cannot count the stars of the sky, the sand of the sea, the flakes of snow, the drops of dew on the meadows, the grains of hail, the blades of grass under the feet of the herds, and the "*horses of Lér's son*" in a stormy sea." ("Horses of the son of Lér" indicates the waves of the sea.)

15. Bress Had Spared His Life

They then had the chance to kill Elatha's son, Bress. Bress said, "It's better to do me grace than kill me."

"How will you reward us if we grant you grace?" asked Lugh.

"If I am spared, Ériu's cows will give milk forever."

"Shall we be gracious to Bress if he gives milk to Ériu's cows forever?" Lugh asked the druids.

"No," said Máeltne Mór-Brethach. "Even if Bress had power over cows' milk, he has no power over their longevity or fertility."

"That doesn't save you," Lugh told Bress.

"Máeltne made a harsh announcement," said Bress.

"How else could you reward us if we grant you the grace?" asked Lugh.

"There is another way. Tell your judges that if I am spared, they will reap a harvest every quarter of a year."

"Do we have to thank Bress if he will guarantee us a harvest every quarter of a year?" Lugh asked the druids.

"No," said Máeltne Mór-Brethach. "There is no reason to have four harvests a year, as even one crop requires work in each of the four seasons: spring for plowing and sowing, early summer for growing wheat, early autumn to finish ripening and harvest it, and winter to consume it."

"That doesn't save you," Lugh told Bress.

"Máeltne made a harsh announcement," said Bress.

"But I could spare you for much less," Lugh said.

"Like?"

"How should Ériu's men plow? How should they sow? How should they reap? When you let us know these three things, you will be spared."

"Tell them," said Bress then, "Tuesday to plow, Tuesday to sow the seeds, Tuesday to harvest."

And with this spell, Bress saved his life. Thus ended the second battle of Mag Tuired.

The Prophecies of the Morrigan: The Happy Age and the Cruel Age

The text of the Cath Maige Tuired closes with two prophecies, launched by Morrigan, the warrior fury of Ireland, to open disturbing glimpses of the past and future.

   1. The Announcement of Victory

As soon as the second battle of Mag Tuired was over and the corpses were eliminated, the Morrigan, daughter of Ernmass, went to the royal heights of Ériu and, among the ranks of the síde, went to the most important lakes and the mouths of the rivers to tell of the great clash and to announce the victory of the Túatha Dé Danann. Thus it was that Badb narrated the lofty feats that had been accomplished.

   2. The First Prophecy

They asked her, "What story do you have for us?" And she sang:

Peace to heaven.
Heaven down to earth.
Earth under the sky.
Strength in everyone.
A cup full of honey;

Amy Hughes

Mead in abundance.
Summer in the winter,
the spear on the shield;
the shield on his fist.
A mighty encampment:
lamentation is banned.
The fleece from the sheep;
luxuriant forest;
cattle horns:
fence on the ground.
Fronds on trees:
a branch bends
heavy for growth.
Health to a son,
son on the shoulders,
bull's neck,
bull for slaughter.
Tangle of trees,
wood for the fire.
Desired focus.
A boulder on the ground,
mooing from the cows
the Boann in its course.
Very long course,

at the mouth the blue current in spring,

in autumn the wheat ripens.

Support for the land:

earth with sharp ribs;

Eternal strength to the woods

durable and extensive.

What story do you have for us?

Peace to heaven.

3. The Second Prophecy

Then the Morrigan prophesied the end of the world and foretold all the evils that would come and all the diseases and all the revenge. And she raised this song:

I'll see a world

that will not be dear to me:

summer without flowers,

cows without milk,

shameless women,

worthless men,

conquests without a king...

Woods without trees,

seas without fruit...

Unjust judgments of the elders,

false record of judges.

Every man a traitor,

every young man a thief.

The son will enter the father's bed,

the father will go into his son's bed,

each will be brother-in-law of his brother...

An unholy age.

The son will betray his father,

the daughter will cheat on her mother...

CONCLUSION

I hope that you have enjoyed reading this introduction to Celtic mythology and that you now have a better understanding of Celtic myths, gods, and legends. This is the third in a series of books that will discuss the myths and legends of various cultures. If you're interested in Norse and Greek mythology, you can look for the first and second book. Thanks again for reading and stay tuned for the next books.

Printed in Great Britain
by Amazon